Also

(Rippe

The Penny Portrait

Short Story

Christmas Scrubs
(Medical Romance)

Maggie's Child Copyright © 2012 by Glynis Smy
Second Edition: March 2015 / New Cover 2015

All rights reserved. No part of this book may be used or reproduced in any manner whatsoever without written permission except in the case of brief quotations embodied in critical articles or reviews.

This is a work of fiction. Names, characters, organization, places, events, and incidents are either the product of the author's imagination or are used fictitiously. Actual place/street names have been used, but not necessarily in the correct map area or town.

ISBN-10: 1481253352
ISBN-13: 978-1481253352

www.glynissmyauthor.com

Cover creation: Jessica Bell Designs

Publisher: Createspace Independent Publishing Platform;
1 edition (20 Dec 2012) USA
&
Anastasias Publishing Europe

All rights reserved.

Maggie's Child

Glynis Smy

DEDICATION

For my children, Darren, Nicola, and Emma, who are always my babies, despite being too old to wear nappies. I hold you in my heart forever and a day.

For my husband, Peter who keeps me fed and supports me 100%.

For Mum, my biggest fan. Thanks for cheering me on.

Heartfelt thanks for support and encouragement go to:

My Beta Readers - thank you for your support.

Jessica Bell for the creation of a fabulous cover.

Author Talli Roland, for spurring me forward yet again.

For family and friends who listen over coffee and cheer me onto another bout of novel writing.

To you, my reader. Without you my dream would not be fulfilled. Thank you.

MAGGIE'S PRAYER

I have never seen your eyes-
nor looked into your heart-
it beats deep within-
the rhythm of life-
tick tiny tick tock-
timing is crucial-
days are long-
waiting-
hoping-
for a
breath of life.

Copyright © 2012 Glynis Smy

Chapter 1

Monday, 13th of October, 1856

Intense pain ripped through Maggie's body in waves. Sweat lay on her brow, and nausea drained her. She bit hard on the stick between her teeth. As she entered her sixth hour of labour—the longest pain of childbirth endured by Maggie—she convinced herself death must be around the corner for her and the baby. In past pregnancies, labour was over within two hours, and the babies slithered wearily down the birth canal. All died within the first few minutes of arrival. This, her fifth pregnancy, seemed different. Unable to pinpoint as to why, Maggie concentrated on the task ahead.

Her body, sapped of energy, gave in to nature. Maggie drew in a deep breath, arched her back, and pushed through the pain. Now came the moment she dreaded, the split seconds when life and death merged. When body and soul would cry out with the pain of loss. Bearing down, she bit deeper into the stick. Never had she felt so alone and helpless.

Damn you, Stephen Avenell. Damn your promises.

A breeze wafted across her face, and Maggie welcomed the cool offering. She placed trembling fingers between her legs, and her hands recoiled when she touched a warm, sticky mass.

With speed, she made out a rounded mound, and with slippery hands helped the tiny body into the world. She tugged gently, and while she wrapped her hands around the small mass, a hand grasped at her fingers.

Maggie inhaled and held her breath for a few seconds; the wet hand had a firm grip. Tiny fingers moved and told her there was hope.

She pushed away the stick with her tongue. The wood left behind earthy flavours. Maggie longed to rinse away the taste, but there were no luxuries surrounding her at this delivery. She spat indelicately onto the ground beside her and, with as much speed as she could muster, pulled the babe onto her belly.

With one arm supporting the child, she forced her body downwards and pushed out the afterbirth. With her free arm, she wiped herself clean with rags laid out in readiness.

Now came the moment of truth. Slowly she lifted her head and looked down at the squirming pink flesh that celebrated life on her abdomen. A sob caught in the back of Maggie's throat when a small squeak escaped from rosebud lips. The cries of her baby were an orchestra to her ears. She had never heard a sound from her labours before today. The vibrations against her breastbone were like church bells on a wedding day for Maggie. A sound to be rejoiced.

She cut the cord with a clean knife from her basket, rubbed the child clean with a rag, and bound a binder tight around the rotund belly. Exhaustion kept her lying on the ground. She comforted the child upon her body with one hand while, with the other, she fumbled and wrapped the afterbirth in the bloodied rags. Maggie put them to one side and reached out with trembling hands to hold her new-born for the first time.

The warmth of its skin made hers tingle.

A red face settled to baby pink when she enclosed her arms around its tiny frame and rested it gently in the crook of her arm. She traced her fingers around the mouth and down the cheeks. Eyes opened and looked into hers. Maggie's whole being surged with powerful love as she looked back into them. Tears streamed down her face and ran along the soft downy head of a blue-eyed boy.

She had a son.

Baby Sawbury, had a mother. Two lives from one body was the only miracle Maggie had ever asked God to grant her. The only child who had managed to find solace in her womb and lived was now telling the world the good news at the top of his lungs.

Sadness crept into her soul when Maggie remembered what was to be done before nightfall. The task to be carried out would be the hardest task of her life. For nine months, she played the role of the happy pregnant woman, despite knowing she would never keep the child. Jacob had been fooled into believing the child was his once she suspected she was pregnant with her lover's baby. Her husband showed no interest, claiming he would only be happy if she produced a boy, live and kicking. Maggie knew that whether boy or girl—if the child lived—Jacob would play no part in his or her life. Telling him was a ploy to protect her and the baby's future. Now that the time had arrived, it was a nightmare—not the plan she had thought simple to carry out. In her heart of hearts, she had convinced herself this baby would die like his siblings.

Now he lived, she needed to face the consequences.

Time was of the essence, and Maggie moved quickly. She spoke to the baby in soothing tones while she wrapped him in linen robes. 'I made these, little one. Your mama made these for you. Every stitch holds my love.'

They were nothing like the delicate outfits she had made for her first born and those who followed. These were simple garments with no embroidery, no identifying motif, but it lifted her spirits to think that at last, the tiny items she had kept secret were to be worn. Maggie would treasure this moment forever. She stopped rushing and gave herself a minute to enjoy her son. To absorb and make a memory of the most joyous event in her life. A twittering yellowhammer flew overhead, and Maggie fantasised it was telling the animal kingdom of a special arrival. Looking down at her son, she marvelled at his perfection and traced a loving finger over his tiny button nose. Both she and Stephen had narrow noses. Maggie's was petite with a slight tilt to the tip. Stephen's was longer. Someone once described it as a Roman nose. The baby's had a stubby shape, fortunately nothing that could be linked with either parent.

His tiny fists punched the air. Maggie drew him close and held her cheek against his downy head. 'Hush, little one, all is well—you survived. God be praised! Know this, I will always love you. My heart will always hold you close. It is torn in two as I look down upon your beauty. Forgive me, but I cannot burden you with my life. When I next hold you, it will be in Heaven when we are reunited in the afterworld. I cannot let you live in my world on earth. You deserve better, and my husband does not deserve you. He is not your blood, and I cannot bring myself to inflict him upon you. Your true father will never know you exist. He made his choices in life, as I have to make mine.' Her voice was soft and tender as she crooned the only words she would ever say to her child.

Maggie wiped away the tears and gathered her belongings. The little boy lay in a wicker basket she had woven from soft wood. She had made a quilt in secret, from rags and old clothing casual farm workers had left lying around over the past six months. From the moment she realised her pregnancy, she had prepared for this day. Each item had to be anonymous—there could be no connection to her or the farm.

She tied a rag around her waist and wedged it between her legs to absorb any blood. It chafed as she moved. She was sticky and sore, and the walk across the field to the roadside was a long and painful one. Each bump of the basket tugged her insides. Now was not a good time to stop and adjust the rag for comfort.

Maggie reached the long main road leading into the centre of Redgrave village. It was tree-lined with large horse chestnut and sycamore trees. A russet carpet of leaves lay across the pathways, and the white tower of St Mary's church was to her left. It indicated the south side of the village and marked approximately one mile away from where she stood.

Maggie turned her back to the majestic building and looked to the distance at a lone, large shape on the brow of a hill. Dark and dismal against the powder blue skyline was the outline of her home. It sat central to smaller buildings and appeared forlorn among the furrowed lines of grey, brown fields and dilapidated fencing. The north side; the side that love forgot. It looked every bit as depressing as it was. Even a bright autumn day could not improve the view. A cruel fact of Maggie's world gave her the nudge forward she needed. There was no turning back.

Shaking off the dark mood that threatened, she scouted around for a safe spot in the shade. The midday sun was not fierce, but it could dehydrate an unattended child quickly, especially a new-born. Gently, Maggie placed the basket with its squalling contents on the ground beside a large wall of greenery. The gorse bush would protect him from stray animals and give him shelter but still allow him to be found. Despite the temptation, she did not touch him again. Maggie knew her resolve would break down. It would be so easy to scoop him into her arms and take him home.

Fight it, Maggie! Fight the urge!

Blowing him a kiss to last a lifetime, Maggie walked away with a heavy heart. Regret and remorse had no place inside the gap he had left at the present time. She would grieve later. Prayers—and hope—were her companions.

Crawling into a small hollow of a hedge, Maggie lay low between the hawthorn and gorse. Her head ached, and she was thirsty. There were only two hours left before her husband would miss her, and Maggie prayed for a swift remedy to her predicament. It would be easier to walk away, but she wanted to see who claimed the child. She needed to reassure herself that all would be well in his new world. Should an unsavoury passer-by pick him up, she would show herself and pretend she was answering the call of nature. Maggie had spent months contemplating how to secure a safe home for her child. To give birth and walk through the village holding a child was not feasible. To give birth, hide a baby until dark, then place it on the doorstep of someone with money was not possible, either. A plan was needed, and this was the only one Maggie could come up with. Not ideal but necessary.

Her nipples tingled with the urge to feed her child. Her blouse was soaked. She fought against Mother Nature.

Her son screamed for his mother. The louder his cries, the more the first breast fluids flowed, and she resisted with all her might. Brambles scraped at her legs; she crouched low and placed her hands over her ears. Tears ignored her inner battle; they flowed, adding to the dampness of her clothing.

Her insides ached with the need to hold him. To inhale his sweet baby perfume one last time. The want was so powerful! Suddenly she remembered something she had meant to tell him.

'Nathaniel,' she whispered on the wind, 'your name is Nathaniel. I forgot to tell you—forgive me.'

The pain between her legs subsided to a dull throb. The tender belly area was not so uncomfortable, but the pain in her heart would never leave. Temptation was building by the second. If she took him home, she could only enjoy his baby life and protect him for a few years.

However, after that, it would be a life of drudgery and aggression. One she had endured since the age of fifteen.

With no consideration for Maggie, her parents had sold her to a widower. A man with no morals or love in his bones. A stray dog showed Maggie more affection with one sniff than Jacob Sawbury had shown her in five years. He lay on top of her and grunted like a pig from the sty in order to reproduce.

If Nathaniel's biological father, Stephen Avenell, knew the truth, he might be tempted to take him from the farm. Their secret would be discovered. If her husband found out the truth, he would destroy all three of them. He would take pride in being the one to bring scandal to the doorstep of the squire. The safest thing to do was to hope someone investigated the wailing sounds. Maggie prayed Nathaniel would not cry himself to sleep.

Keep screaming, my son! I will come for you one day. Dear God, just give me a chance to glimpse who takes him.

She knew she would never take him from whoever gave him a home, but Maggie needed to know where he would spend his years. If she did not recognise his rescuer, she would follow them until she knew where he had been taken. She could make discreet enquiries if he was given a home elsewhere. Locally, it would be easy to trace a newborn.

For fifteen minutes, she listened to the caw-caw of crows, the screams of the child and her heartbeat as it pounded within her chest.

A cart rolled by, and the noise from the wheels against the flint and rocks drowned out the sounds from the basket. Gold-brown leaves fluttered upon the breeze each wheel produced. Maggie watched with trepidation as the driver stopped a few feet away from the area where the babe lay. A large man in working clothes jumped down. He looked around and walked across towards where Maggie crouched.

She shrank back into the hedge. Twigs tangled in her hair and scratched her face. To her horror, it became obvious he was about to relieve himself. He fumbled with the button fly and rummaged around his crotch, freeing his flaccid appendage. She assumed he was desperate to heed the call of nature; it was unbelievable he would simply ignore the cries.

Maggie held her breath as the man urinated. She raised her head a fraction to see if she recognised him. She dared not move too much for fear of distracting him.

Her stomach gave a small flip of disappointment.

Luck was not on her side. The man was Colin Daker, the miller's help. A pleasant man, but he had birth afflictions. He was a deaf-mute. Not one sound would penetrate his eardrums. Nathaniel could scream until he had no air left in his lungs, and Colin still would not respond. Because she had placed the basket in the shade of a bush, Nathaniel would have to cry to be found by Colin. He would never see the child by chance as he was too far away from the bush.

Maggie focused upon Colin, staring at the back of his head as he walked away. She willed him to look to his right and around the bend of the hedge. Hope upon hope was thrown his way in silent, invisible words.

Look, just look down! For the love of England, move around the corner. He's there—find him, Colin! You are a good man; you will do right by him. Please just look.

'Hey there. You, man, move your cart.'

Maggie was shaken out of her trance-like state and shrunk back into the hedging. A deep, well-spoken voice was responsible. While she had been concentrating upon Colin, she had not noticed a horse-drawn carriage pull up behind his cart.

Colin, oblivious to the fact that he had been spoken to, waved back in acknowledgement when he saw the driver wave to him. He climbed upon his cart and pulled away. Maggie's heart sank as the carriage moved forward.

'Wait—stop the carriage!' a female voice called out to the driver through the open window.

It was the voice of Felicity Arlington. The woman read Bible verses in church on a regular basis, enough times for Maggie to know who she was.

'Whatever is it, Flick?' the man who had called out to Colin used a pet name, but Maggie knew it was not the voice of Mr. Arlington; his was much deeper.

The carriage door opened, and a woman in her late twenties climbed down. Her boots were dainty, tan and, Maggie noted, made of expensive leather. She thought of her own black, shabby ones, in need of another repair, and shook her head. Her feet would never house anything so luxurious.

'Shush. Listen! I can hear a strange noise. Listen!' Mrs.. Arlington put her fingers to her lips and looked about her.

A young man about the same age clambered down from the carriage and stood beside her, shaking his head.

'… 'tis a kitten. A cat has a litter around somewhere. It is coming from over there.' He pointed towards the gorse bush that housed Nathaniel, he cocked his head to one side, then nodded and put his finger to his lips to silence those around him. He tiptoed slowly towards the noise.

Maggie squeezed her hands together. Her stomach tensed; her son was about to be found. She raised her head and sent another silent prayer to the wind. This time it was to thank God for sending Felicity Arlington. A good woman with a caring soul. Her family was an upstanding, honest one within the Suffolk community. Nathaniel would be safe in their care.

'Goodness—Flick, come here! It is not a kitten, 'tis—well—a baby in a basket! A tiny baby!' The man lifted the basket from the ground and brought it out from under the bush. His face flushed, he hurried towards the carriage.

Maggie sat mesmerised as the woman gently lifted her son from his bed. His fists clenched, and his arms flayed around him. His cries were frantic.

Felicity patted his back and held him close to her chest. All the time, Maggie was crying inside, and more than a twinge of envy passed through her. At least the woman cared for him—she was affectionate and comforted him.

'Oh, you poor little thing! Who has left you here alone? There, there, do not cry, sweet child, we will help.' She turned to the man who was still holding the basket.

'I cannot see anyone around. Get Dukes to see if the mother is lying sick somewhere! This baby isn't many hours old.'

The two men walked in opposite directions, and for several minutes, his mother watched as the woman stood cradling him. A stranger crooned soothing words of comfort.

'Hush now. Who could have done something like this? Who has abandoned you here? How frightened you must be alone. Never you mind, you are not alone now.'

Maggie wanted to run to her and snatch him away. To declare he was not abandoned; she thought about where he had been placed, she wanted him, but she could not keep him. She wanted to explain how he came to be there, but knew it was wise to stay in her hiding place.

'I cannot see anyone around, madam. The man in the cart was Colin Daker.' Dukes, the driver, stood with his hands behind his back and waited for further instructions.

'Dukes, did you see anything? I haven't noticed anyone walking around.' The young man strode up beside the woman.

'Dukes said he has not, and the man on the cart was the deaf-mute from the mill. He would not abandon a child. 'tis obvious he would not have heard it crying. What are you going to do with the baby? He needs attending to. Thanks to our Lord, *we* found him, and not a mangy dog. For I fear he will not last the day without sustenance.'

Her companion touched her arm and continued speaking to the bewildered woman. 'Let us take him home, sister dear, and consider our options from there.'

Felicity Arlington agreed. 'Yes, we must take him to safety. Help me inside, then pass him to me. Poor, dear thing! Dukes, head straight for home please.' Her brother held onto the baby, brushing his finger across his cheek.

Maggie could see tenderness in his actions. She was lucky; God had sent good people to care for Nathaniel, and he was safe for the present time.

With the vigilance of a soldier, she waited and focused upon the small bundle, broken-hearted, as the man lifted her child into the carriage until she lost sight of him. Distressed but not giving in to her emotions for fear of being found, she curled into a ball and stayed in the hedges until the noise of the carriage wheels subsided into the distance. They were heading in the direction of the church, away from the dark, dismal hillside Maggie now had to face.

Her body ached, and she crawled out of her hiding place. She slumped to the floor and allowed herself the privilege of grief. Her small frame wracked with sobs. If someone came by, she no longer cared. Her world had ended, and life as she knew it had changed.

I loved you so much, Stephen! You destroyed me, and now I will never forgive you. Because of you, I have lost my son.

When her sobs had dwindled to sniffles, Maggie stood and straightened her clothing. She took a small tool from her basket and dug a hole close to the hedgerow. She placed all the bloodied cloths into it and covered them with rocks. The finality of the act brought a fresh bout of tears. She threw bracken on top, straightened her shoulders and headed for home. Her steps were slow and without enthusiasm as she walked past the public grazing pasture. The glorious colours of the autumnal countryside did nothing to lift her spirits. She had a pain in her chest, a reminder of what she had lost.

There was only one thing Maggie was aware of, and that was sorrow.

Chapter 2

The water from the pump struck cold against her skin, yet Maggie endured it while she cleansed her body. She scrubbed and rubbed her flesh until it became sore. An act of erasing the past—that was how she saw the bathing process.

Every now and then, she stopped and stared out the small window of her room. It looked down upon the village, and she could see the church tower in the distance. The white brick building was to be her focal point, the area Nathaniel would be living in for the present. The Arlington family dwelled close to the church, and she knew in her heart that they would look after him until they found a suitable home.

She gritted her teeth and continued her wash-down. The water bloodied as she cleansed between her legs. Tears joined it in the bowl.

With one loud bang, the bedroom door crashed open.

Maggie grabbed a flannel gown and held it in front of her. Wiping away the tears with the garment, she looked up at the large frame of her mean, unshaven-faced husband, who was standing in the doorway. His long, black, greasy hair flopped across his forehead when he removed his cap. He swept it back with his filthy, bruised hands and stared at her.

Maggie did not intend to hold the gaze of his ice grey eyes. His flattened, twisted nose made her think of Nathaniel's petite one and threatened the onset of tears again, so she lowered her head.

'What the ruddy hell are you playing at? The teats on them cows are dragging along the barn floor. Why are you bathing yourself at this time of day? And look at me when

I speak to you.' He moved towards her, his body language threatening.

Maggie lifted her head but said nothing. If he hit her now she would not feel the pain; she was dead inside—numb. He stopped and looked at the bowl. The blood-stained water angered him even more, and he squared his shoulders, moving closer. His steely, cold eyes looked into hers. His voice became a growl.

'You lost another one? *Chrissakes*, you are useless. Cannot even carry a baby in that rotten womb of yours. Well, brace yourself, madam—I want a son. If you cannot give me one, I will find another heifer that will. Get your lardy body out into the barn, and do some work.'

Jacob Sawbury raised his arm as if to lash out at her. Maggie ducked and slopped the bloodied water onto the floor, staring at it as it trickled down her clean legs. A reminder of what had occurred a few hours earlier. She bit her lower lip, determined not to cry; she hated the man before her and would not give him the satisfaction of breaking her resolve. Strength was her champion as long as she could remain impassive against him.

'Clean that up, you useless lump of flesh.' Her husband pushed her at the shoulder and made her flinch at his touch.

Maggie watched him leave the room, not moving until she heard the kitchen door slam shut. Her clean clothes were laid out on the bed they shared. She dressed as fast as she could, not wanting him to come back into the bedroom in an aroused state. In the past, he had taken her from behind with vicious temper, only hours after she had given birth to their second child. The pain lived with her still, and she never wanted to go through it again.

She moved around the kitchen, preparing the evening meal. After which she rinsed out the clothing from the morning and hung it in the yard. As if in a trance, she went from one job to another, each action a routine movement at which she never faltered. Maggie needed to refocus and gain control of her emotions.

She peeled potatoes and lit the coal oven. When the walls glowed red and reached the desired heat, she made a small mound of hot coals in one corner and swept out the unwanted remains into the fire grate. A cooking pot took their place, and she pushed the door shut, making a mental note to sweep the chimney area the next day.

With her indoor chores finished, Maggie walked over to the largest barn. The cows, settled into the long, wooden stalls made low mooing sounds in unison, their noise soothing her. She grabbed a large bucket and a stool, then went to her favourite cow, the one she had named Sophie. The large beast was gentle, and her coat of a warm velvety texture. With the stool in place, Maggie sat and leaned against the belly of Sophie to milk her.

The rhythmic action soothed her nerves, and the warmth from the animal gave the comfort she sought. For over an hour, she moved from one animal to another. Afterwards, she carried the buckets of warm, creamy fluid into the dairy room. Her husband earned reasonable money from their dairy products, and the room was the cleanest area on the farm. He had hired a young dairymaid from the village when their old one had died. Lizzie, keen and eager, took pride in her work. She had a wide smile but was definitely not the brightest flower in the garden, as Maggie's mother used to say. But she was a caring girl, with a heart the size of the county in which they lived. She and Maggie had become close friends since their first meeting when Maggie arrived at the farm.

'Hello, Lizzie. They produced well today; you will have your work cut out now.'

'Maggie, are you sick, gal? You seem pale—are you feeling unwell? You look done in to me. You are nearing your time, it's too much for you carrying the load you do, here—,' the girl spoke with speed as she moved from behind the blue slab counter towards her mistress, '—sit'. Lizzie slid a milking stool toward Maggie.

Maggie formed the words she wanted to say in her head, but they stuck in her throat. She looked down at the floor to compose herself. Lizzie was a friend, and Maggie, being close to breaking point, was ready to confess what she had done. She took a deep breath and sat on the stool. When she did speak, it came out in a croak, an emotional sob.

'I lost the baby a few hours back. Jacob is very angry with me, so be on your toes tonight. He will probably come to you, and his mood is not a good one. I buried her in the corner of Dupp's Meadow along with the others. It is sad, but I feel for Jacob. He does so want a son.'

She used the pretext of having a girl to disconnect her from Nathaniel. Sooner or later, it would go around the village that a boy child had been abandoned. Jacob never ploughed the top half of the meadow; he buried his parents and a brother in what he called *The Family Plot*. He did not believe in the church being the only place to bury people and, several years ago, had made a place for his dead family on the farm. Before washing, Maggie had gone to the meadow, made a mound of fresh earth and laid a posy of wild flowers on top. The mock grave sat at the end of the row with her other children. Only she knew it was empty; at least, she had done what would be expected of her. Jacob would want her to bury his child in the family area. She also expressed her concern for Jacob to Lizzie in a soft tone. She wanted the girl to be able to tell people Maggie was sad and thought of her husband during her loss. The game of pretence was her protection. The few farm hands that worked the farm loved her, and they often made sure Jacob kept his fists to himself. Sometimes he got away from their watchful eyes and gave her a good hiding, but she avoided situations where she would provoke him whenever possible.

Lizzie started towards her with outstretched arms.

Maggie put her hand out to ward her away and smoothed her apron. She could not cope with being held by another at that moment.

'Ah gal, I am that sorry. Aw, Maggie. You do not carry well, 'tis the same with our Henry's missus, Mildred. Lost seven now she has. 'twas your sixth, wasn't it?'

Maggie willed the girl to stop talking. She would not have said anything at all, but she needed their farm workers to know she was no longer pregnant, and to believe the story she had invented.

'Fifth. Not a breath did this one take.' Maggie gave Lizzie a wan smile and went back to her home, crossing the yard. From the corner of her eye, she could see Lizzie scuttle towards the wood barn. The news of their loss would soon be gossip on the farm.

Maggie tidied away the baby items and crib she aired in the back parlour. She had made a show of keeping things normal despite the fact that she would not have the opportunity to use them. She went through the nesting motions in the home to fool Jacob. As she placed them back into storage, the task brought about genuine sorrow. Jacob would expect to see a measure of emotion; she had never held back the sobs in the past, so she didn't do it this time, either. After a few moments of sadness and another bout of tears, she took comfort knowing there was a living being with her blood in its veins. Despite the dull sensation inside and the overwhelming urge to scream, Maggie allowed herself a small smile. There would never be a chance to hold him again, but her son lived—a triumph over Jacob.

A blackbird announced the end of the day, and the light faded. With it came a deeper melancholy mood. While preparing vegetables for a man she despised,

Maggie was thinking about her son and about who would be holding him in their arms right then.

The aroma of fresh bread could not remove the memory of the baby perfume she had inhaled that day. Mutton stew simmered slowly, the meaty smell permeating the farmhouse, but still the memory of the sweet, soft flesh lingered with Maggie.

Jacob broke the spell of silence when he crashed his way into the kitchen. Muddied boots were thrown against the hearth to dry off, and he scraped his chair away from the table. Each sound resonated in Maggie's ears. They sounded far louder than ever before, and the sounds irritated her nerves. The tension in her body made her limbs ache, but if she relaxed, Maggie convinced herself she would explode in temper.

'Managed the cows, did you?' Jacob grunted through a mouthful of bread, his words holding an edge of sarcasm.

Maggie carried the stew pan to the table and ladled his meal into a deep bowl, all the time avoiding his eye. 'Yes, there was a good yield. Lizzie will have plenty to churn for selling tomorrow.'

She sat at the other end of the table. Jacob made it a rule that they ate alone and first. When they had finished, Maggie took the extra food to a rundown cottage across the yard. A simple building where the few farm workers they had ate and rested. Lizzie lived in a smaller building to one side. She was the only female, and Maggie insisted she had private accommodation, although she suspected Lizzie spent a large part of the nights with the men in their beds.

Jacob grunted an approving sound during the slurping of his meal. Maggie hated his crude manners. Her parents may have been poor, but they knew how to conduct themselves at a table. Her husband behaved like the pigs at the trough, all grunts and mashing sounds.

She nibbled at her own meal, though her stomach was in no mood for food. While she chewed, she reflected on her past, back when she was fifteen, and on her parents. She thought back to the reasons why they had sold her to the bully seated in front of her.

***

June 1851

Maggie's father took ill with pneumonia one winter, and it left his lungs weak. He weakened even more when her eldest brother was killed in a farming accident three years later. It was a dreadful incident: the boy was working parring nettles when a bull charged. A field worker for the squire had let it into the field by mistake. After his death and her father's illness, Maggie and her mother ran the farm for a few months.

Maggie, although fifteen years old and fit, found the work of two men, added to her own chores, far too hard. The family struggled to maintain the fields and the barns, yet, despite working all hours of the day, the squire reclaimed them and the main farmhouse for others to manage. He allowed the Eagle family to stay on, rent-free, in a small, one bed-roomed cottage on the edge of his estate. Her mother claimed that, with him being partly to blame for her brother's death, it was his way of clearing his guilt.

Maggie slept on a narrow truckle bed for a few months and earned a meagre wage working the fields for the new tenants. She took on more chores around the home, but nothing she ever did for her mother was right. Despite her hard work and bringing in a salary, her mother labelled Maggie as lazy. A good for nothing. Her father was too weak to argue, keeping quiet and simply turning over in his bed whenever her mother ranted and raved about trivial things. Maggie was surprised when she returned home from work one evening to find the widower, Jacob Sawbury, seated at their table. It appeared he had approached her father about Maggie going to work for him. Maggie, grateful her time at home might be nearing its end, listened to his offer.

'It'll be more than the Squire pays and a free meal thrown in, providing she can cook.' Neither he nor her mother spoke directly to her, and Maggie dared not speak out.

Cramped living conditions, a sick father, and an ungrateful mother were not the ingredients for a happy home. Farmer Sawbury offered her accommodation and work. Maggie prayed for a better life, and now her chance might be just around the corner; however, this farmer had a poor reputation in the village, and Maggie became nervous about her future. Her father tried to say something, but a coughing fit prevented him from asking questions. He waved his hand to her mother, indicating that she should make the decision.

Maggie watched his thin, feeble arm flop onto the grubby blanket. Both she and her father didn't have to guess as to what her mother would decide. Her mother was a cold-hearted woman with little love for Maggie, if any—and money served a better purpose.

'You needn't think you are getting her for nowt. Worth a something, she is. And neither is she staying under your roof without being wed. Marry her, *and* fetch me a hefty bag of coins, and she is yours.' The pair shook hands in a solemn deal, and Maggie stared in despair. Sold for a bag of coins! There had been no point in her protesting, and she did not want to listen to a lecture. She simply hoped life was about to take a turn for the better. Maggie was not going to upset her mother. Arguing might make her change her mind, and Farmer Sawbury was the ticket out of the clutches of a mealy-mouthed woman. As far as Maggie was concerned, her mother was dead. She also knew that, had her father been well, he would have bartered her the same way and probably held out for more money. She was a nobody in the house, merely another mouth to feed.

When I leave here, I will never return. I mean nothing, nothing to them. Nor they to me.

Her mother organised the wedding for the early morning of June second, a Monday. A quiet ceremony would be held at St. Mary's church in Redgrave.

That day, a beautiful sunrise greeted Maggie, but she could not find excitement in the weather nor the wedding. She was tired from her chores of the previous day and from those she had to complete two hours earlier because of the wedding. Also, they were a mismatched couple in Maggie's eyes, and she could not see it to be an ideal arrangement. Her husband-to-be was tall; extremely tall. She was as petite as he was wide-shouldered. Ten years spanned between them. Maggie understood that he had been married when he was her age and his wife had died in childbirth five years after the wedding. Maggie knew no more about the man beside her. She did not even know if he smiled—he had never done so in her presence. His dark eyebrows knitted together across a furrowed brow and mingled with lank, unkempt hair. His face, swarthy dark from working outside in the sunshine, reminded her of the gypsies who moved from farm to farm. He was not a handsome man and most definitely not her choice of husband if romance had been her luxury.

For the ceremony itself, there were no fineries, no gold band, only solemn words. Her parents gave their approval to the nuptials for the official documents. Her mother attended and signed as a witness. When all formalities had been completed, she pulled her shawl around her shoulders and walked away. Not a glance or a word was offered to her daughter. She did not say goodbye or offer her congratulations to her new son-in-law. The woman simply nodded at the vicar and returned home to her husband.

Maggie was left with a stranger.

She looked around at the empty church. Her wedding day—and not one person congratulated her! Even the vicar had taken his coin and left for home without a word of acknowledgement for the young bride.

Bride. Maggie gave an inward sigh. *No pretty gown for me.* Maggie wore the same shabby dress she pulled on every day. To rid it of field aroma, she had rubbed it down with rosemary the evening before the ceremony. It smelled fresher, but she struggled to get it any cleaner. A pathetic outfit for a young girl's wedding attire! She glanced around, trying to make a memory of the day. The light shone through the beautiful stained glass windows and cast shadows of colour across the white stone. It gave her little comfort, but she stared at them nonetheless. A cough echoed around the sanctuary, and she noted her husband beckoned her to leave the building with an abrupt movement of his arm towards the main entrance. 'We've finished here.' His voice resounded and made Maggie cringe. He showed no reverence or respect of where they were. Apart from saying the few words the parson required, he had uttered nothing else. His impatient tone made Maggie feel relieved that he never said any more and just left the building.

Maggie inhaled deeply. *Courage, Maggie. You are a married woman now. A married woman!*

Mrs. Sawbury! Maggie mulled over her new title, shaking her head in disbelief, and stepped out of church behind the man who had given her his name. They walked in silence along Churchway and onto a winding lane that would take her to her new home. Jacob tut-tutted when she stopped to pick a bunch of Stinkwort and Milkweed, but even he could not resist picking a few juicy blackberries. Maggie gathered several for later in the day. The only worldly goods Maggie owned were in a tied piece of flannel: a pinafore that had seen better days, a few strips of rags for her monthly cycle, a pressed flower taken from the garden she had left behind, and now, a few blackberries. The June day was warm, the sky clear, and Maggie in her innocence saw the world in a different light to her new groom. While she collected the juicy fruit, Jacob removed his cap and mopped his brow.

'Ruddy heat, it will bring about a storm, and the crops will suffer.' He kicked a stone into the ditch beside him.

'What crops do you grow, sir?' Maggie was relieved he had broken the quiet spell.

'You can call me Jacob or husband, none of this sir lark. We have wheat, barley, and potato fields. Our cows earn us our squire's rent with their dairy, and the pigs and sheep are the finest around. You'll be in charge of the hens.'

He strode on, muttering, 'Wasted a perfectly good morning because of your mother and her wedding claptrap. That parson was as bad, dragging out his pompous sermon. All for a scrap of a girl to clean for me.'

The more he muttered, the faster he walked. Maggie broke into a trot to keep up with him but found herself lagging behind when they reached the brow of the hill leading to her new home. At the top, she took in her surroundings and let her lungs settle. She had arrived at Windtop Farm.

A patchwork of rust-gold and green fields spread out before her, ablaze with ripened produce that swayed in the wind either side of the meadow. The scene took her breath away. Heads of wheat and barley rippled like waves along the surface of a river. Wild flowers of every colour lined the hedgerows. Various shades of green leaves and stems hosted a rainbow of colours, each nodding their heads in patches woven throughout the meadow. Maggie threw her arms open with glee, releasing the child within. Her fair hair fell from its ribbon and tumbled onto her shoulders. She inhaled the perfume of a summer's day, watched birds swirl their dances on the gentle breeze, butterflies flitting from bush to bush and a rabbit bobbing amongst lush, green vegetation. Below and across the fields, she could see the river Waveney.

'Oh Jacob, it is beautiful! What a glorious meadow! I can see the river—look!' She pointed and called out to Jacob, but he either ignored her or did not hear. He marched on and disappeared down the other side of the hill. Maggie skipped and jumped her way across the meadow towards him.

'Wait for me, husband! Wait for me!'

On the other side of the hill, the view was different. She watched Jacob stride downward towards her new home. All joy drained from her body. Walking slowly down the hillside, she saw a dismal side to the farm.

A large, dark grey two-storey building with a grey slate roof sat central to several outbuildings. Grimy windows with ragged lace glared back in defiance at the new bride. The yard was unkempt, and Maggie knew from that moment her work was going to be hard. Probably harder than the life she had just left. She gave herself a moment to absorb the scene before her.

It's your new home—your responsibility. Maggie Sawbury—wife. You can bring it alive. Make it as beautiful as the meadow. Pull yourself together, there's work to be done.

Not wanting tears on her wedding day, she scraped back her hair into place, retied the ribbon and inhaled a deep, lingering breath, before exhaling, marching down and catching up with Jacob.

Chapter 3

Monday, the 2nd of June, 1851

Large hands pulled her shoulders. Jacob roughly manoeuvred her in front of him and pushed her inside the building. He husband showed no tenderness, and fear tremored through her body and set off a bout of trembling nerves. Maggie stared around the filthy kitchen they had stepped into and shuddered.

Jacob pushed her to one side and said, 'Stop your gawking, woman, and do what I paid for—you cost me a fair coin, and I intend to get my worth. Get this place decent! I 'ain't had time. Not a farmer's job. If you cannot see it, I don't own it. So none of your pesky questions. I will need feeding a decent meal after sundown, but leave me a lunch pail in the milking barn at mid-day. There's a leg o'mutton for the evening meal hanging back there. Make it last the week. I do not tolerate waste.'

With that, her husband waved towards an area she assumed was the larder, turned heel and stomped out of the building, creating a swirl of dust as he went.

Left to her own devices and relieved that Jacob had left, Maggie laid her goods in a cleaner corner of the room and rolled up her sleeves, deciding to go and have a look in the upper floor first. She climbed the stairs, grimacing at the clods of mud dried on every step, the majority of which had the likeness of cow dung.

Pushing open each door she came to, she could do nothing but stare at the clutter and mess facing her. A large, airless room appeared to be Jacob's bedroom. However, Maggie was convinced he housed many an animal there at times. It was filthy and smelled stale. In truth, it stank. She opened the window and watched particles dance in the sunrays.

Then she turned and shuddered when she saw the large straw mattress she assumed she would be expected to sleep on with her new husband. The linen was black and grimy, not one corner indicated the original colour. She could see no other coverings in the room, but Maggie knew she wouldn't be able to sleep in such filth.

How could he sleep with the smell? What a disgusting man. Never mind, this wife will change his habits.

While the sunshine and breeze were in full swing, Maggie ensured she wasted no time. Stripping the sheets away from the thick mattress, Maggie took them into the yard. She dragged the large tin bath from off a hook beside the kitchen door and over to the water pump. She then threw in the bedding and pumped out water with as much energy as she could muster. The water forced dirt away from the material, but they still looked grimy. Maggie took off her boots and trampled over the grey sheets to release more of the dirt, noting the linen had once been ivory in colour. She jumped harder and harder, determined to bring out the cleaner shade—she would prefer a light grey to the blackened mess she had been confronted with earlier. For some unknown reason, jumping on the sheets made her want to sing. She added a lively tune to the first words that came to her and bounced around in water.

'Tra la la fiddle de de, it's the farmer's life for me'. Suddenly she felt self-conscious and foolish. Not knowing who might be around and watching, she stopped singing, stepped out of the bath and dried her feet.

She found a bar of green, hard soap in the kitchen and rubbed it over the washing as hard as she could. Again, the water pump did its job. Prior to starting her chores, she had found—to her great joy—a battered mangle to squeeze out the excess water. It leant beside a barn, and to

Maggie's delight both rollers were in good condition, and the handle turned with ease. She pulled it across the yard and placed it by the bath. Her small body ached as she hauled the wet linen through the machine, but she was determined to get the job done.

'Jacob Sawbury will never sleep on dirty sheets again,' she muttered while working.

There was a long length of twine attached to the house, running across the yard to a large acorn tree. Maggie threw the bedding across the line, and the summer breeze did the rest.

Every corner of the farmhouse was in need of a good clean. Maggie spent her wedding day airing and beating rugs, washing walls and making the house a home. While she cut chunks of cheese and bread for her husband's lunch pail, she made a mental note of chores she would have to complete before winter set in on the farm. Her summer was to be a busy one, inside and out. There was no love in her heart for the man she had married, but she fell in love with her home within a matter of hours, despite its gloomy exterior.

She carried the lunch pail to the milking sheds and sensed a moment of disappointment that she had met no one on the way or inside the vast room. Suddenly, she felt alone and deserted, and the tears threatened to spill.

Maggie girl, stop your nonsense! There is no one bossing you around, be grateful for small mercies.

A sudden urge to bake something tasty to impress Jacob took over, and the tears abated. Maybe something sweet and savoury would make him smile and relax a bit. Leaving the pail in a prominent place, she stepped outside and took in the scene before her.

The chicken pen stood large and rundown opposite the kitchen window. Maggie had watched the hens peck at the ground, earlier, while washing at the sink, and she had made a mental note to consider the repairs required to keep the hens from fox attacks. Glancing towards the back of the farmhouse and beyond the barn, she could see the edge of another building. It looked in need of repair, too, but so did the farmhouse, which was occupied nonetheless. There was a chance this smaller building might be too.

Curiosity got the better of her. It took a lot of energy to push open a heavy wooden door, but behind it, Maggie found the dairy room, which made the effort worthwhile. Strong-smelling cheeses wrapped in muslin cloth sat on a shelf. Blue and white jugs of cream and generous sized mounds that, upon investigation, proved to be pats of butter were covered in the same cloth on another.

Maggie found ideal ingredients for her menu but felt nervous about taking from the room. After a brief spell of contemplating if she should find someone to ask if she could take the items, she reminded herself that she was now mistress of the house and that it was her right. She lifted down an empty pitcher, filled it with creamy milk, and cut a block of butter from a large mound. It was freshly churned and ideal for pastry. As instructed by Jacob, a mutton leg was to be on the menu, and she discovered a pail of fresh vegetables by the back door.

In the orchard, Maggie found a few windfall apples, and with the precious blackberries she had picked on their walk from the village, it was enough to produce a perfect dessert. Maggie salivated at the thought of the sweet pie for their wedding supper. Further investigation produced a jar of clotted cream, and she placed it into her apron pocket.

'What d' you think you are doing, pray tell?' A female voice with an extremely broad, local accent cut through the silence of the room. Maggie slopped the milk over the top of her jug and turned around to face the voice. A large-bosomed girl about her age glared back at her, stern-faced and with her hands on her hips.

'I…I…,' Maggie stammered, a warm flush rising up her neck because the girl sent a wave of guilt through her.

You have a right to be here, Maggie! Tell her who you are! Stand your ground! Fresh start. No bullies... remember?

She pulled herself to full height and retorted back in a voice loaded with indignation, 'I suppose you could say I am the owner of this milk and jug and do not have to justify myself. You, I assume, are the dairymaid?'

She put down the jug and held out her hand. 'I am Mrs. Sawbury, wife of the owner. My husband and I married this morning.'

The girl laughed. 'So you are the poor gal that's got herself trapped up with that great ...'

Maggie watched the girl's face flush. There was something awkward in her manner when she stopped mid-sentence. The smile went from her face as if Maggie had slapped it, her voice softened, 'I—um—wish you happiness on your wedding day, Mrs. Sawbury.'

Frostiness reappeared in her voice when she asked her next question. 'Do you need anything else? Some cheese mayhap?'

'You could start by telling me your name.' Maggie lost the haughty tone she had used when the girl had challenged her. She needed to start afresh; both of them were battling for no reason.

'Lizzie.' The fight appeared to have gone from the girl, and she gave humbler responses now. 'Plain Lizzie, madam.'

Maggie held out her hand. 'How do you do, Lizzie? Please call me Maggie. I fear we may have gotten off with the wrong footing. Friends?'

'Oh, yes, friends is far better than fighting, I always say.' Lizzie held out her plump hand, withdrew it again and wiped it down her pinafore, then shook Maggie's slim one. 'You caught me unawares, see, and I thought you might be a field worker, stealing like, and the boss, well he don't take kindly.'

'I understand and apologise for not finding you to ask you what I could remove to the kitchen. I assume most of this produce is for market?'

'It is, but you come and take whatever you need, whenever you need it—you're the missus after all.'

The two women exchanged chatter for a few moments, and Maggie left the dairy knowing she had made a firm friend for life. The girl had intimated she was relieved her boss had married. Maggie sensed no love was lost between her husband and his dairymaid.

After preparing the meal, Maggie collected eggs, laughing and shooing the chickens from underneath her skirts. Her wedding day had been unusual, but Maggie had loved every moment of finding her way around the kitchen cupboards. Each pan she found, she scrubbed until it gleamed. Her frustrations with her parents gave her the elbow grease she required. The kitchen was her domain. No sour-faced mother issuing orders, no father coughing and spluttering in the corner. Nothing could take away the joy she had found in preparing her home that day.

***

The wedding feast Maggie had eaten that day was heartier than the one she nibbled at now, and meeting Lizzie had been by far the better memory of her wedding day. Her wedding night was most certainly a memory she would rather forget.

Jacob had given her no warning. While she had sat brushing her hair, he had strode over, grabbed her wrist and dragged her to the bed. Maggie had been too shocked to speak. He had stripped off her flimsy cotton nightgown with not one endearing word, had pushed her onto the bed, turned her onto her face, and then had penetrated her without words. He had ridden her like a horse, grunting like a pig all the while. No gentle caress from his hands had landed on her body, no loving words had left his salivating lips. He was cruel, cold and unforgiving. There had been no respect for her virginity, and he had ridiculed her tears. In a pompous torrent of how lucky she had been, he had also boasted his right to take her whenever he felt the urge.

The memory was painful, and Maggie bit hard onto the bread crust she was chewing. His regular bedding ritual led to her first pregnancy before she was sixteen years of age. The joy of knowing she was to have his child was not evident, nor had it kept him away from her for eight months. A few days after she had been delivered of a stillborn daughter, he had forced her into submission again. The pain she suffered gave her sleepless nights, and she was relieved when she realised she was pregnant again. In her naivety, she had hoped it would keep him away from her for a few months. Sadly, Maggie endured the pain repeatedly, but now he was becoming heavy with his fists. She hid the bruises as best she could.

During their summer together, Nathaniel's father—the Squire's son—had noticed the odd scar and fading bruise. His gentle kisses had soothed the ache away, but that was before he had inflicted his own version of pain—before he had broken her heart.

Jacob gave her no time to continue her walk down memory lane. He pushed his bowl to one side and belched, startling her from her daydream. 'What I have done to deserve you as a wife, I do not know. Your mother lied. You are a no cook. You ruin the perfect meat I provide.'

Maggie suffered his insults each and every mealtime. She shrugged her shoulders as her only acknowledgement and set about clearing the table. He never left a scrap on his plate, for all his complaining.

Jacob went to the fire and spat into the grate, then turned to speak to her, but she turned her back. She sensed his eyes watching her every move. The tension in her shoulders made her neck ache. Her body never relaxed when he was in the house.

'I need to wash that pigswill down with a draft of ale. Losing another child should earn me a few free quarts down at the Cross Keys. Do not worry about keeping the bed warm, I will not be in it tonight.'

Maggie turned to share a look of disapproval. With a laugh and a sneer across his cruel mouth, he looked older than his years, and she saw into the future. A senile old man with spite in his heart. It did not worry her he was sleeping elsewhere—she knew he bedded Lizzie when he could—, but Maggie had become crafty. She had learned that the look of distaste she threw him made him determined to carry out his threat. It meant she got an undisturbed night of sleep. He fell for it every time. Lizzie had often hinted that he slept with another woman in the village when he visited the tavern, so she did not always suffer his lustful ways either. Maggie hoped tonight that both she and Lizzie would be left in peace. She gave a loud huff as she picked up dirty crockery.

'Ah, the lady of the house is upset. Cannot abide the thought another woman finds her husband desirable,' Jacob taunted. 'Well, madam, just for that look, I will not grace you with my presence. Or mayhap, I shall return… however the mood takes me.'

Maggie held her tongue. It was best she did not say a word. In an unrushed manner, she collected his clean boots and jacket from the small hallway between the kitchen and the stairs. She sighed; he was hard work, and she only desired peace. A quiet evening was very welcome. The sooner he left the better. If he drank plenty, he would not come home to her as he had hinted. When he was ready to leave, she thought of another way of keeping him at bay.

'Oh, I nearly forgot. I sold several jams and jellies yesterday. There's a copper or two left in the tin. I will not need it for stores this week, so why not take them. Treat yourself and enjoy a brandy tonight? It hasn't been pleasant for you losing this baby either. It was another daughter by the way. A dear little girl. She had your features.' Maggie used soft tones to bring on a melancholy mood. Her husband enjoyed being the centre of attention, so if he could add layers to his sad story he would.

'Another daughter gone? Looked like me, you say? Get the tin down, I deserve a drink for the shock of it all.' He held out his hand, and she placed four coins in his palm.

He took her by surprise when he closed his fingers around hers and squeezed them. A glazed looked came over his face. Maggie didn't move, and wondered if he was considering her or if thoughts of his first wife had emerged. The only woman he had loved, or so she'd found out through one of his drunken speeches.

Roughly, he shook her hand away and left the room. The twilight shadows moved across the yard as he walked by the window. He glanced in and sneered. It made her shiver. Maggie moved away and tried to shake off his image. She lit a candle, and the warm glow added a pleasant ambiance. She collected stockings and flannels for repair. An evening spent mending would relax her. Now was her time to mourn.

Chapter 4

'Get your lazy backside out of bed. I'm home and want food.'

Jacob dragged the covers from around Maggie. Dazed and trying to focus in the darkness of the room, she took a few seconds to compose herself.

She shivered as the damp, cool air assaulted her body. A mix of fear and chill were in the shiver.

'Jacob. What hour is it?' She clambered out of bed and winced when her feet touched the cold floor.

'What hour?' His voice with its whining mockery tormented her. 'You need the time? Time you fed your husband, woman!' Jacob stood swaying at the end of the bed.

Maggie realised he was drunk and had forgotten his threat to stay out all night. He was at his most dangerous now.

She pulled on her loose outer gown, grabbed a cap and pushed her hair into it. There was no point trying to pacify him in this state. She knew she had no choice but to feed him.

'Of course, you are hungry. It is a long walk home from the village. Let me get the skillet hot and fix you a feast.' She chatted while she dressed, and when she walked past him, she prayed he wouldn't grab at her. She was still tender from her delivery and could not risk him forcing himself upon her.

'I've got just the thing for a hungry man. Fresh bacon. Thick slices,' she chattered as she walked out of the door.

'Stop yarning about it, woman, get and cook it,' Jacob demanded.

He followed her down the stairs; she could sense him behind her as they entered the kitchen. Maggie embraced its warmth, and Jacob staggered to the chair closest to the fire. Maggie always ensured it was kept burning, although in the summer months it could make the room too hot. Often they had to attend to animals experiencing difficult labours, and hot water was always called for during those times. Tonight she was thankful she kept the hearth alive. The darkness outside indicated that dawn hadn't broken through, and a wind whistled under the door. The warm room made the early rise bearable.

She busied herself cutting chunks of bacon and bread. The skillet spat and smoked in the hearth. Wary all the time of keeping Jacob out of arm's reach and in a buoyant mood. Maggie laid out the skillet with his food. She smiled as she handed Jacob a mug with a generous measure of warm preserving cider. It was bitter, but he did not seem to mind.

'Mm, there is something special about bacon when it is cooking. Do you not agree, husband?' Maggie kept up the pretence of being happy to cook for him in the wee small hours.

'Stop your chattering, and just cook it, woman, didn't I just tell you?' Jacob took a swig from the mug and sat staring into the glowing embers. Desperate not to antagonise him any further, Maggie rushed through the cooking process.

'Well, here you are then. Enjoy your supper.' She placed a plate of bacon, egg and fresh bread onto the table.

Then she sat in her seat and watched him rise from his chair. He staggered to the table, slumped into the chair and bit into his food. Egg yolk dribbled from the left corner of his mouth.

She could not stand to look anymore. 'I have to go to the market tomorrow, so I might as well make a batch of scones to sell, now I am awake.' She rose from the table.

He enjoyed her scones and would never prevent her from baking them.

Therefore, his next words startled her. 'Sit down, and stay where you are. There is something we need to discuss. What I mean is, I have something to say. Sit and listen.' Jacob spat out the words along with crumbs, and her stomach churned. *Oh, my dear God—please, let it be about the farm and not about babies and bedroom activities!*

She sat quietly while he finished his meal. Her eyes felt heavy as she watched him go through the usual eating routine: wiping the plate clean with his bread, belching and dragging his mouth clean on the back of his shirtsleeve.

'There's word in the village. I heard it in the Key's tonight.' He sat upright; the food appeared to have sobered him somewhat. His face was tinged with alcohol, and his nose became red and mottled. His eyes, although pink, were steady and focused on hers.

'Word? What sort of word?' Maggie was unnerved and shuffled in her seat.

'Word has it a baby has been found. That Arlington woman and her flimsy brother found it along the road to Wortham Ling. Thrown naked into a bush, it was. Cruel, to treat a babe in that way.'

He threw back his head and downed the rest of the mug. Maggie sat stiffly in the seat. Her hands gripped the sides. She dared not to speak. She wanted to yell that the baby had been left by a broken-hearted mother, not naked and thrown into the hedge, but gently placed. She wanted to scream out he was the cruel one, and if he was not such a cruel man, their child would be in her arms at that moment. Had he been a better man, she may not have suffered the loss of baby number three. The kick in the stomach he gave her had ended that poor child's life.

She also knew that if he were a better man, she would never have broken her marriage vows by having an affair with the Squire's son. Nathaniel would never have been born, and she would be asleep in her bed with a clear conscience. How dare he spout off about cruel people?

Knowing she could say none of those things, Maggie gripped the edge of the chair so hard her fingers ached. She willed him with every breath to finish his rant as swiftly as he had started. Eventually she found her voice and encouraged Jacob to tell her more.

'How dreadful. W-was it alive? You said it had been thrown into the bush…' She knew it was a fanciful tale, embellished to make the story more exciting. Only she knew the truth.

'Alive and screaming the village down, by all accounts. Could be heard all the way in Wortham. Unlucky mite has been landed with the Bible-spouting, pious Arlington family. From what they say, he's going to stay there until they have found his family, mainly his mother; she has to answer for her actions. I told 'em. Family? They do not deserve a baby. I had just lost my own daughter; my heart was broken for the child. Generous, them folks were. Sent their condolences to you. Brandies for me. Good folk.' He put his arms on the table and used them as a pillow for his head. He gave a small snort.

Maggie wanted to laugh. She suppressed the urge. If she did, it would earn her a good hiding. His favourite pastime was to belittle and vent his dislike for the villagers, especially those with more money and land than he had. Only those who put coins his way were a priority in his life. Brandy talk had taken over, and he was spouting nonsense. Maggie needed to end the conversation. She was tired and wary of Jacob in his drunken state. He continued to eat, slurping down the food and washing it down with warm cider. 'That was generous of them, you are right. So it was a little boy then? The Arlingtons are good people, Jacob. They will care for him, I am sure. How old is he?' She yawned and longed for sleep. She hoped Jacob would slump sooner rather than later.

'Eh?' Jacob looked up from the table. 'Newborn, 'twas a newborn. Which reminds me? Tomorrow, forget the market, and get yourself down to the Arlington house. They are expecting you.' He put his head back in his arms.

'I beg your pardon?' A chill ran through her body, and Maggie felt faint with what might be coming next. Had they guessed?

'Wet nurse. They need a wet nurse.' The muffled words hit Maggie like a herd of cattle.

'I beg your pardon? They need a what?' Maggie was stunned by his words.

'Titties, teats, whatever you want to call them. They need yours, and I said if they pay the price, they could have them. Mind, I told them it had to fit in around your farm work. Not having slacking off from my wife. No, sir, I told them, my Maggie will have milk a-flowing, what with having just lost our girl. If she can help the boy, she will. And so you will, madam. Oh, you will. The purse is full and will remain so while those do their job.' He pointed towards her breasts and rose from the table, pushing back his chair and approaching her end of the table.

Maggie looked up at him. She trembled.

He stared down at her, daring her to defy him with his demand.

'You mean I have to feed a strange baby? You want me to feed another woman's child?' Maggie could barely speak. Of all the coincidences in the world, she should fall into this one.

Her breasts had been sore all day. Maggie had bound them earlier to delay the flow. Now she was to have his blessing and feed her own son. It truly was laughable.

She jumped when he banged his hand on the table. Her nerves were on edge, and she was tired. His words amazed her. He would never know it was the first time she had ever felt grateful to him since he took her away from her parents.

'You will do as I say. Do you hear me? Morning and night, every day, you will feed that child. You will not disgrace me and let me down. I gave my word to their man you would be there at the start of the day. None of your lazy backchat, do you hear?'

Maggie responded carefully. 'I apologise. I am tired, and you have surprised me, husband. If you say I must, then I must. Very well. Now I have to get some sleep. I will need some if I am to be in fine feeding form for the Arlington family.' Her voice held a touch of sarcasm but not enough to make him angry. Just a touch to make it sound as if she was put out and that it was to be a chore.

'I'm done in myself. We will turn in and talk some more in the morning. No, in fact, there will be no more talking. You will do as you are told, or there will be a lesson from my belt for you.' Jacob left the room, and Maggie listened as he banged around upstairs. She curled up on her comfortable chair and pulled a blanket over her body. The snores from above gave her the opportunity to stay in the warmth, with the wonder of the conversation they had just had going through her mind.

In a few hours, she would see her son. Once again, she would hold him in her arms. She closed her eyes, thanked God and drifted into a comfortable sleep.

Chapter 5

Weak rays of sunlight worked their way into the room and touched her face. Maggie stretched her body. Her back ached, and she would have given anything for a few more hours of sleep. She glanced over at the table. There sat the dirty plate from the meal she had cooked Jacob four hours previously. It had not been a dream.

Wearily she rose from the chair and slipped outside to the water pump. The cold air indicated autumn was well and truly set. Her chores would become harder, and the daylight hours would fade into darkness much quicker. She did not need more work, nor did she need to be away from the farm for hours on end. Maggie vowed she would find a way to make her workload fit in with feeding Nathaniel. Her stomach flipped at the thought. When the water jug was full, she returned with a second. She knew she was clean from the previous day, but she wanted to deal with the chickens and cows before leaving the farm. She was not going to arrive at the Arlington's smelling like one of their animals.

Maggie crushed sage leaves and rubbed them through her hair. She prided herself on her healthy teeth and rubbed a few leaves to clean them. For some reason, thoughts of her mother came to her. The only gift her mother had ever given her was the knowledge of herbs, recipes handed down from her own. Maggie shuddered at the sudden memory of her mother. A woman she had never disliked so much in her life. Had she been a nicer person, someone Maggie could love, she would have taken Nathaniel to her. However, it had not been meant to be, and she suppressed all melancholy thoughts and concentrated upon the task ahead. Her mother was not going to ruin this day.

She looked up at the sky. No rain threatened, which was a blessing since the walk into Redgrave village was a long one. Maggie realised there was a way she could save time. If she moved quickly, she could leave with the others on the cart bound for Diss market. She tidied the kitchen and untied her pinafore.

As she was folding it away, her husband entered the room. 'I'm starving,' he grumbled.

There was no greeting, no morning kiss, just a blunt statement about his stomach and the unsavoury scratching of body parts. Maggie had already set his place and poured his tea into a large mug. She stirred vigorously, and the spoon clanged against the tin.

'Keep the ruddy thing quiet, cannot you? My head is pounding. I work too hard, that is my trouble.'

Maggie bit back the retort that the brandy might have brought it about, but she said nothing.

'Do not forget. You have to get to the Arlington's today.' He held up his hand. 'I want no answers back. I am master in my own house. What I say here, you will obey.'

Again, Maggie said nothing. There was nothing to say.

'Did you hear me, woman? The Arlington house today. Remember?'

Maggie sighed and added a resigned tone to her voice. 'If you insist, husband. If you think it is the right thing to do.'

'Of course it is right. I am always right.' Jacob puffed out his chest.

Pompous fool. If only you knew! Maggie felt a flutter of nervous excitement and suppressed an urge to tell him the truth. To throw it in his face and rid him of his righteous attitude.

She prepared a large pan of creamy oats and a stack of sandwiches. While Jacob sat in silence eating his second breakfast of the day, she took the pan over to the farmhand cottage. Lizzie was already there. Her job was to clean and wash for the men. Lizzie kept their mealtime on schedule.

'Morning, Lizzie. Here, I prepared a batch of creamed oats for breakfast and a lunch pail; I thought it would save you a job. I could need a helping hand with the milking today. Jacob has found me another job in the village, as if I did not have enough on my shoulders. Could you tell the boys to wait for me? I need a ride into the village.'

Lizzie smiled, and her smile bore a touch of sympathy. 'I hear he got you a wet nurse job at that woman Arlington's home. It'll be painful for you, though happen, it'll help take 'way your own heart-wrench.'

Maggie nodded in response. She did not question how Lizzie had found out. She knew it would be the talk of the farm. No doubt, one of the men had been out with Jacob drinking. He had come home, so she knew he had not been in Lizzie's bed.

She went across the room and put the pan onto the fire hook. 'It will be hard, and I am dumbfounded Jacob could do such a thing. I am sure that, aside from the money, he thought it would help me recover. It's a boy. It would have been harder if it had been a little girl. After...' Maggie pulled what she hoped was a sad face.

Lizzie just nodded in sympathy.

Maggie smiled back. She could not say Jacob had given her the most wonderful gift in the world. That her heart was singing with joy.

Lizzie broke her train of thought. 'If you make the oats and lunch every morning, I'll a help you with whatever chores I can. Mind, if Jacob sees, he will not be too happy.' Lizzie helped herself to a portion of breakfast and nodded to the ceiling. 'Better get this down me. They'll be a rattling about soon. Don't you be a wurrygut about me helping you; most of my chores are done. The others can wait 'til this evening. They are peat-digging today, so I will get a bit o' rest. You do what you have to, gal.'

On impulse, Maggie kissed her cheek. 'You are good to me. Thank you, Lizzie. I will see you in the barn.'

Her mouth full, Lizzie nodded. Maggie left to collect the eggs, her steps much faster than the day before. If asked, Maggie would have sworn she was floating on air.

While collecting the eggs, she watched the hens clucking around the young chicks. She envied the simplicity of their lives, wondering if they felt any sadness when the young were removed from their breast. Never would she want any human or animal feel the pain she had felt the day before!

Maggie set aside a few good-sized eggs as a gift for the Arlington household. She wanted to give something, a gesture of thanks.

Her wardrobe was simple. Over the years, she had made a few dresses for everyday wear. They were not pretty but serviceable. Money skimmed from the egg sales helped buy cheap fabric. Today she wore the least worn one and a clean apron. She brushed her hair back into a ponytail and tied her Sunday bonnet in place. It was plain black with a cream-laced edge and a full brim shading her face. Her shawl was warm and convenient for the present climate. She rubbed her boots with a mix of beeswax and lanolin. They were scuffed but as clean as they would ever get. Maggie did not stop to look in the mirror. She knew there would be a shabbily attired woman staring back at her. Not something she wanted to see at that moment.

Jacob called out to her.

'Don't dally around upstairs, you lazy upstart. We are down the river edge for reed and sedge cutting today. The small barn needs thatching. Some of us work for our daily bread.'

Maggie shook her head. The small barn would never be thatched, the reeds would rot beside it. Jacob used the work as an excuse to build muscle and drink away his thirst.

'Don't wear yourself, husband. I am leaving on the cart, so there is plenty of time,' she replied.

A knock at the door indicated the arrival of her transport. She glanced around the room one last time, making sure that her chores were in hand. The better part of her day was yet to come.

When she stepped out into the yard, the sun, although not summer-hot, shone around the hills. It brought beauty to a grey blot on the landscape.

Chapter 6

The dray was full of produce, clucking chickens, three workers, Maggie, and a variety of vessels containing milk and cider. They filled every square inch until it nigh overflowed. The others chattered amongst themselves, allowing Maggie to sit quietly and concentrate on her own thoughts.

What on earth has Jacob got me into?

Excitement, trepidation and the longing to see her son again made her feel queasy. She did not know if she would be able to hold him and not let her feelings show.

What would happen to me if they found out? Jacob would swing for me, that's for sure.

So many questions tumbled around her mind. She tried to focus on the conversation the others were having, but it bored her.

She glanced around as a pheasant ran across their path. A grubby child in nothing but rags followed it. His hair was matted to his head, and his eyes were wild, intent on catching his prize. The cart came to a standstill while they laughed at his antics. The fact that he would never catch it in a month of Sundays had not crossed his mind. He ran around and around the cart until his wind gave out and his scrawny legs could no longer keep up the pace.

Maggie realised they had reached the place she had given birth the day before. Fear built upon sadness, making a mountain of darkness in her mind. It blocked out the sunlight and the laughter they had just enjoyed. The child would be her son in the future if she gave the game away. She had to stay in control. He was better off with the Arlington family. Her own feelings must not mask what was important for Nathaniel.

'Here, lad,' she called out to the boy. 'I think you have earned this for entertaining us this morning.' She handed him a small cob loaf and a jar of jam.

With a mumbled thank-you, he snatched the gift and ran into the trees.

Maggie smiled. 'Come along, our fun is over. He will feast well.'

The entrance to the village was busy. Drovers had their flocks amble down the middle of the street. On the common ground, cows mooed and chewed cud, watched over by young children. Their parents would be negotiating inside the inns and stay there the best part of the day. It was the children who did the work, got a soaking when it rained and missed out on their education for several days. For some, if a chill set in, they would miss far more. Again, Maggie was reminded that this was the life her son would endure.

She clambered down from the cart. Lizzie came to her, and this time she allowed herself to enjoy the warmth of a friend's hug.

'Good luck, gal. I hope you get on all right. Don't you bother yourself about the cows tonight. I spoke with the others, and they are going to help me after dark. Misery guts'll never know. Only tonight, though—can't let you get away with relaxing every day.' Lizzie gave a little laugh at her own joke to lighten the moment.

'Thank you, Lizzie. You are good to me, bless you. Now, boys, get along to Diss, and make sure that lot get sold and keep the boss happy. Oh, look, here he is now. I thought he was gathering reeds today. He must have changed his mind and walked down with the old bull. How appropriate!'

The rest of the group laughed with her. They were her closest friends. All had suffered the spiteful nature of her husband at one point in their lives.

'He'll be in fine fettle in the Key's when he gathers his coins from the sale. The old bull ain't worth but an ale or two. No thatching on the barn roof this winter then, eh, gal?'

'I think you are right there, Lizzie. Same old story.' Maggie clambered down from the cart and bade them goodbye.

Her heart sank when she heard her husband yell from the end of the road, 'Wife! I need a word!' He raised the stick he used to guide the bull through the street.

Maggie could see him out of the corner of her eye, but she made no indication she had heard him. She did not want to meet up with Jacob. He was bound to say something to upset her, and she needed to stay composed, to avoid confrontation. Pretending she had not heard him, she moved quickly along the main pathway and entered a courtyard with narrow cobbled lanes branching from its four sides. A quick glance before she entered one on her left showed that Jacob had not followed and had continued with the bull. She heaved a sigh of relief and slowed her pace. When she reached the large house that belonged to Mr and Mrs. Arlington, she stopped to compose herself. She had passed this way on many an occasion and had admired the property. Now she saw it in a different light. This was the home of her son.

A beautiful red-bricked building stood before her. It was set detached in its own grassy grounds. Green iron railings declared the property boundary, and an ornate gate showed the entrance to a pretty floral garden. Even in the autumn, it shared its colours with those who took a moment to admire them. The path led to a cream-panelled front door. On both sides of the door were large bay windows, and a green iron bench sat under each one.

The delicate features entranced Maggie. Pretty was the word she would use to describe it to Lizzie, later that day. Not handsome, just simply pretty. It was not as large and grand as the squire's mansion but far larger than the farmhouse. The building looked warm and inviting. Ornaments lined the ridge of the rooftops, and Maggie counted three double chimneys on each roof. Fancy cream woodwork trimmed the insides of each one. It reminded Maggie of lace—delicate and pretty. She walked past the front gate and turned around to the back of the property, where she let herself in through a tall wooden gate.

The yard was active with staff, and they nodded to her in recognition. Many of them she had met over the years, some she had grown up with on her old farm.

She smiled back and carried on to the back door of the property. She came across two doors and hesitated. The larger of the two was partially open and, going by the breakfast smells that wafted from it, Maggie instinctively knew it was the kitchen. The other was possibly the meat store.

She knocked against the hard wood of the door and stepped inside.

A plump woman strode towards her; Maggie knew her as Jennie Bowter, the family cook. They had often spoken outside church, and Maggie always sent the first batch of cream for her. The squire's cook was mealy-mouthed, so she got second batch. Maggie had her ways and means of getting even.

'Sorry for your loss, Maggie. Mrs. Arlington told me about it; she also told me to expect you this morning.' Jennie Bowter indicated a chair, and Maggie sat down. 'I shan't give you a hug as I am sure it will bring on the tears. I know it did to me, and Mr Bowter too, come to that, when I lost my three. Your time will come, lass, just be patient. You have a little gem of a baby to nurse today.

A golden child, Mr Arlington called him. It was quite a moment when we were introduced. Nanny is made up. She was missing Master Leonard, sad loss for them all. Well, listen to me gabble on. You stay there, and I will draw a nice cup of tea a'fore you go upstairs. Nanny's instructions. She said you'd be tired after your walk from the farm.'

'Thank you, Jennie. I was fortunate to ride with the staff going to market. I am weary, though. Jacob woke me to tell me the news of this baby, and I was resting after the loss of my own.' Maggie sighed, and Jennie Bowter offered a sympathetic smile. Maggie felt dreadful telling lies to such a good woman, but she could not let her guard down.

While Maggie sipped her tea, two of the young scullery maids dropped in to say hello, and the butler/valet, who was also the cook's husband, patted her shoulder, his only greeting. While Mrs. Bowter finished preparing her dish, shouting orders at her young staff, Maggie glanced around the kitchen. The scullery was off to the left, and the banging of pans as they were being washed, accompanied by a giggle or two, gave life to the room. It was a big kitchen with ivory, tiled walls and red, quarry-tiled floors. Maggie sat at an enormous pine table, which had recently been scrubbed to a rich shade of honey. High-backed, matching wooden chairs sat around it—she counted twelve in total.

The cook worked at the other end amongst a cloud of flour. Maggie guessed meals were a lively event in this part of the house and suppressed a twinge of envy. The black cooking range sat pride of place. When she spotted the icebox, she more than envied the cook. To have such a luxury item in her kitchen would be a dream. A dresser sat proudly with a variety of jugs and crockery, giving a vibrant colour backdrop against the pale walls. The high windows, designed to stop all distractions, glistened as the sun moved higher in the sky.

Maggie was content to sit and watch the staff go about their work. The butterflies in her stomach returned when Mr Bowter spoke to her. For a moment, Maggie had forgotten why she was waiting.

'Right then, young lady. Let us get you upstairs. There is squalling and screeching going on behind one of the doors. I think the young man is not fond of cow's milk. He has kept the noise up all night. Even the sugar rag Mrs. Bowter sent up for him to suck has not kept the mite happy. Nanny is at the end of her tether. She'll be a sight happy to see you.'

The two of them climbed the stairs, which took them into the end of a large hallway. Maggie glanced along its length. Polished oak furniture topped with lace doilies lined either side, each one housing an ornament or a photograph. A long, narrow carpet, red and gold, lay on the floor, and family portraits decorated the ivory walls. Maggie had never seen such a luxurious entrance in a village house.

Three panelled doors were closed onto the corridor, and she wondered what was behind each one. Bowter— the name he told her to address him by when in the house—promptly explained that one was the front parlour, one the back, and the other was the dining room. Mr Arlington had opted to have his study upstairs, at the front of the building, from where he could view the village and hillside while working. He was in finance and needed a quiet environment in which to work.

'This is the back entrance to the bottom of the stairs. Please use this route every time you come. Now let us get you working.'

The closer to the top they climbed, the more and more nervous Maggie became. She tried to focus on the decorative, twisted wooden balustrades, carved with flowers. She did not envy the girl who had to dust them on a daily basis. Their pattern was a very intricate one.

'The master's room, Mrs. A's, guest one, guest two,' Bowter reeled off the names of each doorway they passed. 'Bathroom, stairs to staff quarters. Guest room three and here we are: the nursery.'

Maggie's head swivelled from side to side as she made a swift note of each one. She did not want to walk into one by mistake.

Bowter tapped on the door of the noisiest room in the house. Nathaniel was pitch perfect with his scream. Maggie could not believe her ears. He was most definitely alive and well. Her breasts tingled—she had unbound them when Jacob told her the news, and the milk was now ready to be expressed.

'Come in, come in!' The family nanny stood before them, holding a bundle of clothing. Quality shawls wrapped around the babe's shoulders. 'Thank goodness you have arrived. It has been an arduous night, I can tell you. This child is a strong-willed one. It is no wonder the fairies put you in the bushes; you were too noisy, little prince. Mrs. Sawbury, firstly I am so sorry you lost your little girl. Your husband told Dukes when he sent out for a wet nurse. A tragic event for you. A blessing for us.'

Maggie stood by the doorway. Bowter beckoned her further into the room, but her legs would not move. She wanted to turn and run. The moment had arrived, and Maggie knew the minute she held her son again, she would never be able to let go. It was time for her to confess. As she opened her mouth to speak, the nanny beat her to it, and with gentle encouragement, Maggie stayed quiet.

'Maggie, I can call you Maggie, can I?'

Maggie nodded.

'My dear girl, I know you must be saddened by the task ahead of you. Have you done this before?'

Maggie shook her head.

'Well then,' continued the nanny, 'let us start by making you comfortable. Come and sit by the fire. You can hold the baby and start when you are ready. Thank you, Bowter, I think we will be fine now.'

The butler left the room, nudging Maggie forward as he did so. He gave her a reassuring smile and closed the door behind him.

The cries from Nathaniel sounded louder now the door was closed, and Maggie could bear it no longer. She removed her shawl and placed it over the back of an oaken nursing chair. The room was warm, so she rolled up her sleeves.

'I know this may sound rude and rather personal, but you did wash—er—around the area this morning, did you not?'

Maggie, still at a loss for words, merely nodded. She sat down and held out her arms. The nanny placed her son in her arms. It was a momentous occasion, one Maggie would never forget. His warm body moulded into hers, exhaling a sweet perfume that made her smile down at him. She stroked his lips, pursed in readiness for another bout of screaming. Then, she slowly unbuttoned the front of her frock and bodice, a little embarrassed to do so in front of the nanny. But the woman had the good grace to recognise the situation, walking to the other side of the room and busying herself with the laundry.

The child drew up his knees, and she could feel his tiny body tense. The screams, his red face, and her readiness to serve the one she loved brought forth her maternal instinct. 'Shush, little one. It's all right, the cows have done their work, now give me a chance to do mine,' she said in hushed tones. His screams subsided to gentle sobs.

Maggie teased his lips with her nipple, a droplet of fluid leaking onto his lips. He opened his eyes. Mother and son stared at each other, and love reflected both ways. Maggie hoped instinct would tell him this was his mother, that he could feed from her and that she would nourish him. He mouthed at the teat, and Maggie's stomach tightened. When he started suckling noisily she knew instinct had told him.

The nanny handed her a piece of muslin in case she needed it and stared down at the feeding child. 'My, you have the knack for this, Maggie! A thank you to our God that you have the milk. His lordship there surely appreciates it. Do you know this is the first time he has been quiet since he arrived? I am normally good at settling the little ones, but this little fellow did not want to know. But you—look at the pair of you! God in his wisdom gave you each other to heal your pain.' She smiled kindly at Maggie.

Maggie smiled back, and then looked down at her son. Each moment with him was precious, and she could feel the tears of passion, love and joy rise up. She found her voice and responded, 'He is a beautiful child. I... I understand he is not Mrs. Arlington's baby.' She had to say something, or it would look odd. 'My husband mentioned something about him being abandoned.'

'Hm, poor thing was not so fortunate to have madam as his natural mother. Abandoned he was. Dumped into a hedge by all accounts. It was his lucky day when this family brought him home, I can tell you. Mrs. Arlington lost her only child, Leonard, when he was just two years old. A dear child, and it nigh on broke my heart when he died. The family are meeting today to discuss this little one's future. My prayers are for him to stay. Nanny will look after you, won't she, little man?' She stroked his head so tenderly that Maggie wanted to say 'thank you for caring so much for my son'.

'Madam has instructed Master Leonard's baby items be brought down and into the nursery. A trunk of clothing is being washed and aired as we speak. It will be good to see the nursery used properly again. I was on the brink of despair. Mrs. Arlington told me I could remain here until I found a new position or decided to retire. They have been most generous. Even if it is for a short few weeks, it is good to feel useful again.'

A tear released itself. Maggie could no longer control herself. 'He certainly is a fortunate child. There is a bright future for him in this home. I wish—I hope—' She stammered over her words.

The older woman moved to her and touched her shoulder. 'Ah, there, do not cry girl, be grateful you can help. He will surely help you recover, you wait and see! Now we need to express from you for two more feeds. As I understand it, you are coming down for the late afternoon one. Good, good, he should be content tonight.'

Maggie sat rocking while Nathaniel sated his hunger.

The room was cosy, and the atmosphere comfortable. Maggie was disappointed when Nathaniel stopped sucking and settled into a contented sleep. She brought him to his crib and carefully laid him down, removing his dirty nappy and adjusting his white gown. After she had wrapped him securely, she watched his chest rise and fall, his eyelids twitch and his rosebud mouth make imaginary sucking movements.

'Sleep well, Nathaniel. Sleep tight, little one. I will come back tonight.'

The nanny stood staring at her and said nothing for a moment or two. She had a puzzled look on her face.

'I'm sorry—did you want to lay him down?' Maggie asked.

'No, no, that's fine. He is settled, and that is the important part. I am going to have an hour's rest before his next feed. I think I have earned it. Can I ask something, Maggie?' She wrung her hands as if nervous.

'If I can answer, I will,' Maggie said.

'Well, when you laid him down, you called him Nathaniel, but I thought you lost a daughter. And Mrs. and Mrs. Arlington have not named him yet. It puzzled me.'

Maggie knew she had to maintain control and not falter with her answer. She had made a mistake but had to recover from it without creating suspicion.

'Did I really? The emotions must have gotten to me— forgive me! Nathaniel is the name I gave my first son. I have lost five children, you see, but had only one son. Holding Mrs. Arlington's child made me think of him... I must have said his name aloud. I am sorry. I do hope I haven't caused offence.'

Maggie put on a humble face. She could kick herself for her error.

'Oh, you poor girl! It must be dreadful to lose one child, but five? Nathaniel is a strong name. It brings to mind a handsome man. Think nothing of it. I would have done the same thing in your place. Now run along, and we will see you before sunset. Thank you for helping us, Maggie.'

'It was an honour. I will be back later. Goodbye.'

Maggie grabbed her shawl. She needed to get out of the room before her heart burst. It was full of joy and other emotions. The boards creaked as she moved along the corridor, and she made another mental note of the room she had just left.

Downstairs, the staff were cleaning the many decorations and floors. Maggie slipped down the back stairs and into the kitchen.

The cook, Mrs. Bowter, was rolling out pastry on the large table Maggie had sat at an hour before. She looked up and gave Maggie a beaming smile. 'How did it go, lass? You feel alright, need a hot drink?' She rolled as she talked.

'He took to me straight away and is sleeping sound now. I will not stop for tea; I have to get back to the farm. It is a trek back and forth between chores, so I have to get the timing right.'

'Hold fire, Dukes is going the other side of the village—I am sure he can drop you off at the bottom of Fen lane. If you are quick, you can ask him. Don't be shy. I might not be there later, so take care, and I will see you in the morning.' She went back to her baking, and Maggie slipped out into the yard.

She asked a young boy who was cleaning boots where Dukes could be found. The boy pointed out a man hitching a horse to a small cart.

'Mr Dukes?' Maggie enquired of the extremely handsome, dark-haired male before her. He had a healthy glow. His shirtsleeves were rolled up, and she could see the solid muscles on his forearms. He was most certainly pleasing to the eye. Despite her endeavour to refrain from looking, her imagination moved with each ripple of his muscles. Strong arms to hold a lonely woman.

Stop it at once. He is probably no better than all men—disloyal. Concentrate. Take your eyes off him.

'No mister, just plain Dukes. And what can I do for you, fair lady?' The man continued to organise the driving reins.

'Well, Dukes. The cook said you might be going by Fen lane, and I would appreciate a ride home. I live at Windtop Farm. I would normally walk, but I have chores to do and be back to feed the baby at the end of the afternoon. Would you oblige me, sir?'

Dukes stopped what he was doing and looked at Maggie with deep, brown eyes dressed with long dark lashes. The man turned back to his horse, patted its nose and whispered in its ear. He made a play of listening to the horse. Then he turned back to Maggie and grinned, his smile wide and white, his eyes glistening. 'Roman here said we should offer the lady a ride. She is doing the house a great service. So jump up, I am leaving now.'

Maggie could not help but giggle when he gave a sweeping bow and assisted her onto the cart. They crossed the village green, and she could see the tavern was in full swing. She hoped Jacob would be negotiating over ale and brandy, his favourite pastime although he referred to it as 'business negotiations'. If he had settled into the tavern, Maggie would be able to rush through the rest of her chores, have a rest, wash, and be back holding her son in good time.

Please, let him be in the tavern. Please, let him be in the tavern.

Maggie's thoughts went around her head in rhythm with the cartwheels as they turned at a leisurely pace.

'You are quiet. A penny for your thoughts, Maggie Sawbury.'

Maggie laughed. 'My thoughts are not worth a penny, sir. If you must know, I was enjoying the sounds of peace and quiet. This is a pleasant rest for me. There is no work involved until I reach home.'

'A rest, eh? No resting for you. Look at those chestnuts on the ground. We can't be having them go to waste. I am partial to chestnuts.'

Maggie looked to where the chestnuts had fallen from a well laden tree, and Dukes pulled his horse to a stop.

'The cook loves chestnuts. She would crown me if I passed by and ignored these beauties. Come on, we will collect a few for you at the same time. Hot and roasted is how I like mine.'

Maggie jumped down and joined him. Together, they collected a half-sack full, and Dukes loaded another with a generous portion for her.

'I love hot chestnuts on a frosty eve. Jacob, my husband, is not so keen. He likes his mashed with a slice of belly pork and onions.'

'Well, you have sophisticated tastes like me, Maggie. On the next frosty night, I will enjoy mine and think of you enjoying yours. Now let us get you home. What time are you to return for feeding the new king of the house?' He helped her into the cart again.

Maggie was bemused by his good manners, and his light hearted banter was pleasant. She relaxed in his company. Although she was a little embarrassed that he knew what she was doing at the big house.

'I have to be back before sunset. It is going to make my days longer, but it's a task I am happy to endure.' She smiled, but her smile dropped when she recognised the place they had reached.

Dukes looked at her but said nothing. He clipped his tongue, and the horse broke into a trot. 'We had better get a move on then, or your day will become night.'

The rest of the journey had silent moments, but Dukes kept a flow of entertaining chatter, and the dark moment that had clouded her mind passed.

'If you wait here at four o'clock, I can give you a lift when I pass by. Should it be four fifteen, I will drive straight on and accept you have made your own way. Agreed?'

'That would be wonderful, Dukes, thank you. My husband will not be able to help me today, so I would be most grateful.'

Chapter 7

Maggie made her way along the lane, telling herself she must get used to walking or driving past the bush where she had left Nathaniel. If she allowed the image of that day to stay with her, it would drive her insane. She picked a few red Campion that brightened the hedgerows. Before she made her way home, she took a small detour. After a brief prayer, she laid the flowers on the small grave mounds beside the empty one she had made the previous day.

Thank you, God, for caring for my babies and for giving me another chance to hold my son. Amen.

Lizzie waved to her and called out as she entered the yard. 'Did you cope, gal?'

Maggie just nodded to reassure her friend she was well. She added a smile.

Knowing Jacob would have eaten several pies while carrying out his business transactions, Maggie prepared a cold meat platter, cut him a generous slice of apple pie and set it beside a pot of clotted cream. She covered it and left it upon the table.

Satisfied he could not complain she had neglected him, she went to the hen house and spent time clearing out the boxes. Her bantam chicks ran around like little bumblebees. She loved to watch them scuttle around their mothers. There was something satisfying about watching a broody hen cosy herself down into a nest.

The pigs' swill trough needed scrubbing out, which could not be put off any longer. Maggie had taken on the task after her marriage. She could not bear the smell and neglect. Jacob had been more than happy and refused to encourage another member of staff to take on the task. His words had been harsh: 'It is a fitting job for the likes of you. No need to go adding to the jobs of others, you lazy mare.'

Maggie carried a large bucket of water and a stiff yard brush out to the sty. She attacked the metal with vigour. If she gave it a good scrub, it would last an extra day or two, again saving her time. Time she could spend at the Arlington house.

'It went well today, then?' Lizzie made Maggie jump; she nearly fell into the trough.

Both women burst out laughing.

'Lizzie—look what you did, making me jump like that! It went well, so it happens. The babe is beautiful, he was hungry, and I gained comfort from the fact that I could help him.'

Lizzie found another broom and joined in with the scrubbing.

'I think 'tis a shame that Jacob has not eased off the chores a bit for you. Goodness, only twenty-four hours ago, you lost your own child! Are you all well, you know, down below? Your belly? You look better than I thought you might. I am so glad you are not too saddened by the feeding.'

'I am fine, my dear, dear friend. Stop worrying about me, please. I mean it, I am fine. If the baby wasn't meant to live, so be it. I have to face up to my loss. Right, if we both go now and clean the dairy room, it will leave you time for the milking. I am grateful you are helping me. Once I know my routine, I will take back the work.'

'Why Jacob is so stubborn is beyond me, why he insists you do it alone I'll never know. I asked once and am none the wiser. It just gained me a slap, so I never asked again. Sometimes, we are all free from our work, and you have to cope with twenty milkers.'

The chatter continued as the two friends worked together. Maggie set a pot of food onto the fire of the workers' cottage and left Lizzie to the milking. She went back home to wash some clothing, then hung it out to drip overnight and dry during the day. Determined to find her routine, she worked her way through little jobs. She had a strip wash-down and changed back into the dress she had worn that morning. Finally it was time for her to eat. She was tired and knew she would need nourishment and rest.

She placed the chestnuts onto the skillet and sat it on the fire. Her own meat platter satisfied the gnawing hunger she had begun to feel inside. And a treat of roasted chestnuts finished off her meal. They were tasty. She took advantage of a half hour's rest and savoured each one. While she peeled them, she thought about Dukes. He seemed to be in his mid-twenties, handsome and thoughtful. He had made no mention of a wife and appeared to be a bit of a ladies' man with his banter. Fanciful in her thoughts, she noted he was of similar nature to Stephen, although she doubted he would be as deceiving in love as the latter—he rather seemed a genuine, caring character. He would be a good catch for Lizzie. She must introduce them some time.

The clock in the parlour struck three-thirty, and Maggie gathered her things. She did not want to miss her ride back into town. She had to walk back that evening and knew her husband would never turn up to collect her or think of sending one of the men. So a lift one way was a gift not to be missed.

True to his word, Dukes arrived, and their journey back into the village was another pleasant one for Maggie.

'I have a gift for you. They are wrapped well to keep warm.' Maggie patted a small pail beside the seat.

Dukes gave a grin. 'You roasted me chestnuts?'

'I did while I roasted mine—I thought you might enjoy a few. You will need to eat them quickly if you like them warm,' Maggie said.

Dukes put the package into his pocket. Maggie noted his face was slightly flushed. 'That's the nicest gift I have been given for many a year, thank you,' Dukes replied, his smile wide, and Maggie was pleased she had made the effort for him.

***

Mouth-watering smells from the kitchen greeted her again, as did the staff. She slipped up the back stairs and was about to climb the main ones when someone called her name, 'Mrs. Sawbury, how timely!'

Maggie saw Felicity Arlington exiting one of the doors along the hallway. 'Good afternoon, Mrs. Arlington. I hope you are well.' Maggie dropped her knee in respect. Not really sure of what to say next, she just smiled.

'Come, I would like to speak with you,' said Mrs. Arlington, and Maggie looked down at her shoes. 'Do not worry about those; my husband has marched around with his hunting boots on before now. My girls are used to more mud than you can ever imagine. Now come along, the boy will want his feed shortly.'

Maggie followed the woman, and they entered a room twice the size of her own parlour. It was decorated in blues, reds and creams. Maggie wanted to touch the walls. They looked so pretty with flocked paper on them. Stiff brocade curtains hung at the bay windows, and across the top were fringed, pleated canopies with large, tasselled tie backs. A large, round table stacked with books had a glass dome sitting in the centre. Inside the dome was a stuffed bird. Maggie was not too impressed by it; it was not something she would like in her home.

How gruesome. Morbid.

The white marble fireplace with the black iron hearth was something she coveted more. It was a handsome feature, and the ornaments across the mantle were of fine china. Carpets and chairs decorated with tapestry had many beautiful colours in them. They complemented everything in the room.

'My dear Mrs. Sawbury, your husband told us of your sad news. Mr Arlington and I offer our condolences. However, your loss is a blessing to the young baby upstairs. Nanny Summers has told me you handled the whole situation perfectly well this morning, and he has been content ever since.' Mrs. Arlington sat on one of the seats by the window. She stared out and then looked back at Maggie, who waited for the invitation to speak. 'Nanny also told me you were clean and well presented. I thank you for considering personal hygiene. It is of the upmost importance Nathaniel is kept free from germs.'

Maggie's raised her head and frowned when the woman mentioned the name Nathaniel.

'Yes, we have chosen to use the name you christened him with this morning. Nanny mentioned it as well as the story behind it, and my husband is rather taken with the name. We are going to raise him as our own, and I think it suits him. I hope you are not offended. I like to think it will be an honour to your dear, departed son. Something you and I sadly have in common is that our little ones never lived to see day.'

Maggie took this as her cue to speak. 'Thank you, madam. I am honoured you have chosen the name. He is a beautiful child, and to carry the name of my son pleases me very much. I too am sorry for your sad loss.' She could not believe her ears. Nathaniel—she could say his name out loud and not be afraid.

'It is good it pleases you. Now we have talked enough, but before you go, Nanny has an outfit for you in the nursery. I would like to see you wear it while here at the house. You will change downstairs. I am certain your own clothes are perfectly clean, but I should worry if farm diseases are taken to the nursery. You do understand, do you not—Maggie, isn't it?' Mrs. Arlington rose from the chair.

At last it was time to leave for upstairs. Maggie couldn't wait to see Nathaniel, and she was also curious about her uniform. 'I do understand, madam, and yes, Maggie is my given name. I will ensure my clothes are washed daily, thank you.'

'No need, just leave them for the laundry here. That way they will be ready each day. There are four sets. Time is ticking by, and my son will need his feed, so off you go, and see to his needs. Goodbye, Maggie, and thank you for your assistance.'

Maggie said her goodbyes and went to the nursery. The room was warm; the fire as well as the candles that had been lit gave off a pleasant glow. Nathaniel stirred in his crib. Nanny arranged cups on a tray, and Maggie accepted a most welcome cup of tea.

'He's been dreaming the dreams of a contented angel. You did a grand job, and the top-up settled him nicely, although he did pull a few faces—I think yours is the preferred teat. Mrs. Arlington has sent up a uniform for you to wear. She likes her staff to wear uniforms, even the poor boot cleaner has to wear a stiff shirt and britches. The laundry maid screams blue murder when he gets the black waterproof liquid on his cuffs. Tallow and tar stain terribly. Here, you might as well change over there and take your outer wear downstairs. He will be ready for you when you are finished.' She indicated a loose-fitting, navy-blue gown, white pinafore and sleeve cuffs across the room. 'Wear your own stockings and boots for the present. Madam has said to give you extra in your salary to purchase new ones—purely for here and not the farm, you understand.'

All the time she spoke, Maggie watched her son sleeping.

'I am glad he settled. I met Mrs. Arlington on the way up. She told me about the clothes. It is very generous of her. I will slip it on and do as you say.'

She slipped behind a screen that stood in the corner. The gown was not a bad fit, and Maggie was pleased to wear something other than her dowdy brown one with the frayed cuffs and hem. She re-tied her hair and stepped into the room.

'My word, they are ideal for you. Now get your own downstairs and out of here, then all rules have been followed.' Nanny gave a little giggle, and Maggie knew she was going to like working alongside the older woman.

Maggie slipped into the kitchen. She asked a young maid where she could place her clothes and where she should change on her exit.

While she was talking, Dukes came into the kitchen. He gave a nod.

'Mrs. Sawbury. The youngster happy with his new nanny then?' He laughed at her puzzled face and pointed to her new attire.

'Oh, this. Yes, apparently I have to keep the farm bugs away.' Maggie smiled and brushed the front of the pinafore with her hand. She felt self-conscious with so many eyes staring at her while she spoke. 'Please excuse me, I have to go and attend to him.'

Back upstairs, she could hear Nathaniel's cries and felt the familiar tingle in her breasts. Mother and son were ready to be reunited for the second time that day.

His nanny excused herself, saying she would take advantage of the moment to get some fresh air before the light went altogether.

Maggie settled into the chair and enjoyed another intimate moment. 'Well, Nathaniel, what a turn-up for the books, eh? Who would have thought? Me and you in this situation. That fool of a husband of mine has actually done something good for me, for a change. Lizzie was worried about me. I so wanted to tell her the good news. Of course, I couldn't—we are a secret, aren't we, little man?'

Upon the nanny's return, she handed him over. 'Behave for Nanny, young man, or I will not come back. Do you hear me?' She tickled his nose.

'Heaven forbid, you hear that, Nathaniel? Best behaviour always—we want Mrs. Sawbury to return, don't we now? And tell her she can call me Alice when we are in private.'

'Thank you, Alice. I will probably forget and continue to call you Nanny. So many refer to you by your title, I consider it your name.' Maggie smiled at her new friend. She felt a close bond and wished her mother had the same nature.

The fact that she knew she would be holding Nathaniel again every morning made the evening partings less painful. She changed her clothes and said her goodbyes.

Fresh air blew over her cheeks. The warmth from the fire had made her drowsy, so the breeze was welcome—she still had to walk home, and the daylight had given way to twilight. Shadows moved across her path, trees silhouetted against the skyline looking attractive and elegant. She pulled her shawl around her shoulders and started her journey home.

'You off then?' The voice startled her. She looked around and saw Dukes standing by the gate.

'Yes, that's me finished until the morning. Well, finished here. I have a bigger baby to see to, back home.' No sooner had she said those words than she regretted them. She hadn't meant to say them out aloud.

'Your old man's a bit of a task master, or so I understand.' Dukes leant back against the fencing, puffing on a white clay pipe, his legs crossed in a relaxed manner.

Maggie was about to agree, then she thought against it. She hardly knew the man, and if it got back to Jacob that she had badmouthed him, she would suffer.

'He is my husband,' were the only words she offered.

'Not a good one, I will measure.' Dukes walked over to her. 'I would never have done this to you. He cannot be short of a penny or two. Penny-pincher, that's what they say in the tavern. Tight-fisted with the coins. His farm is run the old-fashioned way. No, I would treat my wife with a bit more respect. Losing a bairn one day and feeding another the next with no choice in the matter. He did it for the love of money, not the child, I'll wager. I was the one who looked for the family, so I know he said yes before you did. He bragged you wouldn't dare refuse. Do not build him up in my eyes; I have my own opinion of Farmer Sawbury.'

Maggie knew what he said was true, but could not stand by and let the man run her husband down. His forthright manner shocked her.

'You have said too much, sir. The job I am carrying out is one I consider an honour.' Her voice lost the indignant tone when she said, 'Holding Nathaniel will never be a hardship.'

Dukes caught the tone change, and he pulled on his pipe and slowly blew the smoke from his mouth. 'Nathaniel, is it? They gave him a name then, or is it one you have chosen?'

'If you must know, it was the name I had chosen for my first-born. My only son. He died. Absentmindedly, I said the name out loud. Nanny mentioned it in passing, and the Arlingtons chose it for their ward.'

She was about to walk out of the gate when Duke's words stopped her in her tracks. 'Ward? He is their son, lock, stock and barrel. That child will want for nothing, not even his real mother. He is there to stay, I can tell you.'

It was time to put an end to the conversation. Maggie was tired and on the verge of snipping back with words. They were on dangerous ground, and she knew it. The indignant tone returned to her voice. 'Well, I haven't got all evening to stand gossiping with you. Thank you for the lift this afternoon. It was most kind of you.'

'Well, you are in luck. I have been informed I am to collect and return you. Morning and evening. Master's orders. So if you are willing to get off your high horse and onto my cart, we can be on our way. On rainy days it will be the carriage, but I prefer the cart for daily journeys.' He strode over to the other side of the barn as he spoke.

Maggie had no time to reply or refuse. She was grateful, but concerned, too, that he would tease her too much and that she would let her guard down.

'It's very good of the master, but I will make my own way home, thank you.'

She walked out of the yard and along the narrow road. She heard the clip of the horse's hooves behind her.

'Do you want me to lose my job?' Dukes called down to her from the cart.

Maggie kept walking.

'If I offended you, I apologise. I promise I will not speak ill of Jacob Sawbury, or of babies, of which I know nothing. Now if you want me to go hungry and penniless, keep walking. If not, please clamber up so I can get you home.'

Maggie agreed to the ride home, but she barely spoke. Dukes gave a whistle or instruction to his horse on the odd occasion, but aside from that, there was little conversation between them. At the end of the lane, she relented. Manners were something she prided herself upon. 'Thank you kindly for seeing me home. My legs appreciate the ride.'

'Welcome. I will wait in this spot each morning at the seventh hour. Goodnight, Mrs. Sawbury.' Dukes spoke in a stilted manner, and Maggie regretted being off-hand with him earlier.

'Again, thank you.' She walked away, hoping the ride in the morning would be less tense.

Snores greeted her when she entered the farmhouse. Jacob drunk and asleep could not have been a better end to what Maggie considered one of the best days of her life. Rather than to ruin the feeling, she preferred to sleep in the kitchen and rise early.

Chapter 8

Refreshed and ready for the new day, Maggie ate before her husband rose and raced through her chores. When she returned from collecting the eggs, Jacob could be heard grunting his way around the room.

'Where the ruddy hell have you been? Been out all night, have you?'

'Morning, husband. You were sleeping well last night, and I didn't want to disturb you. I slept down here. My chores are done. It is uncomfortable sleeping by the fire, but you sounded peaceful after your hard working day. You deserved to be left in peace.' Maggie made it sound as if she was put out. That way, she knew he would not continue the conversation. If he felt for one moment she had suffered in any way, he would be content.

Without looking up at her, he slopped creamed oats into a bowl and sat at the table.

'Did your job properly, did you? They want you back?' He slurped his way through his breakfast.

'Yes. It all went very well. I see you have found your breakfast.' Maggie had no time for Jacob and his manners and did not want to enter into a lengthy conversation with him. 'If you will excuse me, I do not wish to be late with my last chore, nor with the Arlington's. I ate earlier. There is a lunch pail prepared for you by the door. Have a good day, husband.'

'You are running a bit late. Half past the hour of seven was agreed for you to start. It will take you past that if you are walking, and I'll be darned if I am taking your sorry carcass. I will give you a hiding, however, if you lose that job. So get out now.' His voice rose, and Maggie gave a shake of her head.

'The family have arranged daily transport for me. It means I can leave later and spend more time preparing your food for the day. There is a nice bacon-and-egg pie for you today. I know you enjoy them.' Again Maggie resented having to pacify the man she married, but needs must to keep his temper at bay.

'Uh? Yes, go and earn your keep, you lazy mare.'

Maggie left him belching, and she sent up a silent prayer of thanks for her job at the Arlington home.

During the week, her routine had improved with the assistance of Dukes and his ride home. For two days, they travelled in each other's company, speaking only a few words. The words they had exchanged on her first night had added a certain tension between them. On the third day, another glut of chestnuts changed the atmosphere, and they laughed as they collected a half-pail between them.

'I am in favour with the cook, from the last batch. With this lot, I have won my right to a larger slice of plum pie.' Dukes rubbed his stomach, and Maggie laughed.

'Men. All they think about is their stomach. My husband claims I cannot cook yet eats everything I place in front of him. He ate a large apple pie by himself once and claimed it was only fit for pigs.'

'Apple pie, plum pie, give them to me any day of the week,' Dukes laughed with her.

Maggie was relieved their friendship was back on track.

Jacob had a full purse handed to him on the last day of the week, and he threw a few coins across the table.

'Buy the shoes the missus instructed you to buy and some ribbons for your hair. Tidy yourself up a bit. The money is good, and you ain't going to lose it for me.' He put a few coins in the tin on the mantle. 'The rest I will invest in the farm. There is more than plenty there to keep the house running and a draft for me now and then.'

Maggie knew the farm would not see a penny of her earnings. It would be spent on cock fights or in the tavern. She said nothing.

Chapter 9

November 1856

The days had drifted into weeks. Maggie and Jacob rarely saw each other, and it suited both parties. Jacob did attempt to claim his bedding rights one evening, but she reminded him that if she became pregnant, they would lose their extra money. This fed his greed, and he willingly rolled off her body. Relief was great for Maggie; she could not risk losing her time with Nathaniel.

Maggie had been praised by the Arlington family, liked the company of their servants, and now she had been invited to stay for an evening meal with Alice Summers. They had become good friends and enjoyed discussing many subjects while Maggie fed Nathaniel.

She mentioned the invitation to Jacob, and his only concern was his own evening meal.

'Lizzie will take care of your needs,' she reassured him.

He stood with his back to her, spitting apple pips into the fire, leaning with one arm against the mantle. Maggie despised his slovenly ways.

'She often does,' he leered. 'When you are lugging dead flesh around in that ugly body of yours, she takes care of my needs.'

'There's no need to be coarse, Jacob. I am fully aware of your relationship with Lizzie. You mind she doesn't cast her eye elsewhere.' Maggie was furious at his statement. Both Stephen and Dukes had shown her how a man should treat a woman. Maggie resented Jacob and his rough ways more and more.

'Hold your tongue, woman. Forget my supper. I will find comfort with a decent meal at Cross Keys. You, good lady, will stay here and not go anywhere tonight. I will inform the house you are indisposed, and cannot join nanny for a cosy supper. She was only asking you so she could look down on you, anyway. Her chance to play lady of the manor. Laugh at you behind your back, their sort, do you know? I will save you from being fooled. Who would want you sitting at their table anyway? Think, idiot woman—your face is enough to turn the milk sour.'

Maggie slammed down the pot she was holding. The tinny sound resonated around the kitchen. Jacob had gone too far. He was insulting, plus he was removing an opportunity for her to hold Nathaniel. For the first time in their marriage, she fought back with words. 'How dare you! Alice Summers is my friend. We enjoy each other's company, and besides, I have to feed Nathaniel.'

'Raise your voice at me, would you?' Jacob rushed to her side, and the atmosphere was tense. 'Feed Nathaniel? Listen to you! A bastard of a child, left under a bush, and you are more worried about him than about me?' He grabbed her hair from behind and pulled her neck back. Then he spat in her face and twisted his ankle around hers.

The action caused her to fall to the floor. Her arms flailed around her, and she grabbed the back of a chair. It was not strong enough to support her and fell, too. She screamed out when her face hit the cold tiles.

'Think I am without eyes? Do you think I am blind to what is going on? You and that driver! Using a baby as an excuse to play around behind my back! I tell you this, whore: he will not want you after I am done with you!'

His boot hit home. Her knees drew up as it hit her abdomen. He grabbed her hair again and slammed her face down hard. Then he used the ponytail as a pulley and lifted her to her feet. She was winded, disorientated, and couldn't scream for help. His strength was overpowering. He had won many illegal bare-fist fights, enough for

Maggie to know her life was in danger. Each kick and punch burned her skin. Each crunching sound brought about a bout of nausea.

Her words came out in short breaths; she burned with pain. Her jaw felt bruised, and her insides were on fire. 'P-p-please, Jacob. Husband. There is nothing going on between me and the driver. Nothing.'

She knew that if she used Duke's name, it would earn her another kick. 'I will not go. I will stay and cook you a nice supper. Let us stay and enjoy the evening together. We haven't had time together lately. Please Jacob.'

'Shut your mouth, woman. I am sick of your constant whining. *Nath-an-iel* will have to do without these tonight.' She screamed as he squeezed one of her breasts and bit into it, laughing. Then, he slapped her face. 'Good for hysterics, a good slap of the face.'

The room was spinning, and Maggie feared the worse. Her head slumped forward; she saw only blackness.

'Wake up, wench. I've not finished with you yet.' Jacob wrenched her head back again.

Maggie kept her eyes closed. She felt every punch that landed on her face, arms and legs. She tried to fight back, but he held her down.

Again the blackness took hold.

She focused on memories. Of an illicit New Year's kiss. The warmth of a man's arms. Despite his deceptive ways, Stephen had shown her tenderness, something Maggie yearned for at that precise moment.

Unable to focus any longer she sunk into the depths of the darkness. Jacob's cursing grew dim.

All she could hear were whispers. Soft gentle whispers.

Chapter 10

'Is she alive?'

'I'm not sure. Give me a hand to move her head.'

'Oh, it's dreadful! Maggie, gal! Just look at her poor face.'

Maggie could hear Lizzie and Jack, a farmhand, talking. Their voices were faint and in the distance. She tried to call out to them, but the blackness came back and stopped her voice.

'Go and get help, Jack. I'll tend to Maggie. Go to the Arlington house. Tell the nanny what has happened. She's to know, mainly 'cause Maggie will not be feeding that baby for a while now.'

Maggie tried to move again. She wanted to tell Lizzie things were not as bad as they looked. Nathaniel would get his feed. Yet again, darkness filled her mind. She couldn't focus, her eyes felt heavy. She heard footsteps, and the door clicked shut.

Jack, come back! Do not tell them! I will be fine—come back.

'Oh my gal! Dear Maggie. What has he done to you?' Maggie could feel something cool on her forehead but tried to scream out when Lizzie wiped her mouth. Intense pain radiated along her jaw and up one side of her face. Whatever Lizzie was putting on her cuts and grazes stung. Poor Lizzie, she did not know she was inflicting more pain upon her friend, despite all attempts by Maggie to tell her.

When she came round from another faint, Maggie heard Jack, Lizzie, and another voice. Furniture was being moved around, and then she felt her body floating.

The sound of another heartbeat thudded in her ears. The echo of a voice vibrated from within their chest. She recognised it as Dukes's.

'Mr Arlington has sent his men to The Keys. Sawbury will be handed over to the constable for this crime. Evil blood that man carries. You got her things, Lizzie?'

Nausea overwhelmed Maggie as he lifted her up and carried her. Lizzie's voice was a high-pitched, constant chatter; a trait, Maggie knew, that meant her friend was anxious and upset. 'I've put them on the cart. Jack, help Dukes get her comfy, I'll hold the lamp and shut the farmhouse. I reckon Jacob will be held over, so there's no point in waiting up for him. Carry her out, Dukes—careful, mind her head! Oh, look at the blood! Bless her. I'll deal with that. Go. Get her to safety.'

Maggie was in no position to call out that she wanted to stay in her home. Her head throbbed with every step, and she drifted in and out of consciousness. When she was awake, the nausea took over, and she found drifting in and out of sleep a greater comfort.

The wheels of the transport jogged at a rapid pace. She felt every jolt penetrate her body. If someone had held a candle to her flesh, it could not have been as painful. She was powerless and eventually gave in to the darkness. It was a safe place, warm and inviting.

She came to at the sound of Dukes calling for his horse to stop. The stillness was welcome, as was the cool evening air on her face.

Nathaniel! Take me to my son.

She needed to feed Nathaniel. The thought stimulated lactation, and she screwed her eyes up against the pain as the milk flowed through the bitten nipples. She sensed tears rolling down her cheeks, but her hands would not move to brush them away.

A hand wiped them for her—a rough hand wiping with tenderness. Her body was lifted again, and she could smell the aroma of the Arlington kitchen.

'Our Good Lord above! What the dickens happened?'

Mrs. Bowter, help me! Please help.

Pots and pans clanged in Maggie's ears. Her body swung from side to side as she sensed Dukes carrying her through the kitchen and up the stairs. The higher they went, the faster his heart pounded. Maggie focused on its beat. Every one resounded in her ears, feeding her with the need to live.

Dukes' arms enclosed her a little more, his body warmth and the soft smell of tobacco on his clothing comforting her. She heard him mumble something to the cook but couldn't make out the words. They stood for what seem like hours to Maggie, Dukes's heart pounding in her ear. She was helpless and yelling inside. Eventually, the floating sensation came again, and once more the thudding beat was a comfort.

'Dukes, in here. Guest room one has been made up for her.'

Alice! Nanny, can you hear me? I must feed my son. Please, help me.

Softness enveloped her body, but Maggie tried to fight against it. She could hear her baby's cries further along the corridor and struggled to get free from the bedclothes that now surrounded her.

'Still, be still, Maggie. It's going to be fine. You are safe now.' Alice's soothing voice did nothing to stop her. She groaned with frustration.

'Someone shut the door. She can hear the boy, and it's playing on her mind.'

Maggie heard the door shut out the sound of Nathaniel's hungry cries. She tried to wave her arm, but nothing happened.

No. No, he needs me! Don't you understand? He needs me. LISTEN TO ME!

'That brute certainly gave her a hiding. I wonder what she did to deserve the bruises she is going to suffer. Take a look at her little hands! She must have tried to cover her face. Poor lass. And her face, that little fairy face. If he has scarred her, I will kill him with my own bare hands,' Alice said as she bustled around the bed.

Maggie willed her body to move.

The salve being applied to her hands contained lavender. Maggie could smell its strong perfume. Energy left her body, she could fight no longer. Her mind relaxed, and she allowed the dark back inside.

'Doctor Timmis is on his way, ma'am. I asked the master if we could get her attended to as she is a member of the household staff. It's her stomach area, you see, ma'am. The imprint of a boot is coming through in bruises. I fear for her insides. There was blood—forgive me for mentioning such a delicate matter—a lot of blood on the bedding, and I wonder if… well, Doctor Timmis will find out the problem.' Alice talked in hushed, hurried tones.

Maggie drifted in and out of drowsiness and could hear the rustling of fabric. Felicity Arlington's sandalwood perfume wafted around the room. Maggie focused upon the voices. She tried to speak. No sound came. Using all the energy she had, she tried to will the thoughts from her mind.

No doctor. Nathaniel. Just Nathaniel.

'You made a sensible decision. I can tell you this: Mrs. Sawbury's husband is in serious trouble with the constabulary. My husband has had him held over. She will be safe with us. The poor woman, as if she has not suffered enough! A brute indeed, nanny. Let me know what the doctor has to say, please. What will happen with my son? I assume you have made alternative feeding arrangements?'

'There was some of her expressed milk left over from this morning, and we have mixed it with cow's milk, ma'am. One of the kitchen maids has just tended to him, and he appears to be satisfied for the moment. I will tend to him shortly. Maggie has been bathed by me for her dignities sake. I will return to the nursery when the doctor has visited. We will have to play it by ear for the moment and hope she recovers soon.'

'Providing Nathaniel is comfortable and happy, I am sure you can spare a few hours for Maggie. I know you two have become close friends. I must get back to my guests. Keep me informed.'

'Yes, madam.'

Maggie heard Mrs. Arlington move around the room. The swishing of her skirts sounded like a breeze blowing through cornfields. Memories of her wedding day and the meadow flooded back, and Maggie groaned.

'Calm yourself, Maggie, you are safe. We will care for you.' Maggie felt the gentle touch of soft hands over hers. 'Whatever she needs, Nanny, whatever she needs. This is not the result of a domestic dispute between husband and wife. That girl could not say boo to a goose on her farm. I know her from church, she is a gentle soul. On the other hand, I have heard some dreadful things about her husband tonight. This is the result of a violent bully; the act of a coward. She is not to return to that farm until I have spoken with her, you understand?'

'Yes, ma'am. I will see she speaks with you before returning home. A sad affair. Dukes said she looked dead on the floor when he arrived. Quite a shock for him, from what I gather.'

'A shock for us all. A shock for us all.'

Maggie could hear the swishing sounds move out of the room.

Alice sighed. The heavy sigh of someone with a great burden to carry. The smell of lamp oil and lavender wafted around the bed. Night time had come around, she was lighting the lamps.

Maggie strained her ears. She could no longer hear the baby noises that had called out to her earlier. She settled back into the soft mattress. The crisp linen smelled fresh and inviting, and she gave in to the comfort of her surroundings. It was a hard fight to stay awake. Heavy limbs, an aching head, and her abdomen reminded her of the attention her husband had bestowed a few hours previous.

Names entered her mind. People who had touched her life. Those who had destroyed it, and those who had given it to her. Only two of those names had ever received love from Maggie. In the fog of mid-sleep, Maggie remembered.

Autumn 1855: the first loving kiss touching her lips. New Year 1856: the first time she learned that the intimate love of a strong man could bring a woman alive and yet destroy her soul at the same time. Maggie recalled the smells and sounds of that night, drawing comfort from them.

She relaxed, and then she saw him in her mind's eye: Stephen. His smile brought about sensations she had never known until then. He had given his love so freely, and so had she. From their union, Nathaniel had sprung. The child he didn't know existed. The child he neither could nor would ever know about.

Her mind became fuzzy. Suddenly, Maggie was frightened by the night. She sensed the Grim Reaper lurking, waiting to take his chance. Logical thoughts mixed with fantasy swirled around her mind.

Stephen, the killer of love, you disgust me. Dukes, where are you? Please, never forget me. Remember me. Make my life mean something to someone on this bleak earth. Goodbye. Dukes, save me.

Warmth and softness brought about heaviness around her body. Maggie no longer held back. She floated on their comfort.

***

Metal. The taste of metal tainted her mouth. She ran her tongue over her lips. They felt rough, dry, and sore. Her arm had the weight of a heavy laundry basket. It was a struggle, but finally she raised it to her head. Confused, she rested the arm down again. Her pain came from somewhere, but it wasn't her head. She ran her hand across her face. Cloth ran under her chin and around the sides of her jaw.

She lifted her legs. A pain shot through her abdomen, an involuntary gasp escaping her lips. She tried to speak, but someone had tied her mouth. She tried again, and this time she heard a growl. When a second sound reached her ears, she realised it was her own noise.

'She's awake. Thank you, Lord, for my friend. Maggie, you survived.' Alice fussed over the bedclothes. Again the smell of lavender moved with her.

A wet cloth was pressed lightly against Maggie's lips.

'Now suck gently. He broke your jaw, sweetheart. There will be pain, but we have faith. Come, take the water.'

The growl came again.

'No, lie still. Just suckle the cloth. A basil tincture for your sore mouth. Good girl, steady now. There, much better.' Alice stroked Maggie's hair away from her eyes. 'Go and get Mrs. Arlington, Daisy. She wanted to be informed when Maggie came around.'

Maggie looked up into her friend's eyes. She put as much emphasis into her gaze as she could, hoping Alice Summers would understand her question.

'He's fine. He is feeding well. I know that is what you want to hear. I will bring him to see you later in the day, when no one else is around. Now lay back, madam will be in to visit you soon. Oh, and that thug of a husband has been warned you are not returning to the farm just yet. He is to be released with a warning. The girl, Lizzie, she is running things for you, and Mr Arlington sent the daughter of one of the staff here, to help her out. You worry about getting better.'

Maggie moved her eyes, hoping they communicated her thanks.

Felicity Arlington breezed into the room. Her skirts rustled even louder than before. She dismissed all the staff members and placed herself beside Maggie but in full view of her face.

'My dear, you are awake. It is thanks to Doctor Timmis that you have survived this ordeal. A broken jaw and a bleed from the ear are two of the injuries he found. He said you would suffer pains in the head for some time. He has left a sweet woodruff mixture for both your head and body pain. There is one other thing he had to do. Maggie, you were bleeding from inside your body. Your husband said you fell, but the boot imprint shows otherwise. That aside, the doctor had to perform a delicate operation to save your life. I am afraid, he, um…' Mrs. Arlington gave a delicate cough.

Maggie knew something serious was about to be said. She could sense the tension in the woman's voice.

'This is not easy for me to say… rather personal, but I wanted to be the one to tell you. I am afraid he thinks it will mean you will never be able to have children. Given your previous history, this is the most tragic thing that could happen to you. I am so sorry! The good thing is that you are still producing nourishment and can continue to feed the boy. Should you wish to, of course. I am not insensitive and aware it might be too much for you to bear. You are a good woman, and it has grieved me to see you in this state.'

Maggie couldn't believe what she had just heard. She closed her eyes in prayer. She thanked God for the gift of Nathaniel for the second time. For without him, she would have been childless.

The room was warm, calm, and now empty. Maggie let her body relax. She took a few deep breaths and gave in to sleep yet again. It was time for her to remember the good things in her life and the lessons that strengthened her character; time to face her past.

Chapter 11

Saturday, the 14th of July, 1855

'Take these, oh, and these. The men will need a cask of cider. It is warm today. I have never seen so many willing hands.' Maggie gave instructions to the women who were helping with the summer fayre. The flower and vegetable festival was a popular event, and it fell to several of the wives to provide food and drink. Jacob, as usual, had volunteered his wife to set up the tables.

Maggie did not really mind. She did envy other wives of nearby farms because their husbands paid a few coins to hire extra help. Maggie never had the luxury of Jacob paying anyone else to assist her. Fortunately, the families of their farmhands were willing enough to pitch in without payment. Although they did enjoy the free feast and beer Maggie offered them.

'Mrs. Sawbury, do you want me to go ahead with Lizzie? We can set the tables. If it is white cloth, the same as last year, it isn't something you need to worry about. You can follow with the food in about an hour. He will be none the wiser,' with her thumb, Agnes Latchford indicated Jacob outside. He was shouting instructions to the men lifting the cider and wheat beer barrels.

'Agnes, that would be a great help, thank you. Please, I tell you every year, please call me Maggie. I forgot you are an expert at this fayre. Did not your father win the finest potato five years running?'

Maggie wiped her hands on a pinafore stained with a mixture of sweet and savoury foodstuffs. She was grateful for thoughtful helpers.

Agnes puffed out her already large chest and said, 'He did indeed. We lost him last winter. We all miss him, it broke our hearts. Old man Bloomfield cannot believe his luck. He always comes second but sees his chance of the number-one place this year. What he doesn't know is our Henry has been keeping his grandfather's prize crop growing. He is hoping to follow in his footsteps. I cannot wait to see Bloomfield's face when the barrow is wheeled in.'

Laughter rang around the house. Maggie loved to hear her home alive with happy sounds. They were rare.

'Quick, let us toast your family's success. Lizzie, where is he?' Lizzie did not need a name to know who Maggie referred to. It was an understanding amongst them all. If Jacob Sawbury's name was mentioned in full, it tainted whatever event was happening at the time. If he had no name, it was as if he did not exist. A wish of many.

'He's happy right enough; they are taking full kegs to the squire's field now. He'll not be back now 'til he staggers home.'

Maggie poured elderflower cordial and sloe gin into glasses. The women and children, nine in all, raised their glasses to the largest potato, the longest carrot, and the prettiest flower.

The last cart left, well laden with food and giggling families. Arms and legs waved and dangled over the edge of their transport in a relaxed manner. The sloe gin worked its magic.

Maggie opted to follow on foot. She wanted to take advantage of the sunshine and the peaceful atmosphere.

When she reached a small brook that ran alongside the field where the fayre was being held, Maggie took in her surroundings. Lush green vegetation was dotted with colourful splashes of flowers. From across the field, she could hear the sounds of people coming together, laughing, and chatting. Children played tag ran around the perimeter of the nearest field.

The rippling brook was clear, and she could see the pebbled bottom. It looked inviting, so Maggie took the opportunity to paddle. She slipped off her boots and stood with the cool water rippling over her toes. She raised her skirt, enjoying the pleasurable sensation as her feet cooled down.

'A great place to dally and paddle.' The male voice startled her. It was too well-toned to be one of the villagers.

Embarrassed, Maggie dropped the hem of her gown and silently cursed the fact it was now soaking wet. With care, she stepped out onto the small embankment; to slip now would add to her embarrassment. Sunshine glared behind the man and blurred her vision. She could only make out the outline of a well formed figure. Fumbling with the ribbon that secured her bonnet, she said, 'I beg your pardon, sir. I thought I was alone. Forgive me if I intruded upon your privacy.' Maggie slipped her feet into her boots.

'Forgive *me*, good lady. I am the one who arrived after you. A pleasant day for the fayre and for an impulsive paddle, is it not?' Now that the sun shielded her eyes, Maggie could see he had a clean-shaven faced. A face most pleasing to the eye. He held out his hand in greeting. 'Forgive my manners. Stephen Avenell, how do you do?'

Maggie made pretence of shaking out her gown in order to wipe her hands. She was embarrassed. The son of the squire had just watched her paddle in the brook.

Her hand looked tiny in his slender one. His skin was soft, and Maggie was pleased she had rubbed a little lanolin and rose water into hers that morning. The roughness wouldn't be quite so obvious.

'A pleasure meeting you, sir. Maggie Sawbury, wife of Jacob from Windtop farm. It is a pleasant day indeed. Now if you will forgive me, I must be on my way. I have to set the feast with the other wives and have dallied long enough.' She went to her basket and other parcels she had been carrying.

'Allow me—I am heading that way myself.' As he took the parcels from her arms, she melted in his smile, drowned in his blue-green eyes, and lusted after his lean body.

She shivered with the shock of what she had just experienced. He was around her age, certainly no older than twenty-two, and for Maggie, the perfect specimen of a male. His hair had natural waves and a honey-tinged gloss. It sat just above his collarbone, curled around his ears, and shimmered in the sunlight. His skin was unmarked, his jaw line strong, and his neck sleek. His nails were well manicured but not in a feminine way. Maggie tried in those few seconds to find a fault. His voice, had it been a fabric, would have been the purest silk.

'Shall we?' He strode forward, and Maggie, feeling slightly like a naughty child, hung back for a view of his rear. He wore summer britches and a waistcoat. His jacket was slung over one arm. Maggie could see the outline of his shoulders and buttocks as they moved. A stallion horse—she was reminded of a purebred stallion.

Shame on you, Maggie! Oh, just look at the way his muscles move! So powerful! Stop it Maggie, stop your sinful thoughts!

'Have you forgotten something, mistress Sawbury?' He swung a look back at her over his shoulder. The white of his teeth and the soft crinkle around his eyes were the final ingredients Maggie needed in her love potion. She drank it in, the whole picture. Golden field, distant marquees, wild flowers, blue sky, and a god in its midst.

'My apologies, I needed to button my boot.' Maggie caught up with him. She stayed to his left side and side-glanced to satisfy her visual need of his face.

'Is your husband experiencing a good year on the farm?'

'He is, sir. Although I think the modern methods are taking over his way of working. The world moves at a faster pace nowadays.' Maggie did not want to think of Jacob and Stephen Avenell in the same world. One was chipped, coarse granite, the other sculptured, smooth marble. 'How is your father's land faring? I understand he has new threshing machines. I have heard them in the lower fields. I must go and see them working one of these days.'

Any excuse to see you again, my fine gent.

'They are a time-saving piece of equipment; however, there is a lot of resentment amongst the farmhands. They fear for their jobs. He reassures them, but they are nervous.' He swung her a smile, and Maggie experienced a new sensation ripple through her body.

Please go away, you are too delicious.

'I think that is why my husband holds on to the old ways so tightly. The staff certainly work for their wage on our farm.' Maggie wished she could withdraw the last statement. It came out in a resentful tone.

'I have heard your husband has a tough code to work by at Windtop. Oh, here we are, the annual summer fight amongst the hollyhocks.' He threw back his head and laughed.

Maggie joined him. She had enjoyed the five minutes they had walked together. His humour was refreshing, and his appearance intoxicating.

'Where the bloody hell do you… Forgive me Mr Avenell—I did not see you there! I do hope my wife has not been making a nuisance of herself. She has a habit of showing me up in public. A burden I am cursed with for my sins.' Jacob stood before them.

Maggie could feel her cheeks rising to a heat that would pink them a shade more than usual. In all probability, several shades more. She was furious and embarrassed.

'On the contrary, Mr Sawbury. Without your wife, I would not have found my way here.' Her hero turned his back on Jacob and addressed Maggie.

'Mistress Sawbury, thank you for rescuing me from the brook and showing me the correct way across the meadow.' He winked at her, and Maggie found it hard not to giggle.

She dropped her knee as Jacob would expect her to do. 'You are more than welcome, sir. Thank you for assisting me with the packages. Good day to you. I will leave you to discuss the finer points of farming with my husband.' She gave a soft smile of gratitude. She realised he knew her husband was a bully. His quick thinking had saved her from a slap and public tongue-lashing. It was laughable to think the squire's son was claiming to be lost on his own land. Fortunately, Jacob was full enough of ale, so it had not registered with him.

'Dear husband, if you will excuse me, I have to attend to the food. I will save you a plate. Only the finest for my hard working man. Goodbye, gentlemen.' Maggie could feel laughter bubbling up inside.

Jacob's face was one of disbelief. He could do nothing, and she had spoken as if he was a lord. It did not occur to him she was teasing at his expense.

'Very well. Oh, and Maggie, save me one of the meat pies, they will soak the ale, and I intend to sup me one or two today. Now, sir, how is the squire?' Jacob steered Stephen towards the marquee that housed his favourite product: wheat beer.

Maggie entered the largest marquee. Table after table was laden with every type of food in season. Baked pies, pickled fruit and vegetables, bowls of meat jellies, chunks of fresh bread and sweet cakes. Each filled the air with their mouth-watering aromas. Maggie placed her goods around and found Lizzie resting on an upturned pail. She was sipping a rosehip cordial, enjoying the well-earned rest.

'You got a drop of gin in that, Lizzie?' Maggie teased.

'Get away with you. If I have one more, I will sleep forever or sing under the table.'

Both women giggled.

'So who was that fine beast you trotted across the meadow then, Mrs. Sawbury?' Lizzie grinned up at Maggie. She burst out laughing when she saw Maggie blush. 'Ah, a dalliance in the bushes, were it?'

Maggie was anxious for Lizzie to stop her tormenting. If Jacob heard these words, he would hit out first, then ask questions. Even then he would not believe her answer. 'Stop the silly talk, Lizzie. You know full well I never trotted anyone over the meadow. The squire's son, Stephen, found himself cut off by the brook. I showed him the way around it, and as we were both headed in the same direction, he carried my parcels. As any gentleman might. Now you and I both know, if you say things like that in front of Jacob, it will mean the devil will play. I beg you to not mention it again.' She mopped her brow with the edge of her pinafore. She found herself using the same reason as her escort had to her husband. Both had fabricated a story to save face.

Lizzie's voice dropped a level and now had a serious tone to it. 'I'm sorry, gal. I never gave it thought. You know I would never bring trouble to your door for the sake of it, please forgive me. My tongue ran away with me. You are a loyal wife, and it was wrong of me to say any different.'

Lizzie stood up, and Maggie gave her a hug. 'You are forgiven. For the record books, if I was a single woman, that man would not have walked through the meadow before laying in it. In a field full of cattle, he is the prize bull.' She laughed aloud when she saw Lizzie's mouth fall open in amazement. Even Maggie was surprised by her own words. She flounced back into the marquee and joined in with happy-go-lucky friends and neighbours.

Two hours later, it was Maggie's turn to take a break from replenishing plates and serving the gentry. She sat on Lizzie's upturned pail and closed her eyes against the lowering sun.

'It's a busy life you lead, Mrs. Sawbury. A busy life indeed.' The shadowed figure in front of her and the silky voice needed no introduction.

Maggie kept her eyes closed and smiled in a lazy, carefree manner. Her body was relaxed, and she was too tired to jump up and conform to the rules of etiquette. Besides, she had an inclination that Stephen Avenell was enjoying the view. Earlier, she had unlaced the top two sections of her gown, and a fraction of her bosom could be seen. The girl in her decided to enjoy a little flirtation to end the day. A day that would finish in ensuring that her drunken husband kept his hands to himself, and she was back in the usual, dull routine that dictated her life. Maggie decided she was going to enjoy this one pleasurable moment. It was harmless fun.

'Mm, you cannot beat the warmth of the sun going down on one's skin.' She lay back slightly more and crossed her legs, all the while pretending she did not know who stood before her. 'Whoever you are, would you step slightly to one side. You are depriving my body of one of its pleasures.' Still she kept her eyes shut. To open them would now be a mistake. She would not be able to remove her eyes from the meadow god she had been replaying in her mind.

'My sincere apologies, my lady. I for one would never wish to deprive your body of any pleasures. Good day to you, and my compliments for the delicious feast you bestowed upon us today.'

With those words, Maggie sensed his shadow move away from her body. He was leaving. She remained still, barely breathing. Everything about their encounter had been a new experience for her. She had never been so forward with a male before, nor had she broken social class rules. There was no doubt in her mind that the squire's son had felt the same. He had teased, flirted with words, and left her wanting more.

She moved from her seat and watched him walk through the marquee. All female eyes were upon him. Common remarks were bandied about, but Maggie just watched the flanks of the man who, she knew, would be on her mind for a long time to come.

Her thoughts were broken into by one of the women asking if she needed a lift home on their cart. Maggie thanked her and said she had to find her husband.

'Him? You best be home and out of harm's way, my girl. He's full of one barrel and nigh in the bottom of t'other.'

'Is he really that bad, Sarah?' Maggie was not looking forward to the answer.

'He is spoiling for a fight, and you know what he is about when he does that. Anyone will be his punch partner.'

Jacob would need careful handling, and Maggie wanted Lizzie to be safe for the night.

'Leave him to me, Sarah, but do me a favour and take Lizzie home. She will have enough on her plate tomorrow, and I want to ensure she gets a good night's rest. No doubt those who cannot hold their liqueur will give her extra work in the main cottage by the morning.'

'We can take her and some of these baskets, if you like. Then all you have to worry about is the big man himself.' Sarah waved Lizzie over. 'Well girl, you are coming back with me and my lot? Let us take some of these for your mistress and get on the road. We've a journey ahead.'

Maggie smiled. Sarah made it sound as if they had another continent to conquer rather than a ten-minute cart-ride home.

She tidied away all she had to and made her way towards the loud noise coming from one side of the field. She could see the lamps and straw wick lights glowing around a group of men. Some were singing bawdy songs; others were sitting quietly, enjoying the end of their one-day holiday. The majority were debating farming techniques and how they were destroying farming, or improving it, whatever their view.

Jacob was in full form, thigh-slapping and table-banging his answers or opinions. He scorned anyone else's valid import and became louder and louder the more he supped.

'A shilling in the pound tax is what they are after now. A man's money is no longer his own. Scoundrels, the lot of them!'

Maggie sighed. If she tried to get him to leave now, she would only create a problem for herself. She could see Big Joe sitting beside Jacob, who now stood up and leaned back against the edge of their cart, with his foot resting on a stool. He was in full flow, and those who knew him well enough just listened. Joe was nodding and waiting for the right moment to take his leave. He was a good man and could handle Jacob in awkward situations. Maggie surmised it was better if she walked home rather than remove her husband's prop. His audience would see him home. She watched him puff out his chest with importance as he spoke. Compared to Stephen Avenell, he looked unkempt, his body and face bloated with drink. Maggie shuddered.

No point in wishing any different, Maggie Sawbury. What is done is done.

She took a small carry lamp from one of the marquees. She would have Lizzie take it back to the organisers the next day. One last glance at her husband reassured her that walking home was her best option.

Fragrance from the soft meadow grass filled the night air as she walked. It shimmered with the evening mist settling on the flower heads. Her lamplight added to the glisten. It was a beautiful sight. An owl rustled and gave a half-hearted hoot. His day was just about to start. A small bat swooped and played: it too was celebrating the arrival of dusk. Stars popped into view, scattering themselves amongst the sapphire-blue sky. Maggie thought back to when she was a child. Life was much simpler then; she would sit for hours watching the stars, enjoying quiet moments. Tomorrow would grant her a heavy workload and a husband with head pain. Just for once in her life, she wished for a simple moment. To be transported back to childhood and the innocence of youth.

'It's beautiful, isn't it?' Once again, the voice needed no introduction. Maggie stopped walking. Could this be the perfect end to a perfect day?

'Why, sir, surely you are not following me? I agree, it is beautiful. So many stars, so many wishes to make.' She turned to face him this time, fearing he would consider her ill-mannered if she did not.

She had never considered a man beautiful before, but he was just that: beautiful. His eyes sparkled with reflections from her lamp, and she thought that even without that, they would.

He did not smile, he just looked at her.

She became very conscious of her appearance. Shabby clothing and dishevelled hair. In an automatic reaction, she put her basket down on the grass and smoothed her hair back into her cap.

'No. Leave it!' Stephen Avenell reached out and removed her cap. He tugged on the ribbon that held what Maggie considered unruly tresses in place. His finger traced a slow, lingering path down her neck, over her shoulder, and across the top of her breast. A breast that rose rapidly with every stroke.

Mesmerised, Maggie allowed him to take the liberty. Hypnotised by his actions, she shook her hair loose. Jacob had never made a simple, romantic gesture. The man before her changed her whole world with that one, simple act.

'There, much more pleasing to the eye. A thing of beauty should never be tied down.'

Maggie sensed the words were not spoken just about her hair, and her body trembled. If asked to look for her willpower at that very moment, she would not be able to do so. Nor would she be able to find her voice.

'It has been a pleasure meeting you, Mrs. Sawbury. I hope our paths cross another fine day. Good evening to you, and my regards to your husband.'

Maggie said nothing. There was nothing for her to say. The man she could love if given permission walked away. Her meadow god no longer, he had returned to his earthly status, the untouchable son of the village squire. A tear in honour of what might have been slowly slid down her cheek. The owl close by gave a full and enthusiastic bellow of hoots, and Maggie chided herself for her fanciful thoughts.

The journey home was one she would never forget. Her arrival was one she could have done without.

Chapter 12

Screams echoed around the hilltops, joined by loud, frantic voices.

Maggie ran the last, short distance towards the noise. There was chaotic movement of lamp lights, and the screams and voices appeared to be coming from their farm.

The small staff stood gathered around Lizzie's home. She rushed to one of the men and tugged his sleeve. 'Mason, what on earth is going on?'

'Oh, mistress, it's dreadful. Don't go in, please come back.' The man made a grab for her arm, but she shook him off and stepped inside the small building.

'Lizzie. Lizzie, where are you? Lizzie? What is going…'

Maggie stopped talking and grabbed hold of the slim table beside her.

Her friend knelt beside one of the village boys, and it was obvious his body was drained of life. Maggie took in the scene; she had an inkling what might have happened. Her husband had beaten the boy with his bare hands, a drunken rage taken out on a young man who had shown interest in Lizzie. She hesitated to say her thoughts out loud. Jacob was a hot-headed fool, but to kill another man on his farm and get caught was something even he would not do. To say she suspected him to have carried out the killing might influence the thoughts of others. In order to carry it out, he must have left the fayre at the same time she had and raced the cart home. If she had not lingered in the meadow, she might have been able to prevent the incident.

'Where is my husband?' she shouted to the group outside the room. 'He needs to be informed.'

'The squire's men have taken him, Maggie,' Lizzie said through sobs. 'He'll hang for this, to be sure, but—'

'But what? You have doubts? Who saw it? Was it definitely him? Did he kill this boy?' Maggie threw question after question at those who were eager to listen.

'I asked the same, but it appears nobody saw nor heard a thing. I found Peter when I returned from the milk shed. I only left him for about one half-hour. I really am not sure Jacob is in the wrong. He has drunk so much, and the last time I saw him, he could barely stand. He couldn't focus either. Larky said he saw him vomiting in the lane earlier. But the cart is by the farm entrance, so he mustn't have walked. Oh, Maggie, he is a cruel-mouthed man with hard fists, but if he is innocent this time, he should not be made to suffer for somebody else's wrong.'

The room fell silent at her words; those who had entered knew that what she said was true.

'I agree, it would be a wicked thing to do. Now someone fetch a blanket and cover the lad. Has his mother been informed? If I remember rightly, his father passed on a few years ago.' Maggie collected her wits about her and gave out instructions to anyone who stood nearby.

'Mrs. Sawbury?' One of the men addressed her.

'What is it, Larky?' She held Lizzie in her arms for warmth and comfort; they both felt the chill of the night air and the shock.

'One of the squire's men wants a word. I have set him in your kitchen, it is more private there.' The youth screwed his cap in his hands, anxious whether he had done the right thing.

'Very well. Thank you, a wise idea. Now, can I trust you to look after Lizzie until I come back?' Maggie asked

'She'll be alright with me. You go and sort this horrid business out. Now, Lizzie, a cup of tea, I think.' Larky took over, and Maggie slipped out of the cottage.

She addressed those who had no need to be in the yard other than to find gossip to spread in the village. The last thing she needed was a lynch party on her doorstep. With the amount of alcohol consumed that day, there would be many in the village and in the surrounding areas fired up for a lamplight court. An innocent babe would be found guilty by a blood hungry mob.

'This is a sad night for us all. I for one am doubtful of my husband's wrong-doing; he was too drunk. You all know me well enough to know that, if he was guilty, I would be the first to hand him over to the authorities. Now I need you all to focus on the poor boy who lies cold in my cottage and support his mother. I must away to speak to someone, and I need you all back here in the morning. We have work to carry out, and any information you glean, well, I'd appreciate it if you bring it to me first. Goodnight to you all, and God bless.'

As she walked out of the cottage, she nodded to the group who stood to one side and allowed her through. Each one touched her arm, a combination of reassurance and pity.

Maggie crossed the yard, glanced at her henhouse and made a mental note to prepare a chicken for the following day. It then dawned on her that, with Jacob in custody, she would have to carry out his workload, too. Her nerves were jangled; she needed something to aid the shock.

Her world stood still when she entered the kitchen. There at her table was Stephen Avenell.

He stood up the moment she stepped into the room. 'Dreadful business, Mrs. Sawbury.'

Maggie nodded but said nothing. She walked to the fire and added another log, went to a shelf, took down a jug and poured two glasses of cider. She handed one to the man who had unleashed new feelings within her. A want. A need... She raised her glass.

He reciprocated.

The parlour door was ajar, and she could hear the tick of the clock from inside; it was the room she now wished had a fire roaring in its grate. The kitchen was not the place to entertain this man. Lowering herself into a seat at the table, she listened to Stephen talk about the dead boy. She watched his mouth move and longed to reach out and touch his lips. She thought it ironic that Jacob's arrest was a blessing for her in more ways than one.

'My men are fetching his mother as we speak. I wanted to find out more about the situation, about the mystery surrounding his death. It must be a dreadful shock for you. My father is not in robust health, so he asked if I could take his place.' Stephen sipped at his drink.

'Maggie, my name is Maggie.' Her voice came out in a whisper. She couldn't bear hearing him call her by any other name. It was indeed a terrible shock, and Maggie needed some form of comfort, even if it was only to hear him say her name. It was a selfish need, but nevertheless, she needed to break down the barrier between them. To silently give him permission to want her back.

He smiled gently. 'Maggie. Maggie of The Meadow,' he said, and Maggie knew she was his forever.

'Maggie. Do you believe your husband is in the wrong? Do you think he killed that boy?' He leaned across the table and tapped her hand as if to waken her from her trance-like state.

Finally she found her voice. The moment between them had gone, and real life stepped in its path. 'Sire, my husband is a violent man; a bully. He is capable of killing with his fists, but I am convinced he did not carry out this unfortunate beating. You know how much he had drunk during the day. You saw him at the end?' Maggie waited for a response, and Stephen nodded. 'Lizzie said he never sought her out as he is wont when full of ale. Not doing so indicates that he—er—he was incapable of many things. He was seen being ill in the lane by another on the way home, although that puzzles me because he came home on the cart. He must have been capable of clambering up and down without any problem, but I am certain he would not be fit to fight. In answer to your question: no. No, I do not think he is a guilty man.' Her mouth was dry, and Maggie took a long drink of cider. As she watched Stephen sip his and run his tongue over his lips, she fought back the urge to walk over and kiss him.

Concentrate, Maggie. Stop this fanciful nonsense. Your husband's life is at stake.

'In which case we must find out who is the culprit. However, the chances are they have crossed into another county by now. I will return tomorrow morning with the constable. I am afraid he will need to ask all who live on the farm several questions about their whereabouts tonight. I can give you an alibi, and—'

Maggie interrupted. Her voice had a baseline of anger running through it; she could not believe he had the gall to say the words he had. All affection she held for him that day fell away with his offer.

'An alibi? Why on earth would you think I need an alibi? Besides, what will you say? Mrs. Sawbury stood like a street-whore in the meadow while I loosened ribbons from her hair; toyed with her breasts?'

She stood up and walked to the door. The meeting had ended, and it was time for him to leave. 'The workers and I will be here in the morning to answer all questions. I walked home alone and was greeted by each and every one of them after the event. So you see, sir, I have no need of your alibi, and going by your behaviour this evening, it would come at a price anyway.' She looked to the floor; to allow him to see tears would be a sign of weakness.

He lifted her chin and looked into her eyes, his expressing disappointment, a deep hurt. 'Stephen. My name is Stephen, and I ask no price.' His voice penetrated its meaning, and she shuddered with desire. A quick movement of her head released his fingers. Fingers that had burned into her flesh, leaving no visible mark but a definite scald of want.

He moved silently away, and the door clicked shut. Maggie leant her back against it.

Stephen Avenell had pulled at a thread in her heart. He had shown her how a man could turn a woman's head. His gentle flirtations left her wanting more. Her heart had beaten so fast when he stood near her. Each smile he offered made her long for his kiss upon her lips. He had power over her and left her body tingling like nothing she had experienced before.

Her thoughts were stopped by a rapid tap at the door. Maggie, too tired to move, called out, tensing with hope that it would not be Stephen returning to fan her flames and play havoc with her emotions once again. 'Come in.'

With relief, she smiled as Lizzie entered the room, her faced flushed red with tears, her voice hoarse. 'Peter's mother is with him now. T'parson has arrived, and Mr Avenell has asked that all costs are to be invoiced to the squire. Very generous. Oh gal, I hurt so, we were gettin' along so well! He were a gentle soul—who would beat him to pulp? Who could do such a thing? Dreadful. Cruel. I left him there while I finished milking; when I came back, he lay in a blanket of blood. When I went to him, it was to bathe wounds, not to scream over a dead body. A shock, gal, such a shock,' Lizzie sobbed.

Maggie held her in her arms, leading her to a seat. 'Who else have you entertained recently? I am not a fool, and you need to be honest. If you have two admirers, one may have killed tonight. Think, girl, think. As much as I dislike my husband, I need him to run this farm, not hang from a tree. Now think hard.' She put her arms around the girl's shoulders and dried her tears with the corner of her pinafore.

Lizzie came out with one name and clapped her hand to her mouth. 'Larky. Me 'n' him had a bit of fun a while back, nothing of the wrong-doing game, mind. He's not the sort of man for me. No, just a bit of flirting and teasing. Do you think it could be him?'

Maggie thought about the youth her friend had mentioned. Quick-tempered, eager to please, with a weak character. Nothing in his looks would turn a girl's head. In a field of corn, he would be the puniest stem. 'He claimed to have seen Jacob in the lane. I am still not certain that is true. Jacob came home by the cart. If he was so bad that he had to stop and be ill in the lane, I am not certain he would be able to control the horse again. He left the cart at the entrance of the farm. I think he just rode it home as best he was able. Maybe Larky said those things to make it sound as if Jacob were innocent, too drunk to do anything. And he was there to assist him. This would remove suspicion from himself. We all know how much of a burden Jacob can be when he is full of the drink.' She and Lizzie sat pondering over her words.

'What was your relationship with him, Lizzie? What you have told me, is that the truth?' Maggie asked.

Lizzie sighed. 'He can be sly at times, and he follows me into the dairy when he knows no one else is around. He tried to kiss me once, but I wouldn't let him. He told me he wanted what I gave the others. I gave him a piece of my mind and nothing more. Please Maggie, gal. Please believe me. Oh, gracious and all that is good, whatever happened? He is probably happy that Jacob has been arrested. Yet runs around as if it is the most dreadful thing to happen.' Lizzie burst into tears, and Maggie made a decision.

'It does look more and more as if it was him. We will keep quiet at the present time. The authorities are coming in the morning to ask us questions. Before they do, we will speak with Larky in a casual manner. We will try to establish where he was when you milked the cows. He is obliging everyone tonight by making himself useful. I am now in doubt of his sincerity, but I don't think he will run away. He has made a good story and thinks he is beyond suspicion. You will sleep with me—you are in no position to go back to the cottage.' Maggie rose from the table.

'I must go. It is only right that I pay my respects and see Peter's body off of the farm. It is my duty. No. You stay here; it will be for the best. I am going to lock the door behind me. Strange, I know, but under the circumstances, I think it best.'

***

Maggie added her condolences to those of the staff. Peter's mother held her hand, her face a pitiful picture. 'Mrs. Sawbury, they say it was your husband, and he is locked away. I pray it is not so, for you will have a difficult life ahead. I know what it is to work without a man alongside me. I have also heard whisper he is considered innocent. The latter is the preferred outcome, but it will leave a question on everyone's lips. Who killed my beloved son? I curse the girl who enticed him to her bed. You need to watch that one, loose with her skirts, so I hear.'

Maggie stood in silence and allowed the woman her words. There was nothing she could add to them. She did feel, however, that she needed to wipe off the tarnish added to Lizzie's character. Thus, she spoke in soft, but firm tones—with people absorbing every word tonight, things needed to be handled carefully. She might be young, but she was also wise enough to know her words would be the ones most would listen to that night. She needed to leave them with a picture in their minds.

'Peter and Lizzie were not lovers. They were in love and have been courting in secret for some time. I understand they were going to be wed when the time was right. This news came to me from the girl herself. She is distraught and carries the distress of someone who has lost someone precious, so I have no reason to doubt her words. Any slanderous accusations you may have heard came from those who were jealous. Now take your boy home, and leave Lizzie to me. I ask only one thing: allow her the right to mourn your son alongside you. There will be comfort for you both in sharing your love for him.'

Maggie made arrangements for the woman to be escorted home and sent with her a pitcher of milk, butter, and cheese. There would be great need for them when the villagers descended to pay their respects.

Back at the cottage, Maggie had a lot to discuss with Lizzie. The girl was curled on a horse-hair sofa in the corner of the room. She looked so vulnerable.

'Lizzie, I have just told Peter's mother, in front of a large crowd, that you two were in love, not just lovers. I also asked her to allow you to mourn alongside her. Now hear me out. Your character has a stain on it tonight. A man in your cottage, and village gossip will not help you find a husband. Should it be known that you were left by your love through his death, it is a forgivable reason. I need you to show a broken heart.'

Lizzie looked up at her, and Maggie was shocked. The girl would not need to act. The distress in her face said it all; she had indeed loved Peter.

'How long have you been courting in secret?'

'Three months. We thought that if Jacob found out, he would turn nasty. I told Peter 'bout his visits.' She looked shamefacedly at the floor. 'He promised he would not challenge him about them if I promised to try and avoid them. A promise I was willing to make for him, Maggie.'

'Maybe Jacob and he did confront each other. We can only hope that is not the case. Why did you never confide in me? Oh, Lizzie, I am so sorry. I never had a clue. I have never seen you together.'

'That was our intention. We were going to announce our love when the time was right. We wanted to learn more about each other and be sure marriage was what we wanted. It was love—we shared so much. I know all the little secrets he had, about his father and many other things. Facts that will prove to his mother how much we loved each other. Maggie, what do I do now?'

'Now, you sleep. Tomorrow will bring a new batch of problems and situations. I need some rest, and so do you. Come now, bring the candle.'

Lizzie climbed the stairs ahead of her, and Maggie took one last glance at the seat where Stephen had sat. She tried to visualise him there again, but all she saw was an empty chair.

***

Sunday

Morning brought no joy to the farm. The weather of the previous day had moved on to pastures new. A grey mist swirled outside of the kitchen window. An air of gloom and despondency joined the cloud and cast a shadow over anyone who entered the yard. Even the meadow held no joy for Maggie.

Hangovers, bad memories, and fear accompanied the majority. Maggie had instructed the cottage to be scrubbed top to bottom, and Lizzie's things were to be moved into her parlour for a temporary period. Keeping her staff busy was her goal for the day. The more jobs they had to do, the less time they had to stand around gossiping.

She and Lizzie had cleaned the dairy. She paid a husband and wife team down on their luck to deal with the livestock.

In the salt hole set in the chimney, she kept a small pot with money. It was her emergency fund, saved from egg sales. A secret from Jacob; should he know about it, he would drink it away. Now, Maggie put it to good use. A small group of women came to offer their services. Maggie knew they had come only out of curiosity, but as her day was extra busy, she gave them various tasks, one of which was to cook a large breakfast and set it out in the large staff cottage. Eggs, bacon, bread, and pots of creamed oats were loaded onto a table and gratefully received.

Satisfied that all were content and that no dangerous gossiping was carried out, Maggie relaxed with them for a few moments with a mug of buttermilk. She watched Larky going about his business. He moved from one person to another, speculating about the night before and loudly making it known he had seen Jacob in the lane. She judged the right time and decided there was a chance he might be caught out. The more she and Lizzie had discussed their suspicion that morning, and the way he was behaving now, the more she was certain he had killed Peter. The matter had to be handled carefully.

'Larky, was the boss going to or from the farm when you came across him?' she enquired.

'Um, coming to the farm, Mrs. Sawbury. Why do you ask?' Larky frowned.

'And you? Were you heading here or away?' Maggie continued, ignoring his question.

'I was coming here.' Larky pushed his food into his mouth. All eyes were upon him.

'Why?' Maggie persisted with her questions.

'Madam?' Larky gulped down his food, looking uncomfortable.

'Well, you do not sleep here. You live in the village. Why did you come to the farm—did you help Mr Sawbury home?' Maggie placed her cup on the table and stared at him. Her curiosity was getting the better of her. She could see a bead of sweat resting on his brow.

He looked up from his plate. 'I was going to, but he shouted at me. I thought I had better come and warn Lizzie he was in a state and on his way.' His words came in a rush. He stabbed at the bacon slice on his plate and then made a play of cutting it up.

Maggie controlled her voice into a slow, deliberate level. 'Why on earth would you do that? I am the mistress of the farm, I am his wife. Oh, I know Jacob visits the cottages from time to time when he has been drinking. But if he is with someone else, they always bring him to the house. Home to his wife. Why would you even consider taking him to the small cottage? It is well known that my husband drinks heavily, and I am used to putting him to bed. I did not need protection from him, and neither did Lizzie. Tell me, Lizzie, what did you say to Larky when he came to see you?'

Lizzie looked at Larky then back at Maggie. 'He did not come to see me, as far as I am aware, Maggie. I was in the milking sheds for quite some time, so he might have come to see me and found me out. He never came to the sheds or the dairy, though. Peter was at the cottage, as I explained last night. Peter and I are… were in love. We had kept it a secret, but last night we were discussing our future. When I came back from the milking, that is when I found… I found his body.' Tears rolled down her sad, pale face.

The room went quiet while everyone took in what was being said.

A clatter of cutlery and plates startled them. Larky banged his hand on the table. 'No. He was not for you. I heard you both talking cosy in your cottage. I have seen you by the dairy wall. He was not the man for you. He was weak and lily-livered. I was going to marry you. Me. But no, you have to disgrace yourself with him. He deserved it all.'

Shock reverberated around the room. Larky had admitted to the murder with no pressure at all. Maggie spoke first, 'So my husband never made it home? He never saw Peter or went to the cottage?'

'Him? He was so drunk he fell of the cart when it came through the gates. I pulled him up onto his feet and moved him behind the barn. I knew he would be found there, and after I had dealt with Peter, he would be the obvious culprit. Lizzie, I love you. Why did you refuse my kiss? One kiss, and Peter would be alive.' Larky stood up, and the crowd moved in towards him. Maggie knew he was not going to leave without assistance. Every face had anger written across it.

He tried to justify himself, 'If she had loved me, none of this would have happened. She is the guilty one.' His voice was at a loud, high pitch. He was in a frenzied state. His hand trembled when he pointed towards Lizzie.

Lizzie ran from the cottage.

Maggie turned to Mason. 'Keep him here. No one is to touch him. Do you all hear me? Back away. The boy is sick in the head.' She doubted he was, but she did not want more bloodshed. 'Let the authorities deal with him. Not one hair on his head do you touch, understand?' She glanced at her staff.

'Me and two others will hold him until he is taken, Maggie. Go on back to work, you lot. The master will be in the foulest of tempers when he returns—don't give him a reason to use the stick,' Mason addressed the rest of his team.

Maggie sent a man to let the constable know and went to comfort Lizzie. Deep inside, she was disappointed. Maggie realised now that she *could* manage the farm on her own... and guilt gnawed at her over that feeling of disappointment that Jacob would be returning soon.

He is your husband. It is his farm; he has a right to return. You should wish for other things, Maggie Sawbury. Not a life of misery for another. No matter how rotten inside they are.

Their workers would have been supportive. Now, as Mason had reminded her, she would have a grump of a man to attend to and a broken-hearted friend. The mixed emotions the summer fayre had brought her way were incredible. She would never forget the lessons she had learned that day.

Chapter 13

Wednesday, the 12th of November, 1856

The metal taste still lingered in Maggie's mouth. Disturbing noises brought her back to the present day. She could smell a mix of fragrant herbs in the room, and with reluctance she opened her eyes. It always pained her to open them. Slowly, she focused on the bright light that surrounded her.

She wanted to yawn, but the pain was too much, so she suppressed it as best she could. It led to a coughing fit. She groaned. Her body ached so much.

'Hello, sleepyhead.' Alice Summers stood beside her bed. Her smile was welcome. 'I bet you are thirsty. We couldn't waken you. The doctor has been here again. You have been asleep for nigh on a day. We were worried, but here you are now, so all is well.' She fussed with Maggie's pillows, not drawing breath as she worked. 'Young Nathaniel is missing you. He keeps throwing back his other milk. Yours is flowing like the local river, so if it isn't too painful for you, we will draw a little to keep him nourished. But first things first: chicken broth strained through muslin. The cook has boiled some today in the hope that you come around. Mrs. Arlington will be pleased. All for sending for the undertaker, that one, but I told her, Maggie is a strong girl. She's in dream-land now, but she will come back to us soon.'

Maggie tried to smile, but it was an effort. She reached out with her arm to touch her friend. The strain in the woman's face showed. To Maggie it proved that she meant something to her and that the nanny did not use her to play lady of the house as Jacob had suggested.

'I know, darling girl, the pain of it all. I know. My father was a violent man. I understand.'

Maggie moved her head from side to side.

'No? No what, Maggie? What are you trying to tell me?'

Maggie pulled her arm across her chest to her left breast. It was a slow movement, but eventually the nanny understood her message.

'No pain on that side. Ah, Nathaniel. Yes, maybe if we lay him beside you, he can feed from you, but are you certain the bruising will not be too much for you?'

Again Maggie moved her head from side to side. She moved her hand to the right breast, and as she touched it, she flinched.

'No, that one is not ready, my dear. Too much broken skin. It is clean and free from infection, though. The doctor prepared a poultice and instructed it should not be used for feeding for one month.'

Maggie closed her eyes and reopened them to show she understood.

'Lucy is going to come and give me a hand to wash and change you. Things are not wonderful below the bedclothes. We have managed to keep your dignity, but it is time we tried and sat you in a chair and changed the bed linen. It is going to be very painful for you, but it has to be done. Madam doesn't want her son to be brought into the room until it is the case.'

Maggie's heart missed a beat on hearing Nathaniel being called Mrs. Arlington's son. The physical pain was nothing compared to the emotional pains she experienced in her past.

The women washed Maggie while she lay on the bed. She gripped at the bedclothes during the proceedings as each movement sent waves of fire through her body. Two footmen had been instructed on how to conduct themselves, and they lifted her gently from the bed into a large chair. They were thoughtful and gentle and averted their eyes whenever required.

She watched her bed being stripped and cleaned. It was so frustrating for her, a woman who kept busy on a daily basis.

At last the ordeal was over. Maggie and her bed were refreshed. She sat propped by soft down pillows. Despite her condition, she appreciated the luxury of her surroundings. She knew she must have been seriously ill for the family to place her in such a room. Soft, pastel green walls, rich, sage green velvet curtains, and contrasting accessories gave the illusion of a spring morning. Maggie felt like a queen. She imagined the London palace bedrooms to be of similar decor.

The household was a good one. It had been shocked and concerned for her. The Arlington family were not ruled by the strict codes of etiquette. They had their own rules and regulations on behaviour in their home. Those who live there abided by them without question. In the short time she had been amongst them, she had made many friends. They had all enquired after her and sent messages wishing her good health. Small posies were sent to cheer her up, and Nanny said the cook couldn't wait to create tempting dishes.

Alice had opened the window to a small slit, and a fresh autumn perfume filled Maggie's lungs. She sensed a moment of peace in her life. A tap on the door announced a visitor. Nanny opened it and spoke in whispers to whoever stood behind.

Maggie, for some unknown reason, was embarrassed when Dukes walked over to her. He had a big smile across his face and a look of concern in his eyes.

'Mrs. Summers said I could only have a moment. I had to fight her for entry. I know it is not proper, but I wanted to say hello. To see you awake for a change. It has been a dreadful week for us all. You looked near death when I brought you here. It fair bro... well, put it this way, you look much better today, and that does my heart good. Lizzie is beside herself with worry but doing a grand job on the farm. I will fetch here for a visit soon, Maggie.'

Maggie blinked her eyes as a greeting and acknowledgement of his words.

You dear man. Your beating heart saved me. How will I ever thank you?

He said no more and walked from the room. Maggie was lifted by his visit. He was another who had shown true friendship. A little of the ice around her heart melted away. Dukes held a special place in her life. He would never know how his compassion had helped.

'I couldn't hold him back any longer, Maggie. To be fair, he needed to set his own mind at rest, and now he can take the news back to Windtop. Shame your husband hasn't come to make amends. Mr Arlington and the constable gave him a good talking to. They have warned him that he would be imprisoned if he touched you again. Mind, I think Mrs. Arlington has a few ideas for your future, but I will let her speak about them. Now, are you up for one more visitor?' Alice smiled.

Maggie nodded. She was more than ready for this one.

While waiting for Nathaniel to be brought to her, she wondered about the meaning of Mrs. Arlington having ideas about her future. Her future was to feed and leave when she'd be able to. Her husband needed her on the farm. Her duty was to him, regardless of her feelings.

In a month, Nathaniel had grown so much! He lay upon a pillow that raised him to the same height as her breast. His head rested on her body, and he suckled contentedly. She was able to curve her arm beside him, and the warmth of his body mingled with hers. The window had been closed, and she could smell the rosemary and thyme used in his Pears soap, mixed with the lavender of her bedding. Maggie inhaled the fragrance and locked it into her memory. On days when she could not see him, she would remember this moment. She would buy a bar of the soap for that very purpose.

***

A regular routine was established, and Maggie grew stronger every day. During the ten days it took her to walk upright again, her bruising had gone from black to a murky green shade. She had bruising from her brow to her shins. Her gait was unsteady, but she could move unaided from the bed to the window.

Maggie noted the hoar frosts coating the trees with their crystal-white ice. Christmas would be upon them soon. The cosy room was a blessing, but she craved for the outdoors. She longed to walk in her meadow, look down upon the river, and place flowers for her babies.

Alice and the doctor arrived on day eleven and informed her it was now time to remove the support around her jaw. It had been slackened gradually for her to eat soft foods, but today it would be removed for good.

'A great improvement, Mrs. Sawbury. Let me see you walk back to the chair. Wonderful. We will soon have you back to full fitness. Horrid affair, but you survived, and for that we are eternally grateful.' The doctor had a jolly nature, and Maggie enjoyed his visits.

'When this is removed, you will find it tender to eat at first, but it will improve. There now, all done.' While he chattered on, the doctor cut away the strips of cloth.

Maggie felt them slacken away. She touched her face. He was right: it was tender. She moved her lips apart and ran her tongue across them. Slowly, she opened her mouth a fraction.

'Ouch! Hurts!' Her first words were out.

Gentle reassurances from the doctor that all was well were most welcome. He informed her that with daily movement, she would have no after-effects from the break.

'To see her beautiful smile again would be a treat, doctor. Thank you. Madam said would you please knock on her drawing room door as you pass by. She would like a word with you. Goodbye.'

Maggie tried a weak goodbye-smile but had to be content with waving.

Alice patted her hand. 'All in good time, child, all in good time. Now another tea, I think, and then you can rest. By the way, the squire enquired about you today. Quite the talk of the town you have become. It is my understanding that his lordship is to be engaged. Flora Tamworth is to be the lucky bride. Rather a catch, that one, and so is he—the most handsome squire we have had in these parts. What am I saying; his father is the only one I have known, aside from Stephen. It will be a glamorous affair, the wedding. Not that she is any great beauty. Money match, that one, I guarantee.' Alice had her back to Maggie while preparing the tea. Her constant chatter began to annoy Maggie. Alice could not see the tears that fell onto the counterpane, nor the white knuckles of her friend as she clenched her fists. It was the only way Maggie could stop herself from screaming.

As she sipped her tea and stared across the room, her thoughts went to Stephen. If only he visited—there was so much she wanted to say to him! She would take the risk of public humiliation. He was worth it, and she should never have walked away.

No. I do not love him. He is not worth my tears. Nathaniel's arrival has confused me. How could I ever love a man who abused me? He is no better than Jacob. Remember, Maggie! Always remember!

Alice took her cup away and brought Nathaniel in for his next feed.

Maggie held out her arms. 'Hold 'im.'

Her words were not formed, but Alice heard her and handed her the baby. 'While you feed him, I am going for some fresh air again. Will you be alright with him alone?'

'Yes.' Maggie was more than happy they were left alone together. He was the sunshine in her dark, her heartbeat.

She settled back in the chair and allowed peace to wash over her. When the baby had finished feeding, Alice had not returned, so Maggie took her chance and whispered in his ear. The pain in her jaw was minimal, and her words came out stilted, but she knew he would understand them. He was part of her, and they communicated without words.

'You are my son. My flesh and blood. I pulled you from my body. Another woman will be called mama, but I am your mother. I gave you life. One day, we will have to part, but I will always be there for you, watching over you. I love you.' She kissed his brow.

His eyes looked into hers. The son knew his mother. In those few seconds, the bonding process had taken place. No matter what would happen after that day—even though separated, they would be together for one moment in time.

Alice returned and took him back to the nursery. Maggie lay on the bed, emotionally drained. The news of Stephen's engagement had come as a surprise. It was one thing to know he had lain in the arms of many women, and another altogether to imagine him married to someone else.

Life was a miserable friend.

She curled her body into a curve, like a new-born, as best she could and released tears of sorrow. When there were no more tears, she gave into sleep. A partridge released its scratched, high-pitched call in the distance, and she heard the hooves of a horse going through the town.

Gradually, the noises faded, and memories took over.

Chapter 14

Thursday, the 20th of September, 1856

'We have to release the birds this week. Squire wants all we have. He has several shooting parties in November,' Jacob addressed the back of Maggie's head. 'They've bred well. I had Mason make a new pen behind the old one.'

Without turning around, Maggie replied, 'That is excellent news. They will bring in a good income. Maybe you could invest some of the money in new equipment. Goodness knows we could do with some.' She had a belligerent tone in her voice and knew she would suffer for it, but anytime the squire was mentioned, she thought back to her last meeting with Stephen. She had seen him on several occasions when he was passing through town, but they had never acknowledged each other. On the few occasions when they found themselves alone he had flirted openly with words. Maggie had never responded and kept what dignity she could. It had taken an enormous effort to walk away. She could not risk her feelings for him.

'We need more livestock, not machinery. Keep your mouth tight about things you do not understand. Now, I have asked Mason and James to take the birds. I am going into town to negotiate a price for pigs, and we could do with a few more milkers.'

Maggie remained silent. It was the safest option.

'Word has it that Sully has a pair of large, lop-eared swine. We've not had them before. I hear they are docile beasts. Good all round is my understanding. Quite fancy a pair. By the way, Meg's litter is on the move now. The runt is no good. Blind in one eye, I fancy. I was going to shoot him but he might be of use here, to ward off the fox from the pens. The other two are prime specimens. If they shepherd like their mother, we will be lucky. Good girl, my Meg.'

Maggie nodded. She was used to removing runt animals. The majority died within hours of her feeding them. When the lambs made it through, they only did until spring, and then they were slaughtered. It never paid to get too close when you knew they were going to be your Easter feast, but she still shed a tear each time.

One of Maggie's pleasures was a day without Jacob on the farm that she's spend watching new-borns nuzzle around their mother, and she could not wait for him to depart.

Jacob left instructions for the men. She wondered why he bothered. Every year it was the same routine: he avoided extra work and delegated to those around him. The privilege of being the boss. Many farmers pulled their weight around their farm, and they also respected their staff. The workers they had left were her friends, and they stayed because of her. Those not so worried went and worked for other farmers after a few months.

'I will ensure they carry out their tasks, husband. Do not fret. I will take Meg a few extra scraps. She will need them. I hope you get a bargain with old Sully.'

'Don't stand around gossiping. Go and take that runt away. Meg can't afford to waste good feed on a runt,' Jacob snarled back. 'I'll expect my supper fresh on my return.'

'As always, husband. As always. Goodbye.'

Maggie bit back. His meals were always fresh, and she objected to his insinuation that he was served otherwise. She stomped to the barn. He had set her hackles for the day, and she was annoyed with herself for allowing him to ruin her mood.

Her heart softened when she saw the pups. In the corner of a stall lay the blind dog. Meg's tail thumped when she saw her mistress, who rewarded her by ruffling her ear. The dog's thriving pair leapt and jumped, yapping at Maggie's ankles.

'You clever girl, well done. This little one is not going to make it as a herder. He's coming with me—let me take him, and I will do my best.' Maggie lifted the pup, wrapped him in sackcloth and placed him in her basket.

She left the barn and returned to the farmhouse. To her surprise, Stephen was sitting on his horse in the yard. He looked magnificent, so elegant. Maggie took a moment to capture the image. She tried to keep an even tone to her voice. It came out clipped and cold. 'A pleasure to see you, sir. Are you here about the partridge release?'

She watched as he swung down from his mount. Even through his riding jacket, she could see his arm muscles swell. All thoughts of anger against him from his alibi offer vanished with that one movement. If she was hostile and unfriendly, she would never see him again.

'Maggie.' He strode towards her.

Frantically she looked around, not wanting anyone to hear him say her name.

'Mr Avenell, please leave. If you are here for no other reason than to see me, please go. We cannot move forward. I am a married woman, and you are the squire's son. What do you want with me?'

'Invite me inside, and I will tell you.' Stephen moved towards the door. He opened it, and Maggie stepped inside.

She placed the basket on a chair and remembered the pup inside. Grateful for the distraction, she lifted him out and held him in both hands. She put his face to hers, nose to nose. It was cold, a good sign.

'Well, he's better than a basket of eggs. What a dandy-looking little fellow. Is he a weakling?' Stephen ran his finger over the head of the pup. His finger lingered dangerously close to her breast, and Maggie reacted as swiftly as she could to prevent the further caresses she knew would follow.

'Here, hold him for me. He's blind in one eye, I think. I will get him some egg and milk. He is sweet. Two others have survived. Meg had them in the barn two weeks back. Jacob noticed the runt but never mentioned it until today. He chose to leave this little one to struggle.' 'He has a habit of doing that, your husband. Leaving little ones to struggle.'

Maggie chose to ignore the double entendre in his words. She was not going to rise to the bait and slander her husband.

'He is blind in both eyes, I fear. Look, if I move my fingers in front of his eyes, he does not follow. He is useless, I am afraid.' Stephen said.

'Nothing is useless. He deserves a chance,' Maggie replied. 'Here, little one. A feast for you.'

Hungrily the pup lapped and sucked drop after drop of mashed bread and milk. He wagged his tail and disgraced himself on her pinafore. Stephen found it hilarious, and the pair laughed together.

'Just what I need: more washing.' She removed her apron and settled the pup in a box by the fire.

'With you in control of his life, I think he stands a chance. A lucky dog.' Stephen's eyes twinkled with mischief.

'Stop that talk. We should not meet like this. My husband is in town on business, and I think you have been inside with me long enough. The night of the murder was different, but now you have no reason to dally here. I am going to attend to my fowl; you can stay and watch, should you wish. Even better, you could lend a hand.' Maggie laughed at her idea.

'You tempt me, madam. I am here on business, should you wish to know. I have come to inform you that the bottom field has two damaged fences, so do not graze your sheep until your men have repaired them. You would not want to lose a flock. I noticed it while exercising Raven.'

'Gracious, no we do not, thank you. Now, I become Mrs. Sawbury outside this door, you understand?'

She leant against the doorframe, and with one movement Stephen brushed his lips against her cheek. Maggie gasped at his audacity.

'I understand, Mrs. Sawbury.' Stephen winked in a suggestive manner, and Maggie opened the door. The chemistry was too strong for them to stay in the room together any longer.

They walked to his horse, and Maggie had the pleasure of watching him remount. How she wished she could ride off with him, leave the farm and Jacob! To sit behind him and wrap her arms around his slender waist. To lay her head on his broad shoulder while the wind whipped through her hair. To fly through fields and towns on an endless journey.

While she collected eggs, Maggie tried to imagine life away from the farm. It was easy enough to imagine it without Jacob, but not without the farm. Windtop was dull and grey to look at, but it was her home. She had made it a comfortable residence, and her heart was in every brick.

The sound of hooves brought her out of her daydream. She peeped through the gap in the henhouse door. Stephen had come back to the farm. She straightened her pinafore and composed herself. He always made her feel flustered. One look or one movement could set her off; he had a way about him.

'Mr Avenell, you return. What have we done to deserve two visits in one day?' Maggie felt the first spots of rain upon her face. 'You have brought rain with you, sir, perhaps you should get home before it sets in for the day.'

If you stay, I will not resist you. You are a danger to me. Please go.

'I came to tell you I have set two of my men to repair your fence. They were found in need of work. Lazing in a barn is not my idea of work,' he added as an afterthought. 'It is more of a pleasure.'

'Thank you. It was very kind. I will mention it to my husband upon his return. Now please excuse me, I have a pup to attend to before he creates more laundry.' Maggie smiled and started towards the house.

'It will need an inspection in one hour. I think you should carry it out before the sheep are led in to graze.' He looked at her with such intensity that she realised there was a second meaning to his words.

'In one hour, it will be either my husband or I who comes to inspect the work. Thank you again for your troubles.' Maggie was shocked at her boldness. If she went to the field to inspect the fence, she would be paving the way for their friendship to advance further. A dangerous game to play. One half of her hoped Jacob would return and have to carry out the inspection, the other half hoped she had another chance to spend time with Stephen, away from prying eyes.

She left him so that he could turn his horse and depart, not daring to look back in case one of the workers had been watching them. She had to behave in a normal manner.

The pup took his second feed, and she carried him out to the barn where the dogs were penned in while Jacob was not around. His siblings were playing, and his mother sat watching. He ran towards her and tried to nuzzle under her belly, but she lifted her top lip and showed a row of white teeth. A low growl warned Maggie that the pup was not welcome. Meg was normally such a placid dog, but nature had its own methods, and Maggie decided to keep him back at the house. It was going to be tiring getting him to feed and sleep during regular hours. Plus he had to be kept away from Jacob; blind in one eye was one thing, to be totally blind would be considered a burden. Maggie wanted him; she needed something to love and nurture. She would try her hardest to fight his corner.

On her return to the house, she made a carry pouch to hang around her neck. The makeshift sling rested on her chest, and the pup settled to sleep in his new cocoon. The staff laughed when they saw what she had done.

Lizzie was impressed by Maggie's idea. 'You have a great mind for inventions, Maggie. Maybe you could invent a machine to produce the perfect man.' She grinned. It was good to see her smile, a rare event since Peter's death.

'I am sure there is one out there, Lizzie. He has just got to hear about you first,' Maggie teased.

'He would look at you over me, which is a fact I am sure of, Maggie. You have a glow about you today. Will we see a swelling in a few months?' Lizzie stroked the pup, and her question hung in the air until Maggie interpreted its meaning.

'No, Lizzie. No baby due. The last one was exactly that, I fear. Sadly I am only destined to be the mother of a runt, blind dog. No children will run this farm, and if he doesn't keep out of Jacob's way, nor will he.' A sad atmosphere settled over the two women.

'What have you called him? And he is going to make it, Maggie, because he has the best mother in the world. You will protect him from harm. He seems healthy enough, and if you train him well, he will find his way around. Come on, give him a name, that way he will have a place on earth.'

'Oh, I am at a loss. I will think of one later in the day. I have to be away to the house, then to the bottom fields for a fence inspection. The squire has sent his men to repair them, but apparently we have to check them before the flock can enter.' She made it sound a chore when, secretly, she hoped Jacob was delayed. To see Stephen again would make it the perfect day. Whenever she found loneliness overwhelming her, she thought back to the day at the brook and the evening walk home.

Just when she was leaving the barn, she was struck with inspiration for a name.

'Brook. I am going to call him Brook. It suits him, don't you think?'

'I most certainly do. An unusual name, though. What made you think of that one?' said Lizzie. 'Hello Brook, welcome to Windtop farm.'

'A pleasant moment in the past—no other reason,' Maggie replied with a flippant air. 'Brook just seems appropriate.'

***

Maggie spent the hour cleaning chamber pots, plus the tools Jacob had instructed her to wash down. She looked at the sharp blade of the castration knife and wondered how many women would be tempted to use it on their husbands. She giggled at her private thoughts. Something had changed inside of her since meeting Stephen. He brought out a person who had been suppressed. Would she have been bolder and more daring if she had stayed with her parents or had married off to a different farmer? She checked the hour and decided that Jacob was not going to return in time to go to the fields.

She placed Brook back into his sling and took a slow walk through the lane. Inside the first field, she could see their flock grazing with an easy manner. They moved as if one animal through the lush grasses. Their heads lifted to watch her pass by, and she watched as they chewed lazily. Red paint on the hind was a statement. They had bellies full of new life. Lambing in springtime would be a busy one. Maggie envied them, shook off the feeling, and gave Brook a tickle around his ear. He stirred and whimpered.

Not wanting him to christen the front of her gown, she lifted him down onto the floor. He waddled a few paces and squatted to do his business. The sheep watched him with curiosity. His pink tongue hung from the side of his mouth as he bumped and staggered his way around a large stone. Maggie was enchanted by his stumpy legs and the fat belly wobbling from side to side. She scooped him up, and within seconds, he was asleep again. Seeing him take his first steps and avoid obstacles with his constant sniffing had made her smile. He was a determined dog.

There were no signs of the men when she reached the bottom of the field. Freshly sliced wood planks and woven willow threads showed there had been considerable damage. She was surprised that Jacob had not noticed it on previous occasions, although she suspected he knew and was waiting until the farmer on the adjoining farm fixed them. It would keep the coins in his pocket. His penny-pinching habits were an embarrassment. Fortunately, Stephen had dealt with the issue on time.

Brook squirmed, and Maggie took him out and placed him on the floor. He waddled away, and she watched again as he manoeuvred his way around. His nose rummaged amongst the grass, and his fluffy tail wagged continuously. Maggie sat on a large boulder, pretending she was not really sure why she lingered.

Maggie Sawbury, you know why you are killing time here.

Not disappointed, she saw her reason ambling along the opposite field. Tall and relaxed, Stephen waved to her.

He is so handsome. Look at his body; those thighs!

Maggie stood up and nodded a greeting.

'Mrs. Sawbury, what luck. I was just coming to inspect the fencing, but I see you have beaten me to it.' Stephen strode toward the fence and made a play of inspection.

'There is no one else here, Stephen. Your men have finished their work. A fine job they did too, thank you.' From the corner of her eye, she could see the pup settle into a mound of grass.

'Brook, you have worn yourself out. Come along, time for another sleep.' She went over to where he lay.

'He has a name. An unusual one, I must say. Does it have reference to anything in particular?' Stephen asked.

'It may, but then again, it may not,' Maggie giggled.

Stephen clambered over the fence and lost his footing, falling onto his back. Maggie laughed and placed Brook on his stomach. Stephen pulled her to the ground, and before she could protest, his lips engaged hers. Passion raged through her body, and only the fear of being caught brought her to her senses. She pushed him away and stood up.

Stephen remained on the floor and rolled onto his back. The pup took the opportunity to investigate. He crawled along, sniffing and licking. Stephen played with him for several minutes. It was a heart-warming scene. A black and white bundle of fur and a grown man, rolling around in play. Maggie fought back the urge to join them—the kiss had lit a flame of desire—, but she knew to do so would be foolish. Brook found his voice, gave a yap, and chased his tail.

Stephen stood up and grinned. 'I forgot what fun a puppy can be. Ours are reared for hunting, not play. He will bring you joy; his blindness will not hold him back. He is the possessor of a strong character, like his mistress.'

'Your teasing and flattery will get you nowhere. I should not be here alone with you. If Jacob came now, how would we explain ourselves? A married woman and a single man.'

Stephen brushed his clothing free of grass. What she had said was true, but she could see he resented her words. He startled her when his voice cracked with emotion.

'Listen to me. You are trapped in a marriage; goodness knows how he snagged you. He does not deserve to rise in the morning and see your face, your beautiful face.' He cupped her cheek with his hand. She nestled her face into his palm for a few seconds before reality struck home, and she pulled her head up abruptly.

'This is wrong, Stephen. I am going to leave now. Please accept our thanks for repairing the fencing. From now on, if my husband is not home, leave a message with Lizzie. To see you is a painful reminder of what I cannot have in life. You are not available and out of my social class. You have a flirtatious manner, and if I fall for it any further, I will be left with a broken heart. I bid you good afternoon and goodbye. I was foolish to come alone.'

She turned and walked towards the farm. Inside her chest, she held a pain so fierce she could not fathom out what would take it away. Without Stephen, her life would return to the mundane. There would be no daydreams. Yet she knew that if she turned back now, it would be the start of a dangerous courtship.

Stephen called out after her. 'You cannot deny the chemistry between a man and a woman. If they are the right mix, there is nothing that can be done. That kiss should have proved it to you. Walk away, but you cannot hide from your feelings—or me mine. Chemistry.'

Maggie continued to walk, and the pup bounced against her chest.

Do not look back, Maggie; his kiss is not worth the pain of discovery!

There was no delight on the walk home. The rain that had threatened earlier fell heavier and heavier. She met with the men bringing home the cattle and sheep. Questions were answered, and instructions given—reminders of where her duties lay: with Windtop and her friends. With her husband and the memories of stillborn children. This was the map God had given her to follow; he had offered her no side roads, something she knew she should never forget.

Chapter 15

Monday, the 15th of December, 1856

'My dear, you cannot possibly return to that dreadful man. It is not five weeks since he broke nigh on every bone in your body. And only the dear Lord knows what he did to your insides. You must see reason. Nanny, speak to her, and I will return later in the day. My son also depends on you, please, never forget that fact. You have an obligation.'

Felicity Arlington had a face as scarlet as the dress she was wearing. For over half an hour, she had sat sharing plans for Maggie's future within her household. In her considered opinion, Maggie would be a good candidate to step into Alice Summer's shoes upon her retirement.

After she had left, Alice pleaded with her friend. 'Maggie, she is right. You should be wary about returning to the farm. Your husband could undo all the good the doctor has done; the man is unstable. I am nigh on fifty years. Nathaniel is tiring as a babe. I will find him even harder work when he walks. You settle him better than anyone else; you have a gift. This is a wonderful opportunity—take it, and enjoy life here as I have done.'

Maggie looked out over the town, her mind in turmoil. There was so much to think about. She was walking with the aid of a stick, and her bruises were subsiding. Her jaw had healed completely, but the mental scars had not. Jacob had once visited the Arlington house to demand that she return home. Mr Arlington, always the gentleman, had intervened and told him it was against the doctor's orders. If he wanted his wife home, he had to show more consideration for her plight. He was, after all, the cause of it, and for however long it would take for her to be back to full health, she would stay with them. Her husband had slunk off with his tail between his legs, so she had been informed by Dukes.

'Alice—if I stay, it will bring trouble to all involved. Jacob is fully aware he needs to be more careful around me now. Lizzie mentioned that fact on her last visit. Oh, how I would dearly love to watch Nathaniel grow and share his life adventure with you! Life here is such a pleasure, something I agree is lacking in my life.' Maggie stood and paced the floor; her legs were stiff through sitting for too long. 'This stick reminds me my physical health is not at its best. My face I can bear to look at now. I accept that a child will not be born from this body. What I cannot cope with is leaving Windtop farm. My friends are there, I cleaned that place on my wedding day. I made it my home, regardless of who I have to share it with.'

She stopped to smell flowers in a vase that sat on a dresser close by her bed. She stroked the counterpane and sat on the edge of the bed. There was so much to lose if she left, but Jacob would not let her rest there for much longer. His visit had just been the beginning; he would make a nuisance of himself until she gave into his demands.

'I will speak with Jacob. If Dukes can take me to the farm, I will try to persuade my husband to grant me until the New Year. Nathaniel will be weaned from me around that time, and life will move along for all of us.'

***

Dukes assisted her through the house, and Maggie was grateful for his support and once again was reminded of his strength.

'I never realised how weak I have become. Having a strong arm to lean on is more than welcome.'

'You will soon be back on your own two feet, but until then I am more than happy to be your leaning post.' Dukes smiled down at her as they walked slowly across the courtyard.

'The support of good friends brings joy to my heart, Dukes. Thank you.' Maggie looked up into his face. His smiling eyes always gave her comfort.

Dukes assisted her into the enclosed carriage Mr Arlington had instructed that she was to use. Mrs. Arlington was anxious Maggie should be kept warm and free from chills. They could not afford for their son to contract a winter cold. Maggie was touched by their concern and felt every bit the lady as they jogged along the lanes.

Word had been sent to Windtop that she was paying a visit, and the farmhouse was to be warmed through. Maggie and Alice giggled at the thought of Jacob being given instructions to treat her like royalty. Dukes was instructed to stay by her side at all times. At no point was Jacob allowed to raise his voice or fists. Mrs. Arlington had been all for Mr Arlington attending, but her driver had reassured her he was more than capable. Should he need assistance, the staff at the farm were far more loyal to its mistress than master.

Brook came bounding over to the carriage, yapping as she called his name. He sniffed frantically and took great leaps to get to her.

'My, how you have grown! Oh, Brook, I have missed you so much! You are the reason I need to return. Has he cleaned your eyes?'

'What do you think? Brook has found a new mistress, not one who lingers in silk sheets on a daily basis!' Lizzie's voice rang out.

Maggie swung around and faced her friend. 'Lizzie! Oh, Lizzie, how lovely to see you! Thank you, he looks so well.'

The two women hugged, neither one wanting to release the other. Eventually, Dukes gave a subtle cough before reminding Maggie she needed to get in the warm. 'I cannot afford to lose my job, Maggie. Go inside, and I will find your husband.'

'He is out with the plough. It's stone picking day for the others. I am so thrilled you came to visit, Maggie, I got out of that chore. I was instructed to tend to the farm and dairy. He would have me out there breaking my back if he had his way. You, out of all of us, knows what he is like—mean. He will not spare a penny for extra help. Come on, gal, you look tired. Let us get sat in the warm.'

While Dukes went in search of her husband, Maggie took the opportunity to gather a few personal effects from the bedroom. She was determined to persuade him to honour those extra months. She would use money as enticement, it was his weakness, and the very mention of a few more months of supplementary pay might change his mind.

One of the items she put in her bundle was a small coin with a hole in it. She had found it while walking into town one morning. It had sparkled when the sunlight flashed over it, and Maggie had picked it up, intending to use it as a lucky charm. She had forgotten about it, but today she decided she needed all the luck she could lay her hands upon. Plus, if ever she got the chance, she would pass it on to Nathaniel, a keepsake from his mother. Not that he would ever know that, but Maggie liked the idea that he would have something of hers.

She heard the door slam shut and Lizzie talking to Dukes. Maggie lingered a short while. She wanted her two friends to have some time alone. It was still her aim to bring them together. Dukes was a special man, his kind nature and rugged looks were a good combination. Maggie had become fond of him and wanted him to have a good woman in his life. If she could persuade her two best friends to become a couple, it would be a job well done.

Another slam of the door made her jump. Inhaling three times for courage, she brushed down the front of her gown and prepared herself for the meeting with her husband. Her foot faltered on the top step.

Come on, Maggie. Dukes is here to protect you. Jacob won't touch you while he is there. Courage, girl, courage!

The two men were sat at the table, and both glanced her way when she entered the room.

Dukes stood and pulled out a chair. 'You look done in, sit.'

Maggie did as she was instructed. It smarted that her husband had not shown her this courtesy. She could feel the tension between the two men and wondered if they had argued outside.

'So you're back then? Lizzie changed the bedding, not that she made any of it dirty,' Jacob scowled. He reminded Maggie of a sulking boy.

'It was kind of her, on both counts,' Maggie retorted with a touch of sarcasm. She looked around, but her friend had slipped away.

She fidgeted on the chair. It was now or never. 'I am not completely back to full health, but I am much improved. However, the child still needs nursing and will do for a few more months. I am fully aware you are keen to have me back at your side, husband.' Maggie held up her hand when Jacob tried to speak. 'Allow me to finish please. I mean no disrespect, but I tire quite quickly.'

Jacob gave a low growl of consent. He appeared to be struggling with his temper, and Maggie knew she must act fast.

'The money will come in useful, and while I can still feed him, we can earn.'

'Your place is here with your husband. I have rights. Those namby-pamby folk down there can try and tell me what to do, but I have the right to my wife beside me in bed.'

Maggie was embarrassed he should bring up such a delicate matter in front of Dukes, who to him was a virtual stranger. He had already embarrassed her by mentioning Lizzie's refusal to share his bed. She needed to convince him to allow her to stay, one way or another. She was in no position to allow him to bed her.

'Dukes, would you give us some privacy, please? I have something to discuss with my husband, and it should be said just between the pair of us.' Maggie watched Dukes as he went to the door. He turned and spoke to Jacob. 'You stay in that seat. No matter what she says or does, you do not move. Do you hear me?'

'Threaten me in my own home, would you?' Jacob's face turned to the man, and they locked eyes.

Maggie had to diffuse the situation quickly. 'Dukes, I think he will behave. And Jacob, to be fair, you nearly killed me. He is only concerned your temper will injure me again. Now a spell in prison over someone as low-ranking as me is not worth it; I am sure you will agree.' She let out a sigh when Jacob looked back at her.

He nodded. 'You are right there—to do a spell in prison over you is not worth the time. What is it you have to say? I am a busy man, even more so now you are not pulling your weight, so get it said.'

Dukes slipped outside. Lizzie must have been lingering close by, because their muffled voices drifted into the cottage. Maggie was touched that neither of her friends had moved too far, should she need them. Life on the farm with them in her life would be a happier one than she was used to.

If only things were different. I am tired of Jacob and his tantrums.

Jacob slapped his hand on the table and made her jump. Maggie knew she must tell him her idea swiftly.

'The doctor said I will most likely not be able to carry any more children, and if I do, they will be weaklings. The kick you gave me caused some kind of internal trauma. It is my regret I have never given you a child, but I am sure you would not want to risk me giving birth to a deformed one. So this is what I suggest. We take the time to earn money and get me to full strength. You find a clean woman outside of town to satisfy your needs and leave Lizzie alone. In four months' time, I will return and keep house again. Lizzie will return to the dairy, and we will employ a girl to tend to the house. You will also leave her alone. You have one paid companion for your needs. Do you understand?' Maggie had no idea where her inner strength came from, but she could hear her voice was stronger and more commanding than usual. She drew strength from the fact that she had the support of the Arlington family.

Jacob sat still and stared at her, his eyes showing no signs of emotion. Maggie waited for him to explode and was ready to call for assistance. Instead, he looked at her as if he was meeting her for the first time. 'Well, well, well, my wife has a bite to her. Surprisingly, I think what you have said makes sense. The money will be useful to pay the cleaning girl. Help will be most welcome.' He waved his arm around in a circle, and Maggie flinched. 'This place costs a fortune to run. You have no idea.'

'So it's settled. We will both benefit in the long run. It is sad we never had a child. I am sorry, Jacob. Things may have been different between us. I was so young when my parents sold me to you.' Maggie had a moment of nostalgia, and the memories of carrying her children overwhelmed her, but she held back the tears. She could not weaken. Jacob agreeing with minimal fuss was a relief.

In true Jacob-style, he ruined the moment. 'Sold you? Forced me to take you away. You are no good to man or beast. Talking of beast, you can take yours with you. If not, I will be rid of him.' He stood up. The scraping and clattering of his chair brought forth a tap at the door.

'Stay there, I am fine,' Maggie called out to Dukes.

'Yes, she is fine. It is me who has no son and heir, no wife in his bed. Oh, yes, she is fine and dandy.' Jacob went to the door and yanked it open with such force that it creaked on the hinges. 'Take her away. A man in a black gown saying words from a book made her my wife by law. If that law could be changed, I wish it for the morrow.' He stormed out of the house.

Lizzie went white. 'Maggie, he be furious. Please do not leave me here with him. I have avoided him as best as I could, but he will take it out on me soon, I feel it as sure as day.' Lizzie held Maggie's arm; the girl was frantic and looked frightened.

'Don't fret, Lizzie. I have warned him away and given him the opportunity to look elsewhere. Another will suffer his brutal ways, I am sad and pleased to say. Should he turn nasty—call for Mason. Plus our friend Dukes here will assist you.'

'Lizzie, I will come by each day to check on you. And if you will excuse my frankness, from what I gather by Maggie's words, Jacob will be in the tavern tonight looking for a new lady-friend. Shocking for Maggie to have to live with, I know, but a brave, bold move on her part. It protects both of you. Calm down, and I will speak with Mason on your behalf,' Dukes reassured Lizzie, and Maggie's heart went out to him. He obviously cared for her friend.

She hugged Lizzie goodbye and went to the carriage. Looking back at her home, she felt sad. She did so love the farm but knew she was not in a fit state to return for a few months. In the yard, Dukes stood talking to Mason, and Brook sat by his feet with his tail thumping up dust.

Maggie turned to Lizzie, who had followed her outside. 'It's funny how dogs know who to trust. I've never seen him do that to Jacob.'

They both watched the dog sniff the air then move whenever his new friend did. Maggie felt a twinge of jealousy mixed with a touch of self-pity. Everything she ever loved always found somebody else. She was destined to be alone forever.

Dukes strode over and addressed Maggie. 'I have arranged with Mason to bring Brook to the yard tomorrow. He will be fine there and safe. Plus I think he will do you good. I can see how much he means to you.' Had Dukes given her a gold sovereign, Maggie couldn't have been happier. There was a temptation to kiss his cheek in thanks.

Instead, she clapped her hands. 'Oh, you most certainly have made me happy, but will the Arlington family tolerate him?' Maggie did not want to get her hopes up.

'Don't you worry about them. They love to take in waifs and strays.' Dukes touched her shoulder, laughing at his own joke.

Maggie, embarrassed by such a public gesture, shrugged him off, but she did so laughingly. 'So am I the waif or the stray?'

Dukes turned to Lizzie, 'What say you, Lizzie? Is your mistress one or the other?'

With great indignation, Lizzie straightened her back and said, 'Maggie is none of those things. She is just the unluckiest woman I know. If she had married a different man, she would never have the need to be taken in by anybody. Now if you will excuse me, Mr Dukes, I have work to do. Maggie, I will come and visit you on market day, if it pleases.'

They watched as she flounced off towards the dairy. Mason laughed and muttered something about hot-headed women.

'There, see what you have done with your joking. Upset our Lizzie. She is sweet on you, I am sure of it. You would not do wrong making friends with her, she is a good person. Her luck is as great as mine, yet she never fails to think of me,' Maggie reprimanded Dukes.

'She is not for me, Maggie. Too feisty. I will make it up to her when she visits next. I will introduce her to a young groom who has noticed her. Sam asked after her the last time she came over. He's a good lad. Time is ticking along, let us put Brook here in his pen and get you back to yours.'

Maggie took a last glance at her home, noting how sad and drab it looked. If only Jacob would allow her to have a floral trellis around the door, it would brighten the front view from the lane. She had wanted to put a window box outside the kitchen window with a few colourful blooms to make a dull day vibrant. Jacob had dismissed the idea, never giving a reason. She wondered if his first wife had ever looked at it in the same light and whether he had dismissed her wishes so flippantly, too.

'That was a great sigh.' Dukes helped her into the carriage.

'Yes, it was rather. I was daydreaming. I would love to see this place allowed to come alive. It has beauty but a suppressed life. There is a melancholy air about it.'

Dukes closed the door. He looked into her eyes. 'Just like its mistress. Both held back by Jacob Sawbury.'

Maggie put her head down. He was right. She and her home were exactly the same, shabby and owned by Jacob.

Chapter 16

Sunday, the 8th of February, 1857

'Brook, you scallywag, bring that back at once.' Maggie chased after the bouncing ball of fluff. He had sniffed out a shoe from the cleaning room and was enjoying a game of fling, sniff, and fetch.

'You would never think he had no sight in those doleful eyes, would you?' The boot boy held the shoe in triumph, and Brook sniffed around for more. 'Dukes suffers the worse, his shoes have more teeth marks in them than lace loops.'

'He has a fondness for Dukes, and with Brook's sense of smell, all items are in danger. It is a good thing Dukes holds a placid nature. Even Mr Arlington has taken to Brook. I found him playing a tugging game with an old sack the morning last. He was most embarrassed to be found larking about the yard.' Maggie manoeuvred Brook into the makeshift pen that had been erected for him. During the night, he had a cosy kennel inside the locked barn. He had entered the heart of everyone in the house with his mischievous ways.

'He will miss this place when you return to the farm, Maggie.' The boy had settled down to his boot shine, and Maggie sat shelling broad beans for the cook. She liked to sit in the cool air; if she did not, her return to the farm would be a hard one. She could not stay by a fire every day like she could at the present time, should she choose to do so. A lady's life was not for Maggie Sawbury.

'We will both miss the place, Will. I for one have been treated like a princess these past months. My husband came yesterday to remind me I have only three weeks left here, and I have to get back to my old life.' Maggie dreaded the thought of returning but knew she had no choice.

Jacob had made it quite clear during his visit that her duty lay with him and the farm. She had asked him why, if all was running to his favour at Windtop, she should rush back. He had no need for her anymore. The venom in his voice had been enough to make her agree to return. The fact that he did not want to be made a fool of in front of the village should be reason enough for her to understand. She could continue to attend to the boy, but she was to live at Windtop. If she chose to disobey, he would create problems for her and embarrass her present employers.

She tried the money tactic again, but it no longer worked. She was desperate for ideas to make him change his mind. Her time with Nathaniel was now more precious than ever; he was growing, and she did not want to miss one moment of his life. Alice Summers had become tearful at times. She had said it was worry about Maggie and selfish pity. She would be losing a friend and companion. Now that Maggie was no longer dependent upon a stick, they took long walks with the perambulator. They had an easy-going friendship, one that slipped into a niche all of its own. Their evenings were spent stitching for the baby and chatting about various subjects. Both avoided their past childhood, although this was their common ground. They had both opened up their hearts to each other, and then the subject had been closed. No further words were needed; only trust and support.

Chapter 17

1867

An arrangement between Jacob and the Arlington family kept Maggie in their employ until Nathaniel reached the age of ten. Alice Summers passed away in her fifty-third year, and it was a natural progression for Maggie to step into her shoes. He had a governess for his education, and Maggie to see to his basic needs.

Jacob was happy, but the farm never saw many benefits from the extra income. Maggie never questioned him but suspected he gambled it away. She still had duties on the farm and was more than happy to carry them out. Brook and Dukes took her to and fro. Dukes was as much a loyal friend as her dog.

During the summer prior to leaving home for boarding school, Nathaniel spent much of his time with his father or Dukes. One particularly glorious Sunday in August, Maggie suggested they picnicked by the lake. Dukes and Nathaniel carried a well-packed hamper basket, and Maggie carried blankets. Brook sniffed around their heels, his tail wagging in anticipation.

'I do hope the cook put in some of the game pie left over from last night,' Nathaniel said.

'All you think of is your stomach, Master Arlington,' Maggie replied. She hated calling him by his adopted name but had got used to it over the years.

'He's a growing lad, and not one of feeble mind. He knows a good pie when he eats one,' Dukes joined in the conversation. 'I think this is a fine spot, what say you, young sir?'

Nathaniel indicated to Dukes to lower the basket. 'It will be fine, Dukes. A grand spot.'

Maggie listened to them chatter about cricket. Not a sport she was interested in, but she enjoyed hearing Nathaniel's well-spoken voice animated by something he loved.

She and Brook rested by the shade of a willow tree. Her eyes were heavy from eating and from the warmth of the sun. Splashing noises woke her from a short doze, and Brook started yapping loudly.

'Hush, boy. They are swimming. Come and feel the water on your paws.' Maggie went as close to the water's edge as she dared. Dukes and Nathaniel were in full battle, spraying each other with handfuls of water.

'Maggie. Be careful. Nathaniel has the devil in him today,' Dukes shouted.

'He had better watch his step, or I'll inform the cook no more pie for the master,' she called back. 'Look, Brook is having a paddle.' She pointed to the dog splashing around in front of her.

Dukes swam over, and Maggie's heart missed a beat as he stood up. He had removed his shirt and wore an under-vest that was now clinging to his body. She could see the outline of muscles across his broad chest. He had kept his pantaloons on for dignity's sake, and they too were wrapped tighter around his thighs. When he clambered to the bank, Maggie had to force her eyes away. Dukes was an even finer specimen than Stephen. For a brief second, Maggie imagined herself in his arms. Dukes had stirred something in her that she had not felt for many years.

Oh, to lean my head against your chest and hear your heartbeat once more… The heartbeat that saved my life. Honest arms to hold me tight.

'He certainly is enjoying himself.' Dukes brought her back to reality with his laughter. Brook was swimming towards Nathaniel as the boy called to him.

'He is not alone. You appear to be a strong swimmer, and Nathaniel is having fun.' Maggie hoped her cheeks did not burn as red as they felt.

'I have enjoyed my afternoon immensely. Earning a living watching over the young man is not what I consider hard work.' Dukes rubbed his body with a blanket as best as he could and replaced his shirt. 'I will dry off on our walk back. It is so hot today—I do not envy you in those clothes. You should remove them and cool off with a swim. I'd like to see you swim… er, enjoy yourself.'

Maggie burst out laughing. 'Dukes, I think you should retract that statement. It is not something to be said in front of the boy.'

Dukes put his hand to his mouth when he realised his error. 'I am such an idiot. Forgive me. How inappropriate. I am sorry, Maggie. I didn't mean anything improper by it. Although it is not such a—'

Maggie shot him a warning glance then added a soft smile when she realised he was just teasing.

Nathaniel joined them, and Brook shook himself dry over the whole party. Laughter rang through the woodland area.

Maggie poured fresh lemonade into glasses. 'I raise my glass in a toast. To one of the finest afternoons this summer, and to the best company a woman could ask for. Thank you, gentlemen, for a wonderful picnic.'

'Hear, hear,' Nathaniel and Dukes said at the same time, then chinked their glasses in salute.

Nathaniel raised his glass high. 'To a special nanny. I am the luckiest boy alive. What say you, Dukes?'

Maggie watched Dukes swallow hard; she too had a lump in her throat but one that had come about with her son's words.

'I think anyone who comes in contact with Maggie is extremely lucky. A special lady indeed. A fine toast, young man.'

'Thank you, Dukes. How lovely. Thank you.'

'The truth, only the truth, Maggie.' He smiled at her, and Maggie returned it.

'Well, the afternoon has come to an end. We must head home. Come along, Brook.' She shook the blankets free from grass and twigs. 'Nathaniel, do you want to wrap yourself in this? Or are you going to dry off like Dukes?'

'Dry off in the sunshine, Maggie,' Nathaniel said.

'Very well, but when we get closer to the house, you must put on your shirt,' Maggie instructed.

She watched the two of them swing the nearly empty basket along, with Brook yapping around them. If a stranger passed by now she fancied they would think the trio a family. She was fortunate to have them both in her life. A perfect picture to end a perfect day.

***

Maggie returned to the farm when Nathaniel left home. Her son had become a handsome boy with a loving nature. On his return during the holiday breaks, he made it his duty to visit her. He enjoyed the farm. Maggie watched him grow from boy to man. During harvest, he helped and pulled his weight, as if the place was his own. Even Jacob enjoyed his company and often took the chance to snipe at Maggie of what might have been. She never regretted giving Nathaniel up; she knew things would have been much different between him and Jacob, had they lived together.

Nathaniel's relationship with his biological father had developed due to the friendship of his adoptive parents. He had joined the hunt and had been raised as a friend of the squire's daughter. Maggie had been present while they played alongside one another. Brother and sister shared the same blood but would never know. Stephen and his wife, Flora, had taken over the duties of the great hall when his father had died. Maggie watched both events from a distance. Stephen bore the same face on his wedding day as he did at his father's funeral. She knew then that it was a marriage of money matters, but no doubt he would find another to amuse him.

The day the village celebrated the arrival of the squire's daughter Ruth, Maggie took Nathaniel for a walk to the place where she had left him as a baby. She let him play amongst the bushes with Brook. Both animal and boy were free of all restrictions.

'You have a sister and no doubt a playmate for the future.' Maggie whispered the words in the same way she had when he was born. 'She has half your blood. I wish you and your father could know the truth.'

Nathaniel was too busy running with a stick and picking flowers to heed her words. Maggie had never forgiven Stephen for his transgressions upon her body. His only saving grace was the son she had born. Now he would spend all of his affections on his daughter, while his three year old son played in ignorance of their father's love.

Nathaniel should be the rightful heir to the great hall when Stephen passed. Maggie had prepared letters telling the truth many times and thrown them into the fire. There was no profit from the truth. She would not be believed, and it would only harm a family who had saved her life.

Chapter 18

1873 – 74

One summer, Nathaniel arrived at the farm. Tall and handsome, with a wide boyish grin, he brought to mind Maggie's brother. She was secretly pleased that he took after her side of the family. He strode towards her, and his companion had trouble keeping up with him. She trotted like a young foal, taking skittish and delicate steps.

'Hello, Maggie. I have brought Ruth to show her the farm. She is curious about life outside her home. I thought I would bring her here to taste some of your homemade goodies.'

'Hello again, Mrs.. Sawbury.' The pretty young girl held out her hand.

Maggie took one look at her son's face, and it told her something she had never considered before, something that gave her cause for concern: the pair had gone beyond childhood friends. They had fallen in love.

'Come in. I have cordial and fresh scones ready for you, young man. Ruth, I do hope you will take care of your gown. A farm is not the place for such pretty fabric.'

Maggie busied herself in the kitchen, and her nerves jangled every time she saw a look pass between them. Panic set in. She would have to find a way of preventing the pair from taking their love any further. Never had she given incest a thought until the moment their eyes met across her table. The atmosphere was ripe with love and want. A dangerous combination.

***

Throughout the summer, they were seen in the village with Ruth's governess. They were closely chaperoned on farm visits, and the staff encouraged their return.

Lizzie and Dukes could not understand why Maggie, although polite, was not enthusiastic about the young couple's relationship.

She made feeble excuses. 'They are young. Look at me, I was tied down at fifteen, and Ruth will not be much older if Nathaniel's plans go ahead. Only this morning, he was talking about marriage. Their parents are eager for the match. Myself, I feel he needs to see more of the world.'

'It must be hard to watch a child you have had a hand in raising grow up. You and Nathaniel have a close bond, but it is time to let go. Not that you have any say in the matter,' declared Dukes. He gave her a sympathetic smile.

Lizzie was excited by the romance and the thought of another glamorous village wedding. 'I think it is a romantic love story. You are jealous, Maggie Sawbury— he is not going to love you as much as he will his little beauty.'

'Stuff and nonsense, Lizzie. I am just concerned for his future. He is too young to earn good money and keep her in her fancy attire,' Maggie sniped back.

Lizzie guffawed loudly. 'I do not think he will ever have to worry about money, Maggie. Think on it. She is the squire's daughter, and he is the son of Arlington parents. Money to money. Admit it: the golden child is not going to want your kisses when he can have hers.'

Maggie dared not speak. She closed the conversation with silence and continued with her chores.

***

Wednesday, the 14th of August, 1867

Maggie and Dukes were chaperoning the young pair while Ruth's governess took a walk around the fields during her relaxation time.

Laughter rang out from the meadow as they were chattering under a tree a few feet away from the adults. Maggie became agitated. 'No misbehaving, you two! Stay where we can see you!'

Dukes chuckled loudly then plucked a blade of grass to chew upon. 'You can't stop young love, Maggie. And they are a pair in love, if ever I saw one. Love is hard to dismiss with a stern warning'

'There is no harm in reminding them of their position,' Maggie said and playfully pulled the blade of grass from his mouth. 'It is bad manners to talk with your mouth full.'

'Beg pardon, madam.' Dukes doffed his cap. 'Not my place to offend the lady of the house—err—meadow.' He leaned back against the tree and patted the ground. 'Relax. Sit a while. Enjoy the enthusiasm of youth.'

Maggie sat beside him but could not relax. The body language between the young couple was of great concern, and she knew she would have to speak with Stephen as soon as possible. He had a right to know he planned to wed his daughter to his son.

How on earth do I approach him? Oh Dukes, if only I could confide in you. I know you would help me.

'Dukes,' she ventured. 'Dukes, if I—'

A shout silenced Maggie and the laughter. A woman's scream echoing around the valley.

Nathaniel and two of the farmhands working in the next field ran towards the sound. Dukes jumped to his feet and headed in its direction, too. 'Stay there until we find out what is the problem! I will send Ruth to you.'

The girl settled on the edge of a haystack with Maggie. Lizzie had arrived with a small food basket. 'What is going on? Who screamed?' she asked.

'It sounded as if it came from where Miss Clements walked,' Ruth replied.

They tried to strain for a better view.

'Look, here she comes now.' Maggie pointed towards the governess and Nathaniel. The woman was leaning heavily on his arm.

'Is she injured? I wonder why she screamed. It is most unlike her,' Ruth said. 'She does look pale. Where are the others?'

'No doubt we will find out soon enough. Lizzie, go put the kettle on, and get the brandy Jacob saved from Christmas. As Ruth said, she looks shaken up, and Nathaniel looks no better,' Maggie instructed Lizzie. 'Ruth, you go with her, and we will follow on as soon as I find out what the problem is. Don't worry about Miss Clements; she will be safe with me.'

The governess rushed through the gate towards Maggie.

'Mrs. Sawbury! Oh, it is too dreadful for words! I feel quite faint at the thought.'

'Hush now; calm yourself, and tell me: whatever is the problem?' Maggie put her arms around the woman's shoulders. 'What on earth made you scream like that?'

But the governess made no reply. Maggie turned to question Nathaniel. He looked as pale as the governess. Before he could answer, Maggie spotted figures moving across the meadow towards them. She could see Dukes and the two farmhands with what appeared to be two long poles between them. As they came closer, Maggie could see it was a makeshift carrier, and Jacob lay upon it.

'Oh, my husband has been found drunk in his hiding place, I see. No wonder she screamed—he is not a pretty sight drunk. Very drunk if they have to carry him home.' Maggie walked towards the small group.

The governess groaned and moved swiftly away from the scene to the farmhouse. Nathaniel snatched at Maggie's sleeve.

'Maggie, wait. Jacob is not drunk. He's dead. I am afraid your husband has been killed. He is not a pleasant sight. His face was trampled upon by one of your shires. I am so sorry. Jacob had mentioned he wanted to plough over the small field you left fallow last year. I tried to persuade him to try the squire's new machine. He declined, not too politely I must say. Unfortunately, your wooden one has seen better days. Today, it snapped mid-seam. He must have stumbled and startled the pair.'

Maggie stared at Nathaniel and back at the rescue party. She tried to say something, but her mind was numb. Everything seemed like a dream, and she was not sure what to say or do. She had a dead husband. Jacob was dead. A man she had disliked with as much hate as she had love for her son lay on a wooden frame, his face covered in sacking, and not a breath left in his body.

She started to laugh. Everyone around her stopped and stared. Maggie did not refrain from laughing; in fact, she laughed louder and louder.

'Dukes, do something!' Nathaniel appealed to his driver.

'Shock—she's been taken by shock. Get her into the house. I will deal with him and the horses.' Dukes nodded at the stretcher.

Nathaniel took Maggie home and was thankful the governess had informed Lizzie of what she had seen. Her friend rushed to Maggie the minute she walked into the kitchen. They held each other tightly. Neither spoke; there was no need for words, both knowing the thoughts of the other. They were free, their tyrant was dead.

Maggie made herself busy around the chimney breast. All eyes were upon her. The governess hiccupped. She had sipped two tots of brandy according to Lizzie, and Maggie was concerned for her well-being as the governess had suffered a dreadful shock.

Eventually Maggie had found what she was looking for and addressed her son. 'Nathaniel, you take my dray and get Ruth and her governess home. I know it is not the finest of transports, but I think it is for the best they both get home and settled; they are in shock. Inform Ruth's father of the situation, and give him this purse. It has money for the rent; I need to secure my place here at Windtop. Tell him I will organise a meeting with him as soon as Jacob has been laid to rest.'

Nathaniel took the purse. 'Slow down, Maggie. Take in the news—you are in shock, too. Look how you reacted when you first heard of Jacob's death. I am so sorry for your loss.' He broke all rules and hugged her.

His tenderness was too much for Maggie, and she fell into his arms, sobbing. The governess and Ruth ignored the inappropriate action and sipped their brandies. Maggie had been his wet nurse and nanny, after all, so it was natural for Nathaniel to care for her.

'I will be fine now. Thank you for your comfort. You are a good boy, Nathaniel.' Maggie could not tell him her tears were not for her dead husband but for him. Her next meeting would be to prevent his marriage, and it broke her heart. He was in love, and she had known that feeling for a short time in her life. She also knew the pain endured when love is taken away again.

'Go now, the three of you. I am so sorry you suffered such a dreadful event. I need to attend to my husband and to the formalities. Nathaniel, please take the ladies.'

The visitors left, and Maggie stood watching them until she could no longer see their dark forms in the distance. She closed the door and sat at the table. Lizzie handed her a glass of brandy, the house was silent. Neither said a word, they raised their glasses in unison, chinked them together and downed the liquid in one gulp.

Dukes came back to the house and told her he had informed the undertaker and that the man would collect Jacob later in the hour. He laid at rest in the cottage, with Mason watching over him.

'Do you have any instructions for them when they arrive, Maggie?'

'Just to ensure the coffin is nailed tight, and dig the hole deep,' Maggie responded with the boldness of a second glass of brandy.

'Maggie!' Lizzie was shocked at the frankness of her friend's answer.

'Come now, Lizzie. You are not going to tell me you are not a little relieved he has gone? Here I am a widow, and it is the happiest I have been for years. He was a cruel man. You two are my dearest friends, and this is the only chance I will get to say these words, so allow me to speak my mind.'

Dukes went to her and took her in his arms.

'In which case, while we are throwing etiquette out of the room, allow me to embrace a strong woman. I for one am pleased to know you two are safe from harm now. I no longer have to threaten him to keep his hands to himself.'

Maggie pulled back and stared at him, a questioning frown on her brow.

'Oh, yes. Many times I have found him staggering home, worse for wear, and warned him off.'

A tapping on the door announced the arrival of the undertaker. Maggie handed them Jacob's best suit of clothes. They gave her a message from the parson, who would pay a visit in the morning. He wanted her to consider when Jacob would be laid to rest in the local cemetery.

'His parents are buried on the family plot that he made. Our children rest there as well. It is not consecrated ground, nor ground for paupers; however, the previous parson blessed it, after a threat or two no doubt.' Maggie ran her fingers through her hair. She had a decision to make, and it disturbed her.

Dukes listened intently as she spoke.

'His parents would have deserved to lie on church land, but he denied them that right. He does not deserve such a blessing.' She noted the startled faces of the undertakers. 'Forgive me, what I mean is, he was a non-believer, and they were church-goers. He deprived them and my babies, in my eyes. The parson is a good man and comes to say a prayer over their graves once a year, for my peace of mind. He made it a holy place for me; I see it as sacred ground. Jacob should be buried with his parents and children. However, I do not want Jacob to be buried against village rules. This is difficult.' She made it sound as if she was thinking only of him, and doing right by her husband. Then, with a loud sigh, she added, 'I think it would be best for all if he had a village funeral. Yes, we will lay him to rest in the churchyard. A wake can be held in The Cross Keys—he was well known there.' She hung her head as if in deep thought. 'Indeed, I think that would be most fitting for my husband, to be laid to rest in the village.'

The men nodded, and Maggie smiled inwardly. Dukes and Lizzie both spoke at once. 'Most fitting.'

Inside, Maggie smiled. She had kept her dignity and removed Jacob from the farm, away from her babies. She would sleep well tonight.

***

Lizzie was washing windows when Maggie came downstairs the following morning. After the undertakers had taken Jacob, Lizzie had collected her clothes and moved back into the house with Maggie.

They talked for hours about the future of the farm. It was decided that if she could continue renting, Maggie was more than capable of upgrading and running Windtop. She would keep all staff and permanently employ a husband-and-wife-team who helped out on an irregular basis. Lizzie said she would give up half her wage to help pay for them. She needed only a small payment to purchase personal items. She agreed to move into the middle-sized bedroom in the farmhouse, and this way, the couple could live in the cottage. With the woman cooking for the workers, Lizzie's working days would be easier. Maggie was grateful for her friend's offer of a cut in salary. Until she knew what her financial situation was, she could do with all the support she could gather.

She went to the sink and waved at Lizzie on the other side of the glass.

'Morning. The water is hot. I am cleaning these before the sun comes around. There are eggs in the basket and a rasher or two for frying in the skillet.' Lizzie called as she peered through one of the small panes.

'Oh, Lizzie, where would I be without you? We are an odd pair. Best friends yet both Jacob's women.' Maggie poured tea into her mug and stood leaning in the doorway, watching Lizzie rub grime away from the glass.

'We are not that anymore. We are who we are. Have you thought any more about having a wake here for you know who down the road?' Lizzie continued rubbing the glass clean.

Maggie grinned at the way Lizzie avoided saying Jacob's name. Neither of them held back on their feelings about him when they were together. They did show a bit more respect when the other staff members were around.

Mason waved to them, and Maggie walked over to greet him.

'Lizzie, I have thought about this, and the wake will be held at the Key's tavern. The following day, we will hold a private party for the staff here in the farm. No one else. I don't want them to drink on that day. I do not want them caught up in the tavern with the fools he drank with. However, the following day, I will let them enjoy his brandy, ale, and cider without restrictions after the morning work,' Maggie said as she walked past her.

'A good idea. Clear the mood, and refresh the farm.' Lizzie nodded in approval. 'Poor old Mason, look, he is so worried about Brutus—look, see?' She pointed towards the horse and groom walking into the yard.

'Morning, Mason. How are you today?' Maggie stroked the horse's muzzle. He snorted his approval of her gentle touch.

'I am not so bad, madam. Not so bad. Just giving the pair a clean; fair spooked they were this morning. I spotted blood on the straw and thought Brutus was injured but realised it was from yesterday. It must have been his hoof that killed the boss. He is not a dangerous or aggressive horse. He is normally so calm and gentle.' He shook his head from side to side.

'The horse is not injured? That is a blessing for sure. If his master had had respect for him, he would not have been made to pull a broken, worn-out plough. Poor Brutus, you must have been so scared.' Maggie spoke softly and continued snuggling into the horse, giving him a final stroke and wiping her hands down her apron. 'I have the squire and parson visiting today. Put the horses in the stables after grooming. Out of sight, out of mind. Jacob was killed in a ghastly accident, but should someone want to place blame, it is not going to be at these fellows. You can guarantee that fool of a constable will come along to puff out his pompous chest. He will want to make a mountain from a molehill just to sound important.'

Mason gave a snort of approval. 'I most certainly will, Maggie. Can I ask a question? Do you intend to find a manager to run the farm? The others are concerned about their jobs.'

'I will speak to everyone after the funeral. The day after, we are going to have a private wake here on the farm. Just us, away from prying eyes. I will have answers for everyone then. I can give you one now: Windtop will stay with me for as long as I can run it. Should the squire feel otherwise, I will get a written guarantee for the new tenant to keep you all in work. Lizzie will put you in the picture about my request for all staff attending the funeral.'

Maggie left him whistling and grooming. She heard the clop of Brutus's shoes against the flint floor of the yard and gave a small smile. She had a fondness for that horse. Even more so now that he had brightened her future.

Her next visit was to one of the men who had a skilled hand with wood. She instructed him to make a window box and hang it in front of the kitchen window, plus make a porch around the back door, with a trellis of willow to assist a climbing plant. Both tasks were to be finished by the day of the farm wake.

Lizzie had finished the windows and was cleaning out the hearth.

'Reach into the salt hole, and fetch out the two tins you find there please, Lizzie,' Maggie called out to her.

She emptied their contents onto the table and went to the parlour—making a mental note to cover the mirror—and found the leather pouch where Jacob kept his spare leisure money. She fetched his outer coat from its hook and found a packet of money in a pocket. She had always suspected he carried secret money.

'There is nigh on seventy pounds here, Lizzie. Where on earth did he get that much money from?' Maggie counted it over and over. Her figures always came out the same.

'My, my gal, that's a fair sum of money! Not egg money for sure.' Lizzie looked down at the notes and coins.

'The dairy brings in a fair bit, but he pays that over for the rent. It is a tidy sum and will pay for a good send-off, plus leave enough money to replace the plough. It is my intention to buy one of the new metal ones. Mason said that if he went direct to Ransom's of Ipswich, he would be able to purchase one at a reasonable price. The sooner we can get the team working again the better.'

She put the money back into the pouch and placed it into the larger of the two tins. Now that Jacob was no longer around, she would not need to hide money from him. She placed the tin on a shelf behind another containing tealeaves.

'When I have time to think, I need to organise my finances properly. Nathaniel has a good head for figures— I will ask his advice.'

'Good idea, gal, good idea.' Lizzie glanced out of the window. 'Best get yourself up the stairs to tidy your hair. Your visitors have arrived. I'll let them in. Go.'

Maggie slipped upstairs. She needed time to compose herself and change into a black outfit.

She listened to the voices below. Stephen and the parson had arrived together. She was not in the mood for either man but had to play her role as the grieving widow.

When she entered the room, both men stood. The parson ventured forward and offered his condolences. 'Mrs. Sawbury, I am sorry for your loss.'

Stephen hung back. It was an awkward moment for them both. He spoke first, 'Mistress Sawbury, my condolences. My wife sends hers alongside of my mother's. It is a dreadful time for you here at Windtop.'

'Gentlemen, thank you. Please sit. Has Lizzie offered you refreshments?' Maggie could feel her hands shake. Stephen looked so distinguished. She was thankful

Nathaniel did not look like him. He had the features of her family. To see him with the face of a traitor would be more than she could bear. Standing before Stephen now, she saw him in his true light. Lord of the manor, an arrogant man with money. Within seconds, Maggie knew her feelings for Duke were stronger than any she might have for Stephen. He was the village squire, no more than that.

She turned to the parson. 'Have the final arrangements been made for the funeral?'

'We will bury your husband on the hour of eleven, tomorrow. I am pleased with your decision to give him a resting place within the walls of God's house.' The parson laid his Bible upon the table. Maggie stared at the worn edges; it was black, drab, and tired-looking. Standing there in her widow's weeds, she felt like the cover. Full of good intentions on the inside, yet shabby on the outside.

'I feel it is where he belongs. Please, while you are here, would you go with Lizzie and say prayers over his parents and our lost children?'

The parson preened himself. He was a man who liked to feel important. Another arrogant male. 'Why, of course, if it helps you in your darkest hour. God's word will comfort all.'

After they had left, Stephen found his voice again. 'How are you bearing up, Maggie?'

She bristled at the sound of him saying her name in an informal manner. He had lost the right to do so the minute he lay with another after her.

'Squire Avenell, I am now a widow. Widow Sawbury. I am not of high spirits and have a funeral for my husband to attend. I am bearing up well under the circumstances. Thank you for your enquiry.' Sarcasm rolled off of her tongue. She bit back the words 'We have a son who is in love with your daughter!'; instead, she enquired after Ruth and her governess.

'They are upset with the events of yesterday, but Ruth has the support of her family to help guide her,' Stephen responded stiffly.

'I understand. I have also noted Nathaniel Arlington and she are growing fond of each other. It is not many years ago they toddled around in play. How time flies. Is it presumptuous of me to ask whether you anticipate a marriage between them?' Maggie wanted to find out what Stephen's intentions for his daughter were.

'They are showing signs of nest building, I agree. Both families would be more than happy if a union came from their friendship. Between you and me, it is hoped that an engagement will be announced in the near future.' Stephen pulled out a leather-bound book from his pocket, and his tone changed; he gave a cough and tapped the book. 'Business matters. I have more important things to discuss with you than a pair of young children in love. The farm.'

Maggie sat down. She had not been prepared for him to talk business so soon; it was something she knew she would have to face but surely after her husband's burial. She was going to jump in and offer her plans and ideas to move the farm forward but waited to hear what he had to say.

'You sent a purse of money to pay rent. One thing we do for any of our female tenants who are newly widowed is waive a month's rent. 'Tis only fair—you have a lot of outgoing expenses during the mourning period.' He handed the purse over to her. She took it and stared down at the worn leather.

'Thank you, sir. It is most generous of the estate to consider its tenants in this way.' Maggie held out her hand to offer her thanks, yet Stephen never accepted it and continued to speak. The words that followed shook her world. They changed everything.

'I am confused by the rent you wish to pay. I checked our accounts, and it is not money for a field outside of your boundary. Perhaps you could confirm: why do you send me rent?'

Maggie looked at him, his words confusing her. 'I beg your pardon? I do not understand. I paid you rent to secure my home for a few months. It is my intention to run the farm with the staff I have and another reliable couple, should you agree.'

'Maggie, this is the part I do not understand. You own the farm—why on earth should you pay rent? Your husband bought the place a year after you started working at the Arlington residence. He asked that it be kept quiet, he did not want people asking him for money, should they think he had some to spare. We understood his fear and kept our silence. Never in my days did I think he would have kept it a secret from you. I was wrong; I can see that much is obvious by your face. Windtop is your farm; you own all ten acres, including Dupp's meadow.'

Maggie sat staring at him. Her chest felt tight, she could hardly draw a breath. Stephen kept talking—she knew that as his lips were moving—, but she could not hear his words. Her thoughts overcrowded her mind. Jacob had spent their money wisely after all, but had chosen to keep it a secret from her. Why? Was he going to remove her from his life? What was the reason behind his secretive ways? Within a flash of seconds, it hit her. It no longer mattered. The answers were irrelevant. Within twenty-four hours, she had become a widow and a landowner. In a few days, she would be thirty-eight years of age, and she had become the mistress of her own farm.

'Is it true? Your words are not in jest?' She managed a whisper, her throat constricted with emotion as she struggled with the news.

'The farm is in both your names. I have copies of the paperwork; the solicitor, Markham, has the originals if I am not mistaken. For all his faults and stubborn ways, your husband was a wise investor.'

Maggie gave a small chortle. 'This may sound callous, but he would have bought it for his vain self. He coveted what you have. If he had cared for the farm, his gambling money would have been put to better use. No, Jacob owned the farm, but he never worked it to its best. I on the other hand, along with the others, worked day and night to keep it going. The future will be different now. I intend to bring Windtop out in its full glory. There was a difference between my husband and me. I love the farm; he lived on it and saw only soil. He never could see what grew in the soil, only the money it provided for gambling.'

She drew in a deep breath and continued. Stephen would hear every emotion held inside with regard to her husband and her feelings for Windtop Farm. 'He suppressed my ideas, ridiculed me as a human being and, like most men I know, abused me, physically and mentally.' She noted Stephen's face flushed at her words, and he had the good grace to look to the floor.

Maggie raised her voice a notch. 'Windtop will flourish, and I am grateful for the chance to see it through. You might look at me as an ungrateful wife, but believe me when I tell you that I deserve this farm. You heard I nearly lost my life through that man. Every kick and punch earned me an acre.'

Stephen had listened out of respect to her words, and Maggie could see he understood her feelings. She had nothing more to say and remained silent.

Stephen spoke with softness to his voice. 'You are right, you do deserve Windtop, and I wish you good luck for the future. Should you need assistance, please feel free to approach me. I will train your staff on our machines; you can have use of them for the next harvest.'

Maggie nodded with gratitude. 'I had intended to ask Nathaniel to assist me with my finances. I will now ask him to work with me through the farm ledgers. I will make use of your kind offer until such time as I can afford my own. Thank you for taking the time to inform me, Mr. Avenell. Now, if you excuse me, I have a farm to run. I ask you to please keep this between us; mention this to no one. I will inform the staff tomorrow when I have other ideas to put to them. We are holding a private wake in memory of my husband, and this news will round off the event.'

As Maggie moved to the door, Stephen turned to her, and his words chilled her. She knew he was not referring to the death of her man, so they came eighteen years too late.

'I am sorry, Maggie. Truly, I am.'

'Thank you, it is not going to be easy being a widow.'

Maggie pretended she had understood him to talk about Jacob. She was not going to let him back into her life on a sorry. She was her own woman now, and Stephen Avenell was not going to try and slip between her sheets. He was her past, and Windtop was her future.

She sat at the table for over an hour, thoughts raging around her mind. She needed air, she needed to be outside, so finally, she ran to a coat hook and grabbed her black bonnet. Maggie vowed to wear mourning for the shortest period; she could not mourn the passing of Jacob, and he didn't deserve the respect of black widow weeds.

Dupp's meadow shared its full glory with her. Gold, yellows, reds, pinks, and every shade of green surrounded her. She pulled off her boots and bonnet, hitched her skirt and ran around amongst the flora and vegetation. It was hers, all hers! Had Jacob bought it for her or just wanted to own it? He knew she loved this place—had it been his intention to destroy it or keep it untouched? The answers were ones she would never know.

'I am free. Free to love you, dear meadow, free to breathe, free to speak, free to live my life. Thank you, Jacob. Thank you for dying. I hope you find a place in Heaven. I will not miss you; I have Nathaniel and the farm. My true son and my own business, they have my love—love you could have enjoyed. Or Stephen Avenell—he was the only true love I had known until I had his son. Neither of you had any respect for me. Well, I am going to gain respect, Jacob Sawbury. Windtop farm and I say goodbye and good riddance!' Maggie shouted to the clouds as she twirled and skipped.

She felt sixteen again, agile and innocent. Her mind slipped back to the day she had married, the day her hopes had died. Maggie sat to catch her breath and knew that in that short emotional burst, she had released all the pain from the past. The future was hers, and she was going to grab it with both hands.

She looked down on the farm and smiled. Already a transformation had taken place. Mason and the carpenter had fixed the window box in place, and the arch sat against the wall. Maggie could not wait to see the farmhouse come alive. She began to consider other forms of decoration and practical matters.

The barns need re-thatching, and the hens could do with mobile arks, not those dilapidated pens. Two or three could go on the bottom field. It is going to waste, and I can expand the poultry side of the business.

So deep were her thoughts that she never noticed the figure leaning against the meadow gate.

Chapter 19

The black trail of mourners weaved their way through the cemetery. Maggie watched them and wondered if any one of them had liked Jacob. Liked him as a person, not for his gambling losses, their gains. Stern faces stared at the coffin as it was lowered into the ground. The parson offered her a handful of soil, but she lifted a handkerchief under her veil and walked away. Lizzie stepped in and dropped it into the grave. Others thought it was distress that prevented Maggie from carrying out the task, but she knew Lizzie would understand. For her friend, throwing a handful of soil on the coffin was a final act; Maggie's was walking away, never to return.

Dukes approached her when the last of the mourners had spoken with her. 'Are you ready to leave? They are all heading for the tavern; I gave the landlord the money. I must say his wife has laid out a fine feast. They will all love Jacob from the bottom of a glass and an empty plate. I hope I leave more than that as my legacy among friends.'

His voice sounded so wistful that Maggie looked up at him. 'Do you suppose my life meant anything at all to Jacob? I wonder—would he have cared about our babies had they lived? Would life have been different for us all?' Maggie had not expected to feel so sad. Watching the lowering of the coffin had opened a wound. Four of her babies had entered heaven via the same portal, a hole in the ground. It was them she mourned, not their father.

Dukes handed her a large, clean handkerchief as the tears flowed down her face and soaked the front of her gown. His voice held gentle reassuring tones. 'Maggie, through Nathaniel I can see you would have been a wonderful mother. Jacob would have cared. I am certain he did care; he just couldn't cope. Remember, children have two people to create them. Maybe he felt guilty about their deaths, the same as you do.' He wiped away her tears with his handkerchief and handed it to her.

Maggie took it from him and composed herself. 'Thank you, Dukes, you are a dear friend. Whenever I eat chestnuts, I think of you. Now, your words will be added to that memory box. Come, you must be starved.'

When they reached the carriage Felicity Arlington sent her for the day, she turned to him. 'What is your real name? You have never said. I do not understand why I need to know today, but I do. Maybe it is strange emotions that trigger the unusual.'

Dukes grinned. 'Maybe that's a fact. William. It's William, Maggie.'

She smiled. 'No. You will always be Dukes to me. I cannot imagine you as a William. Tomorrow, as you know, I am holding a private wake for Jacob up at the farm. Please attend. I owe you so much and would like you there with us at the final farewell. Nathaniel is coming, and Mr Arlington has agreed you can join us should you wish.'

'Thank you, Maggie. I will escort Master Nathaniel. I will be there.'

***

Maggie scrubbed the pine table. She had baked pies and sweet pastries for the afternoon, and they sat cooling on another table, the one she and Mason had dragged in from the dairy. Lizzie and the others were about their business as if the previous day had never happened. All kept to their word and not drunk heavily. They were saving it for the private function with the widow as instructed; such was the respect they had for her.

Although their gathering later in the day was an unofficial wake, Maggie thought of it more as a birthing party, the start of new life on Windtop. She and Mason had rearranged furniture in the parlour. He also filled her window box with bright flowers as a surprise. When she saw them, she was touched and cried at what he considered a simple gesture. He would never understand what the window box meant to her. She was blessed with good friends, and she could not wait to announce her news.

'My word, it smells delicious in here. Jam pastries, so tempting!'

Maggie turned to see Dukes standing in the doorway. He held a large, wooden box.

'The cook was instructed to make and send these for Jacob's wake. She sends her condolences, too. Now, where shall I put them?'

'What a gift, how lovely! Thank her for me. Take them into the parlour, would you, please?'

They unloaded fruit jellies, tripe dishes, sliced hams, and tongue, plus many more plates of delicacies.

'The table is groaning with all this delicious food. What a shame the one man who would have appreciated it is not here. Jacob did enjoy his food.' Maggie rearranged a plate or two while she spoke.

'We must ensure we do not waste a crumb in his honour then. Today will be a day to make merry. I for one cannot mourn his passing, he was a cruel man. However, it is a shame he died to provide you with a party, Maggie. I bet you have never celebrated your birthday in style, being married to him.'

Maggie lifted her head. 'As a matter of fact, Dukes, today is my birthday. How is that for coincidence? It is why I wanted a private event here. Please do not tell the staff, though, it is their day to get over Jacob. Promise me?'

'Many happy returns, Oh Secretive One. I promise my lips are sealed. Enjoy your day to its fullest,' teased Dukes with a bow.

'Get away with you. I must say, I could do with a short break. What say you?'

Dukes placed two chairs out into the yard, and they sat out to enjoy the warmth of the sun. They sipped at cool elderflower cordial, and Maggie thought back to a fayre and the day she had paddled in a brook.

'Do you think Nathaniel will marry Ruth?' she asked Dukes.

He leaned back lazily in his chair. 'Mm, I am fairly certain it will go ahead. They both seem to love each other, and the parents are all for the union. He would become squire should Stephen Avenell die, and I think Mr Arlington is keen; it would be a good marriage.'

Maggie thought of Nathaniel as the squire; his rightful title. Should she ruin his chances or choose to ignore what would be incest. Today was not the day to think about it; she would tackle it later.

Laughter rang around the yard, and they both watched the farmhands working together.

'That never happened when my husband was alive. Life was never cheerful when he was around, that is most definite.' She looked to the hillside, still finding it hard to imagine she owned it all. It was time to move forward. 'One thing I am certain of: sitting here and enjoying your company is not getting my chores done, Mr. William Dukes. That sweet pastry you sneaked away needs replacing.'

Dukes looked so funny when he realised he had been found out, and Maggie laughed at his sheepish grin. 'There is no need to pull that face, it is not so innocent. All naughty boys get found out in the end.'

'Oh, dear, I had better take my leave, or I will find myself ploughing fields to make amends. I will come back to taste more this afternoon. With the appetite master Nathaniel has on him, I would bake a batch or two more, they are a tasty treat.'

***

Maggie stood by the sink and looked out to her beloved meadow. The afternoon had bloomed into a perfect English summer's day. She could hear a collared dove coo its gentle song, and a Skylark fluttered in circles and shared its trill with anyone who cared to listen. The honey perfume from the sweet alyssum wafted in through the open door. Unsettled and no longer wanting to be indoors, Maggie gathered her staff and instructed all chairs and tables were to be moved into the yard. She sent Mason and Lizzie to town for bright fabric to cover the tables. Small jars were filled with wild flowers and decorated dull corners. Old shepherd crooks were cleaned, driven into the ground, and lanterns hung from them. A keg of ale had been brought up from the local inn and placed upon an old upturned one.

Satisfied with the cheery look of her surroundings, she spoke with her friends. 'Finish all basic chores, and return home to rest a while. Mason, please continue with your tasks as I know you have a few jobs to finish. Tomorrow, you will have the morning off. A well-deserved break.'

'That is most generous of you, Maggie. I am much obliged, I'm sure. Thank you.'

'You are welcome. Now go, all of you. We will talk plenty later in the day.'

Maggie went back inside and upstairs. Her room still had the smell of Jacob despite a large pot of lavender in one corner and the windows wide open. Another job was added to her mental list. The room would have to be scrubbed top to bottom until he lingered no more.

She looked at her clothing laid out in preparation on the bed, and something snapped inside. For years, she had

had to mend and make do, made to feel poor. During all that time, Jacob had known they were landowners, and the money she had found secreted in various places during the course of the day made her realise she could have had finer gowns than those she wore. Granted, as a farmer's wife she did not need satin and lace. However, sturdy boots for winter and a thicker cape would have been welcomed.

She raced downstairs and grabbed her bonnet. Lizzie was shelling peas, and Mason tacking the trellis frame around the porch.

'Mason, please hitch up the cart. I need to go into town. We will be gone no longer than a hour.—Lizzie, you were instructed to rest. Go and do so, and please inform the staff they are to wear their best clothes. The brighter the better! No mourning items for this afternoon, please.' She raised her hand to silence her friend. 'No, Lizzie, I will explain everything later on.'

***

Still the weather held in their favour, and Maggie glanced out of the window. She could see her staff milling about in the yard. They had done as she instructed and were wearing their Sunday best. The six men were still in black, but their neck scarves were red and blue ones, adding a dash of colour. The ladies, three in all, were wearing simple gowns. Lizzie was clad in a deep green with a full pinafore, Mason's wife in a brown one with a half-apron in cream, and the new dairy girl in a simple navy dress, two sizes too big, with a white apron on the verge of grey.

Maggie thought back to the Arlington and Avenell households. Their staff had smart uniforms, each indicating their status in the workforce.

She looked at herself in the long mirror she had purchased on her trip into town. Her gown gave her courage, and she smiled at the reflection.

Time to start a new life, Maggie Sawbury!

***

She showed no expression on her face as the staff stared when she walked into the yard. Dukes and Nathaniel had just arrived and were helping themselves to ale. Both stood with their mouths agape.

Maggie had donned a gown of deep crimson. It was edged with ivory lace around the collar and cuffs. She had a soft cream lace cap keeping her hair in place but had pulled forward soft tendrils by either ear and across her brow.

'You can all close your mouths now,' she said with a smile. 'It came to me today that I have worn widow weeds—or rather rags—since the day I married. This gown is the dress I would have chosen for my wedding day, had I been given a choice. Are we all here, and do you each have a glass in hand?'

Nathaniel handed her one, and she raised it high above her head. She spoke loud and clear. 'Here is the final toast to my dead husband. Please do not be shocked by my behaviour today. I respect the dead, and I respect Jacob for the legacy he has left me. Although I feel he may have hoped I left this earth before he did. Goodness knows, he tried hard enough many times to ensure I did, but I am stubborn. A fact I am sure you are all well aware of... and goodness, please sit down, and close your mouths unless it is to sup his ale.' She laughed. 'To Jacob Sawbury. The end. To Maggie Sawbury the beginning.'

Maggie took a long gulp of her drink. The time had come. She looked at their loyal faces and loved each one of them. She knew they would never damn her for the clothes she wore or the words she had spoken.

Mutterings of 'To Jacob!' went around the tables, and all eyes focused on Maggie when she chinked a spoon against her glass. The elderberry wine had made her bold;

it was time for her to share her news. 'Ladies and gentlemen, I have an announcement to make.'

She smiled. 'Today you are looking at the owner, yes, owner, not tenant, of Windtop Farm. It appears my husband bought the place the year Nathaniel was foisted upon me.' She waited while a trickle of laughter rippled amongst them. 'I understand he invested the money I earned by caring for this young man and forgot to inform me, his wife. The squire told me the news yesterday when I tried to pay him rent. Maggie Sawbury is your new boss. For those of you who will find it hard to work for a woman, I suggest you take your leave now. For those of you who enjoy hard work without a beating, please feel free to stay.'

Breathless she sat down and grinned at Dukes, who had remained standing. He too had a large grin across his face.

No one spoke as they absorbed every word she had said. Mason started clapping and rose to his feet. The others joined in.

'It is the best news I have heard, Maggie Sawbury. I for one will never leave your side while you'll have me. I think I speak on behalf of us all when I say that it is about time you had some good in your life. To Maggie Sawbury!' He raised his glass, and Maggie was touched when her name rang out around the yard.

'Thank you all. Your loyalty is appreciated. You are dear friends, and I want to tell you of my plans. Windtop will be reborn. It will have repairs carried out and new machinery brought in. This will be a gradual process, and the squire has arranged for you all to be taught on his machines until we purchase our own. Ted and Lillian, should you wish, there is a permanent position for both of you here, and you can move into the cottage. Lizzie is going to live with me until I organise better living accommodation for her. The rest of you will continue as we have always done. Your quarters will be improved over time.'

The group around her came alive, clapping and cheering. Mason threw his cap into the air. All thoughts of Jacob and his wake had gone.

She shared their joy. 'Nathaniel, I wonder if you would consider assisting me work through my finances. It appears I have some now.' She threw back her head and laughed.

Dukes refilled her glass. She raised it to him in a silent toast.

'Katie, there is a basket by the back door, please fetch it for me.'

The new dairymaid stood up. 'Yes ma'am,' she said and curtsied.

Maggie put out her hand and gently restrained the young girl. 'Katie, I am Maggie and always will be. We are equal, a family on this farm. No more curtsies, please.'

Katie nodded and fetched the basket. Packages in cobalt blue were lifted out.

'Wrapped inside each of these neckties and pinafores is a list of items waiting for you in the appropriate shops in the village. You will also find a sum of money. This money is yours to do with as you wish. You will receive a rise in wages to match those in the farms around us. My husband never respected your worth—I do.'

She looked around as they opened their packages. 'There is twenty pounds for each of you. The blue items are the colour of Windtop. I want us to stand out and gain the respect of the village. The items waiting for you are working clothes and footwear, appropriate for your jobs. Today we start afresh. Now come, enjoy the food! Some of it is a gift from our neighbours and friends.'

She walked over to Dukes.

He still sported his grin. 'Well, well. Old Jacob was a sly one. I am pleased for you, Maggie. Very pleased indeed.'

'Thank you. I am still coming to terms with it all but so wanted to give back to them.' She swept her hand around, indicating the people who had stood by her through the dark days.

'One step at a time, Maggie. We all have to take one step at a time. Come sit, and tell me your plans for this place. I see you have your window box and trellis porch. That's a grand start.' He led her to a table where Nathaniel was in deep discussion with Mason. They were talking about the new plough design, steam engines, and the benefits of machinery over man. The favourite topic of many farmers and workers around Britain at that present time.

Nathaniel had the enthusiasm of youth. His face was animated with the desire to be heard and agreed with. Maggie felt a surge of motherly love. It took over. 'Nat, come now. Man also needs man. Think, if we had nothing but machinery on this farm, would all these wonderful people be here enjoying my food?'

'But Maggie, the profit from using these labour-saving devices is admirable!' Nathaniel bounced in his seat. He enjoyed nothing more than a good debate on farming issues.

'Maggie will tell you that money is not always the key to it all. A combination of money, machine and man, *that* is a workable solution. One I think she is striving for,' Dukes joined in, and Mason found the courage to have his say.

For the first time, he was listened to, and his valuable ideas were noted. 'Them steam trains are taking surplus produce to London more and more. Our milkers are some of the best in the area. You cannot grumble at a slice of Windtop cheese. I was a-wonderin': if there is money in the pot, why not increase the herd. I remember, in the forties, it was a bad harvest. We had one of the wettest summers. Personally, I would have finished with grain crops. The bottom field did nowt but grow poppies last year. Why not plant it up for good grazing and send the milk on a regular basis to the city? My missus will have a good part of her day to spare, and I know she would help with the milking.'

'Mason, I think you have hit the nail on the head. More milkers—could you run to it, Maggie?' Dukes was fascinated by the opportunities presented to her, so he joined Nathaniel's enthusiastic approach.

'It is a good idea. I was going to use the bottom field for hen arks, but extra cattle will be far more beneficial. We can make new pens around the edge of the yard for my project or use the smaller barn. Herd improving. Yes, Mason. A grand idea. Nathaniel, would you look at the ledgers so I can consider my options?'

Nathaniel nodded, and Maggie continued, 'First, we will expand the herd with a new bull. Jacob sold our old one several years ago. Twenty-odd years ago, to be precise, and he never replaced him. I would like to purchase a good one before we bring in more heifers. Our own milkers were served by Lark's Farm bull, and he charged a large sum, did old Lark—one reason why Jacob allowed the herd to recede. I tried to persuade him to replace ours, but he dismissed the idea. Dairy is the way forward. Windtop is going to be a strong dairy farm, I feel it in my bones. Now I declare it is time for Ted to fetch his fiddle. No more business today.'

The evening moved into a perfect night. Jacob was never spoken of during the rest of what became a lively party.

Nathaniel promised to visit the next day; he was keen to get her back onto her feet.

Maggie and Lizzie sat watching the shadows move in the moonlight. Both had enjoyed more than their usual one or two glasses of ale, so they were in a relaxed mood.

'Do you think you would ever marry, Lizzie?' Maggie asked.

'After Peter was killed, I vowed I never would, but Samuel has grown on me over the years. Dukes is crafty in his ways. He arranges Samuel to be around whenever I am. It has been nigh on seventeen years since we first spoke. We talk about everything around us but never marriage. We are content enough. I, like you, am not a breeder of children; I would have produced one by now if that was the case. What with Jacob and a couple of local lads—oh, do not look at me like that! You must have known I was no innocent when you first met me.' Lizzie poured herself another drink from a jug. Maggie watched her, had the girl been so devoted she had not married a man she loved?

'If he asked you, would you marry him?' she asked.

'Not now, no, Maggie. I am too set in my ways. Men annoy me. Believe it or not, I love my life here. With old misery out of the way and you in charge, gal, it will be so much better. I am content as I say. Never worry over me, I truly mean it. My life could be worse.'

'What about Dukes? I often wondered if you two would ever match.' Maggie looked for giveaway signs in Lizzie's face. She saw only a wrinkling of her brow.

'Dukes? Are you blind, gal? Maggie, open your eyes, he is fond of you. Have you never noticed? He joined the same rank as Brook and followed as a loyal friend. He would lie down and die for you. 'Tis a wonder you've missed the glances he gives, the way he watches your every move. I thought you knew.' Lizzie sat bolt upright. 'Me and my big mouth. Poor you, poor Dukes—you will never look at him in the same way again. Forget I spoke.'

Maggie also sat upright. She had never noticed the things Lizzie mentioned. Dukes was Dukes, her friend.

'How can I forget? How will I look him in the eye thinking he has wasted his life watching me? I am without words to describe the shock of what you have told me.'

'I told you in confidence, Maggie. We all said—'

'All? Who is *all*? The staff members in both houses know of this man's feelings for me? Of my ignorance of it? Is that who?' Maggie's voice rose several octaves. She was more disturbed by Lizzie's words than by Jacob's purchase of the farm.

'Dukes means a great deal to me. We have become close companions along the way, but I never dreamed that he harboured any feelings of love for me. What do I do with this knowledge? How do I react when I see him next? Oh Lizzie, what a worry you have given me.' Maggie paced the yard. Her movement sent a breeze past lanterns, and they threw dancing shadows against the walls.

Lizzie started to laugh. 'Calm down, Maggie. He is still your friend. You do nothing—unless…'

'Unless what? Unless I avoid him for the rest of my life?'

Lizzie jumped to her feet. 'Maggie, sit down. Come on; do as I say for a change. The ale has addled your brain. Treat him no differently to any other day gone before this one. Do not let my words spoil your friendship. I will never forgive myself.'

Maggie smiled at her. 'Sorry, Lizzie. You are right, nothing should change. If he feels for me the same as I feel for him, I am lucky. He is a good man, and I am very fond of him. If I am honest, I love him but do not intend to do a thing about it. We are close friends. Nothing should ruin that. Come on now, we must be to our beds. Another day to get through tomorrow.'

'Dukes is a good man and deserves your love. I hope you find a way to get a life together.' Lizzie walked away touching Maggie's shoulder as she went. 'We gave Jacob a good send-off, that's for sure. He would have enjoyed himself. He never deserved you as a wife. Night, Maggie.'

Maggie felt the hairs stand up on her arms. She had forgotten the reason they had gathered together. Just the mention of her dead husband's name was enough to send a chill through her bones.

She looked to the sky. 'If you are looking down on me now, Jacob Sawbury, you must be feeling very sad. Windtop is mine, and one day it will transfer to my son. Not our son, my son. My *secret* son. That is my new dream.'

A noised behind her made her turn around, and to her horror she saw Lizzie standing in the doorway. Realisation passed over both faces. A secret had been released. One woman had to trust, and one to understand.

'I will explain tomorrow. There has been too much talking tonight. I need sleep. Trust me as I have to trust you. I will tell you everything in the morning,' Maggie spoke softly and touched Lizzie's shoulder. She leaned in and kissed her on the forehead. Then she made her way upstairs, and when they reached the top she said, 'I promise you the truth. But you must promise me your silence. It is the only way.'

***

Both women worked together clearing away the debris from the night before. Lizzie said how strange she found it now that she did not have to rush through one job after another. When both were satisfied their work was complete, Maggie sat and told Lizzie about her past.

'Nathaniel is due to come here this morning. You must promise me no hints go his way. I am Maggie, nothing else. Felicity Arlington has the title of mother.'

Lizzie nodded and said, 'your secret is safe with me, gal. I do have one opinion to offer though, for what it's worth. Stephen Avenell should be made aware. The pending wedding hopes could be a problem for them. Not that anyone would ever know, but for the sake of future children. I hear there can be deformities if same blood mixes.'

'That is a hurdle I have to jump. My conscience is pricking me daily over this since the moment I saw the pair together. I am going to speak with his wife in confidence. I cannot speak to Stephen. Besides, men are no good over matters such as this. It needs the head of a sensible mother to do what is best for her daughter. She will not want a scandal and will probably remove the girl from the situation.'

Maggie heard Nathaniel calling out to Brook and panicked. 'He is here. Now remember your promise, Lizzie.'

Lizzie pulled her into her arms. She squeezed her tight, confirmation of a promise sealed. She let Nathaniel in and went about her business in the dairy.

'Hello there, Nathaniel. How's your head this fine morning? Excuse me for one moment, and I will be with you.' Maggie had her back to him; she needed a moment to compose herself.

'I am well, Maggie, and yourself? It was a good time spent amongst friends. Dukes enjoyed himself and sends word that he will visit in a few days. Now let us look through these ledgers you mentioned. You know me well enough; if there are figures to be played with, I am at my happiest.'

Maggie went to a large cabinet in the corner of the room, where Jacob had kept his farm records. It was awash with loose papers and leather-bound books.

Nathaniel looked at the pile of papers before him and shook his head. 'I think we need a few hours to work through these today. Did you keep up with your reading lessons, Maggie? You were doing extremely well before I went away. I think I might need some help here.'

'I can read slowly and understand numbers. Unlike you, I am not highly educated but know my basics. I can help if required. I understand most things about business.'

They worked side by side for over three hours. Only the tick of the clock and the bubble of the kettle could be heard. The occasional word between them or a tut-tut from Nathaniel were the only other sounds. They shared a plate of bacon sandwiches and cups of tea. Maggie could not imagine a finer time in her life.

The last ledger snapped shut, and Nathaniel leaned back in his chair, placed his hands behind his head, and stretched out his back.

'There were some interesting findings there, Maggie. I can tell you this: your husband was not the poor farmer he led you to believe. You are a wealthy woman. Sadly, some of his money did not come from honest trade. The large black book over there is proof he was a moneylender. Not a fair one.'

Maggie looked to the book. She lifted it over and browsed its contents, disgust etched across her face. 'How could he? These are honest people, down on their luck. Lend them the money, alright; but to take double in return is very wrong. I understand he wanted to make a profit from the loan, but his demands would have crippled some folk. How many?'

Nathaniel counted the names in one book, and reached over to another. 'Twenty-one in total. Two have paid back the loan, but still have the—how does he word it? Out-of-pocket interest, to pay.'

'Out-of-pocket? He tried to make out he was doing them a favour and putting himself out of pocket. Sly man. We must visit these people. I want all loans wiped out. Those who have paid them in full, cross them through.

They have fulfilled their obligation. The others can help me in the summer for the cost of supper in return. I will not be continuing this side of my husband's business. No cash will change hands. We have ample, certainly more than some of the names I see listed here.'

Maggie was upset by what she had read. Her own finances were more than she could ever dream. She did not need to take food from another's table.

'Will you help me, please Nathaniel? With you beside me, it will be so much easier.'

'It will be my pleasure. Any time you need assistance, I will be there for you. Without you, I would not have had life, as I am often reminded.'

Maggie thought how true his words were, although he was referring to the nourishment she had given him; she thought about the day he was born.

'I have an errand to run. Take the ledgers, or work here, wherever it pleases you. All I ask is that you do not mention the loan system my husband had set up, to anyone. I find it rather distasteful.'

'Rest assured, I find it the same. My lips are sealed. If it is fine by you, I find it easier to work here. I will make a list of names for us to visit tomorrow. There are some who are worse off than others. It might be better to visit them first. I will work out an order to work from and return with Dukes tomorrow. We will ease a few burdens together. You have a good heart; the world is blessed with you in it, Maggie.'

Maggie turned away so he could not see her tears. He might not feel the same when she ruined his future marriage plans.

Chapter 20

Maggie knew her visit to the squire's wife should be discreet. She had asked Lizzie to take a message and wait for an answer. She had mentioned that it was of a delicate nature and their meeting needed to be kept a secret, even from the squire himself. Lizzie returned during her time with Nathaniel, with a note stating that although unusual, Mrs. Avenell would receive her at two in the afternoon. She would ensure they were not disturbed.

Wearing her mourning outfit—despite her resolution not to wear one, she felt it fitting to wear black in the company of the squire's wife—, she asked Mason to drive her to the mansion. He would not find anything unusual in their journey, given she was now a business woman.

'Begging your pardon, Maggie, but I have heard about a few people in the village willing to give up their milking cows. I took a walk this morning to some I know and who own one or two. I also took the liberty to tell them we would give them fresh milk in exchange. No money changes hands; they get the milk they need without feeding livestock. We could place them in the lower field. I know of a scrawny Friesian belonging to a family that would be glad of the exchange. Fed up, she will fill a pail for years to come.'

Maggie was impressed. She knew he was a thinker but had never heard him talk about farming so much as he had in the past few days. She admired his ability to look ahead.

'Mason, you impress me. I think we should take up the opportunity. Give them dairy products in exchange, not just milk. I also think you should be granted a sum of money, purchase my new herd, and employ two new hands to help. You will manage and be in sole charge of their care, herd and help alike. What say you? It comes with a raise in pay. On top of the one you should have been given years ago. Plus I will see about converting a barn into a private accommodation for you. Herd Manager will be your title. I want all stock to be branded with the same blue in your scarf. It is going to be our symbol colour.'

Mason chuckled. 'It would be an honour to manage your herd. I have visions of better times ahead. Livestock is the way forward for us. Turn the farm to dairy and beef. Jacob wanted his finger in every pie. Granted a few sheep and pigs, but for farm use only. Let us use the extra grazing for the cows and bull. Our sheep are good stock— keep back some, and exchange the others. Listen to me. 'Ours, us'—anyone would think I own the farm. I do love the place though. It grows on you. Jacob would never have let it. It was his burden, he would say.'

'We will talk some more on the way home. Come back for me in one hour, please, Mason.'

Maggie climbed down with the assistance of a footman. She remembered the last time she had stepped through the doors of the large building in front of her, and felt a deep sadness.

She was lead to a large drawing room. Instinctively, she looked to the ceiling. There was a carved rose in the centre. Shivers ran down her spine.

'The one in the library is pastel green, with my husband's great-grandfather's initials engraved into a petal. Quite the feature, do you not think?' Flora Avenell entered the room and held out her hand. 'I am sorry for your loss, Mrs. Sawbury. A dreadful business, my husband informed me. Now, what is it I can do for you? I am intrigued by all the secrecy, and trust me, I have not mentioned anything to the squire.'

She indicated a chair, offered refreshments, and listened while Maggie stammered out her confession.

When her story ended, a cup hit the floor, and Flora Avenell fainted. Maggie ran to the door to call for help but could see no one. Flora Avenell had indeed ensured their privacy. Maggie saw a bell pull and tugged on it firmly.

A footman came into the room, took in the situation, and ran for the woman's maid. They laid Flora onto a chaise longue. Maggie dismissed the staff assuring them she would call them if needed; their mistress had merely fainted because of the heat. Slowly Flora came round. She sipped a glass of water and beckoned Maggie over to her.

'I am dreadfully sorry about that, how embarrassing. Please help me up. You have given me quite a shock. To find out my husband passed his time away in the granary with other women, one of whom became pregnant with his child, is not pleasant. Then to learn his illegitimate child wants to marry his legitimate one is most distressing.' She fanned herself with a delicate hand-painted fan.

'We, or should I say I, have a dilemma, my dear. You want to stop a marriage, and I want one to go ahead. Only a confession can remove the dilemma.'

Maggie looked at the pale-faced woman. She could not imagine how she must be feeling. 'I am sorry, Mrs. Avenell. It pains me to hurt you so, but you can surely understand my predicament? Do you need me to confess to your husband?'

'Very difficult, Mrs. Sawbury. Painful? I am not so sure. Hear me out'. Flora Avenell settled into a seat opposite Maggie. 'The granary was where I let him take me for the first time too, you know,' Flora continued talking. Maggie tried to stop her; she did not need to hear the woman's memories. She had done enough damage to her present.

'I instigated the whole thing. Oh, he thinks he seduced me, but I let him believe what he wanted for the sake of his ego. Men have large egos, do they not?'

Maggie wasn't sure whether she should respond or not, so she gave a half-hearted smile with a short nod of the head.

'We had been pushed together by our parents. There was no excitement for me. I did not want to be his bride, I loved another. Sadly, he was not a man of means, and I have been rather spoilt all my life. I like the finer things and enjoy spending money on fripperies.'

Maggie could not believe she was listening to the confessions of Stephen's wife. She needed to get the conversation back to Nathaniel and Ruth. To encourage the girl's mother to take her away and hope their infatuation would subside, but the woman continued talking, giving no opportunity to intercede.

'I had to bed him quickly, to make him want me… well, you know.' Flora Avenell swallowed hard. 'I was in a rather delicate position—if you understand my meaning.' Flora's fan moved faster and faster as she spoke. Maggie watched while she absorbed the woman's words. Flora Avenell, nee Tamworth, a daughter of society and strict upbringing, had been pregnant with another man's child? She allowed Stephen to think it was his, and this in turn moved their marriage along?

At last Maggie found her voice. 'Ruth is not of Stephen's blood. Is that what you are telling me? Our children are not related in any way?' She sat wringing her gloves, trying to make sense of what she had just heard.

'Yes, you understand correctly. Now we need to be clear on what has been said here today. We are women with dangerous secrets. Secrets that can ruin lives. I promise you my lips are sealed. Nathaniel is a fine young man, and I am saddened you have to live on the edge of his life. Ruth is a beautiful young woman, and I adore her, as does her father—the squire. My secret relieves you of a burden of conscience, does it not?'

Flora rose from her seat and went to Maggie. She knelt to the floor at her feet. 'I am begging you to keep the secret to your deathbed. There will be no gain for anyone should you speak openly.'

Embarrassed by the open plea from such an important woman, Maggie helped her to her feet and spoke with earnest, almost breathless, honesty.

'You have my word. I would never want to hurt the Arlington family. They have been good to me. This is the reason I have never spoken the truth. Your words have given me great joy in my heart. I *promise*, like you, my lips are sealed. We will speak of it no more. Nathaniel will inherit Windtop when I die. It will not be a surprise, because I hope he will help me manage it, and therefore he would have deserved it. Besides, I have always told the Arlington family I would find a way of repaying their kindness to me one day.'

The two women embraced and shook hands to seal their secret pact. Maggie left with the knowledge she had overcome yet another hurdle in her life.

When she stepped outside, she was surprised to see Dukes waiting for her. His wide smile was just what she needed to see. The news she had heard made her forget what Lizzie had shared with her the night of the farm party. It came flooding back.

'What did I do to deserve this honour, kind sir?' she teased.

Dukes bowed. 'Mason sends his apologies. Apparently, he has been given a free rein to buy cows, and he heard of a bargain purchase in Rickinghall. When I called to speak with Nathaniel, Mason asked if I would collect you. So here I am.'

Maggie climbed onto the cart. 'I spent a pleasant afternoon with Ruth's mother. I worried about the girl and her governess, and felt I should call to enquire after their health. I understand there is to be a wedding, and it will be announced shortly. They make a fine pair.'

Dukes gave her a side-glance. 'You approve of the marriage now? I thought the young master was too young to wed in your opinion. What changed your mind?

Maggie laughed. 'A woman is entitled to make changes whenever she pleases, is she not? I changed my mind while watching him handle my finances. The boy is a man now. More than capable of making his own way in the world. It is my intention to leave him Windtop farm when I die. He will become a man of means. I have no family to leave it to, and he understands the importance of running a good business. Plus he would be a kind, generous man to his staff.'

Dukes clucked the horse to pick up speed as they came to a small hill. He gave her another side-glance, and she felt her face flush.

'Do you not think it a wise idea? It cannot harm the boy, surely. Besides, he will be a man with a family before it is my time to leave this green and pleasant land. At least I do hope that will be the case.'

Dukes said nothing except to slow the horse down. They ambled along at a slower pace, and Maggie could not bear the silence between them. 'Before that happens I have plans for Windtop.'

'Dairy farming. Yes, Mason informed me. A wise idea, Maggie. You have a good foreman with Mason.'

Maggie waved her hand in dismissal of his statement. 'No, I have other ideas. I plan to build on the land beside Dupp's meadow. I want a small house of my own built there. It is the most beautiful place in Suffolk in my mind's eye. I dream of waking and looking across at the river and farm. A beautiful scene in any season.'

Dukes nodded. 'An interesting idea. What would you do with the farmhouse?' He grinned widely. 'I mean before you die.'

Maggie giggled. 'I intend to ask Nathaniel if he would like to live there. He loves the farm, and if he marries Ruth, it will be years before he becomes squire. I have plans to enlarge the house, and when the building is brought back to good health, it will be a marvellous home. A modern farm would be a wonderful start for a young man's career. Should he not want to take it on, then I have no idea beyond that hope. No doubt, fate will lend its hand; it usually does.'

The horse whinnied, and Dukes settled him with a click of his tongue. Maggie marvelled at how gentle he was with both animal and man.

He pulled the cart to a halt and turned to her. 'So a house on Dupp's Meadow overlooking the farm would allow a mother the joy of seeing her son on a daily basis. I think it is a marvellous plan.'

Maggie stared at him. His face was expressionless, and Maggie went back over his words, not sure if she had misinterpreted their meaning. He climbed down from the cart, and she realised it was where they had collected chestnuts on their first meeting. He walked forward a few paces and stood by a bush. The area had changed very little.

Maggie's stomach churned, and she was convinced the blood had drained from her face. He stood in front of the place she had laid Nathaniel the day he was born.

'I found him here. Your son. I heard his cries. When you were brought to the Arlington home, I watched you with him, the way you bonded, how you held him, and I knew he was yours. Over the years, I also learned why you left him to be found. Jacob would have been a cruel father, and Stephen would not have taken his duties seriously. He would have abandoned you—did abandon you. Yes, I knew about your affair. I stumbled across you in an embrace not meant for friends. I have admired your strength from the day you held the boy and fed him. You were at death's door but nothing mattered. Only the survival of your child.' He walked back to her and looked straight into her eyes, Maggie listening with horror as he relayed facts she thought were secrets. 'I watched you recently in Dupp's meadow. You looked so alive—and to hear you shout out your painful past was exhilarating. To watch you come so far is a gift for me.'

It took all the courage she had to remain standing in front of him, Maggie wanted to run, to turn back the clock. Instead, she stood, statue-like, and listened to his words. He had been with her every step of the journey, from the day of her son's birth to her day of freedom. He had saved her, picked her up, soothed her, and never once asked a price.

Jacob she had never loved. Stephen she thought she had, but now she knew he had been an excitement in her dark days. He had dallied with her, made a pretence of not wanting anything from her, and all the time had been merely using her for his selfish needs. Dukes, on the other hand, had lingered in the background of her life. What she felt for Dukes whenever she saw him she had put down to friendship, an acceptance he would always be there for her. Looking at him now, she knew it was something more. Something deeper. She walked towards him and took his hand. His strong, muscular hand.

Her voice came as a whisper but she had no energy left. Her emotions were spent. All she had left was for him, the man who kept secrets and asked for nothing in return. 'I love you, William Dukes. It has taken me a child's lifetime to realise it, but it is the truth. I love you. As a young girl, I felt something but had no life-experience to understand what it was. Now I know, and all I can say to you is: this woman loves you as much as—no, more than that young girl did the day she met you.'

Dukes smiled and reached into his pocket. He pulled out a small cloth and unravelled it, then held up a shrivelled chestnut.

'I hold this every day. It reminds me of a day of innocence. I fell in love with you the day you roasted me chestnuts. I could not bring myself to eat the last one for fear that if I did, the magic I felt inside would disappear.'

He walked to her, and she dare not move. She gave no argument when he held her in his arms. Maggie raised her face, and their lips touched with the gentle kiss of new lovers.

When Dukes released her, she looked to the hills. There was no more grey blot on the landscape. In its place was a landscape of colours; a brighter future.

The End

February 2015

A note from the author.

I wrote this novel while living in Cyprus. I dreamed of Maggie and her life. She haunted me for days on end until I gave in and wrote her story.

All research of Redgrave village was done so via the Internet. Even when I lived in the UK, I had never visited the village.

Whilst researching my mother's maternal family tree in February 2015, I came across an exciting fact. The family line was strong and went back to the 15th century. The family originated from Redgrave and Walsham le Willows. An ancestor was named (actual spelling), Nathaneal.

Did Maggie exist and was she a distant relative of mine?

I now like to think that is the case. She certainly has taken me on a road of discovery! Now I live back in the UK, I will be taking a journey to visit a village that has strong ties to my writing and private life.

***

Thank you for purchasing my novel. Without a reader taking the time to buy my work I would not enjoy the thrill of knowing my dream has been fulfilled.

Please enjoy a sample from my other novels. I have also included a free gift of a few short stories and poems.

Ripper, My Love

(Book I Ripper Romance Suspense)

Growing up in late nineteenth century East London, Kitty Harper's life is filled with danger and death – from her mother, her beloved neighbour and the working women of the streets.

With her ever-watchful father and living surrogate family though, Kitty feels protected from harm. In fact, she feels so safe that while Whitechapel cowers under the cloud of a fearsome murderer, she strikes out on her own, moving into new premises to accommodate her sewing business.

But danger is closer than she thinks. In truth, it has burrowed itself right into her heart in the form of a handsome yet troubled bachelor, threatening everything she holds dear. Will Kitty fall prey to lust – and death – herself, or can she find the strength inside to fight for her business, sanity and her future? And who is the man terrifying the streets of East London?

Chapter 1 (sample)

The Walk Home

Despite the damp air and the arrival of twilight, Kitty, as always, was reluctant to leave her mother's graveside. The caw-caw screech from black hooded crows echoed from the surrounding trees. Their eerie call made her shiver. Dark shapes lined branches; their presence unnerved her. She pulled her shawl around her shoulders and chided herself for not wearing a thicker cape. August appeared to be cooler than in previous years. Kitty brushed her hand lovingly across the top of the gravestone. An hour passed while she stood in St Mary's Cemetery, talking about everyday things. She spoke to the brown mottled slab, wishing it could be the peach-cheeked woman she remembered.

'It is time to go home now, Mama. I cannot believe five years have passed us by, it seems only yesterday in my heart.' She traced her fingers over the engraved stone:

Lilly Harper. Wife and Mother. Born 1848. Died 1883.

She hurried through the cemetery and chose the quickest route home via Angel Alley. Arthur, her tutor, would be waiting to start her reading lesson, already an hour late the shortcut became the better option. Her usual route added an extra half hour.

An oval roof of dark brick made the alleyway claustrophobic. The damp cobblestones were slippery underfoot. Four large shadows lined the walls. Even the gas lamps added nothing to the uninviting ambiance. The black domes gave the impression they were looking down at her, like the crows at the cemetery. She knew them to be harmless, but her brain failed to communicate the fact to her legs, and they began to shake.

A bat swooped around her head; Kitty squealed and ducked. In doing so, she stumbled. She reached out to steady herself, and her slim fingers recoiled as they touched the cold slime of algae coating the wall. She twisted her ankle slightly and it throbbed, her dainty button boots were not made for long walks. Her gown would almost certainly be ruined when she balanced against the wall.

What on earth possessed me to wear my best velvet to sit by a graveside?

She had come too far to turn back. On hindsight, she should have visited the grave the following morning, and not altered her routine, although she shared many thoughts that day with her mother and did not consider it a waste of time. Such precious moments. Death snatched her mother from her life, but not the love from within her heart.

Foggy light made her squint. The mustard haze reduced her vision to a few yards ahead. The area underneath the gas lamps attracted several moths. They cast more shadows, this time moving ones. Kitty's skin tingled; flying insects unnerved her.

She walked past a wooden stairwell and a muffled cry caught her attention. Before she could investigate further, someone grabbed her arm and nipped the flesh under her clothing. Whoever held her made her arm sting. She spotted the glimpse of a black felt hat, overloaded with wilting, torn silk flowers. Her attacker pulled her around until they stood nose to nose, the flowers flopped across the highbrow of a toothless woman. She wore a dark stain around her lopsided mouth; smudged red grease paint.

'Oi, wadcha doin' on my patch madam, there's no room for you 'ere.' The foul stench from the voice blew onto Kitty's face. A mix of gin and rotten teeth. Bile threatened to rise. Kitty swallowed hard. If she did not fight it, she would most certainly vomit. Kitty realised she had stepped into the workplace of a prostitute. A Bow Bells whore, with a true Cockney twang, *and* a claim on a dank corner of an inner city alleyway.

'I am not working your patch. Please let me go, Miss. You are hurting my arm. Let me go and I can get out of here - out of your way. I am not a threat, believe me.' She heard the plea in her voice. Kitty could not muster indignation, and thought even if she did it might antagonize her attacker. She opted for the weak, trembling voice. The woman continued to grip Kitty's arm. Her fingers held on vice-like with the strength of a man, not an easy opponent for Kitty, half her size.

The whore belched. A revolting, drunken, unkempt specimen. How any man could spend money satisfying himself with her puzzled Kitty. Her clothes were made from cheap calico, and smelled stale, unwashed.

'With a voice like that, I believe ya. Git your posh rear end outta 'ere before I kick it to Kingdom come.'

Her broad London accent sounded much stronger than Kitty's. Under normal circumstances to be called posh would have made Kitty smile. Never one for being told twice, when the woman released her grip, Kitty ran as best her boots and sore ankle would allow. Their clip-clop sound and the whore's husky laugh rang around the alley. She fought back the tears and concentrated on a small speck of light yards ahead; the much anticipated exit. Kitty focused and put to the back of her mind there was still a long walk to face. At this precise moment, even the company of Arthur in one of his moods would be most welcome.

Come on, Kitty Harper. Stay focused on the light.

Kitty's heart pounded the more frightened she became, her chest hurt, passing out most definitely threatened. Lying on the ground here was not an option. She bent to allow her lungs the luxury of oxygen. While they filled and the ache subsided, she watched a rat chew on the dead carcass of another. For some strange reason her thoughts turned to the local gossip and the talk of a recent murder, a local woman. Zach, the ragman, told her the woman had been hacked to death. Gang members were responsible. Her friend Brady said he thought the job appeared to have been carried out by a professional. Kitty wondered to what sort of professional he referred. Quite possibly he meant a surgeon. The type of doctor who had removed her mother's ulcerated leg. Yet surely a medical man would never murder? They were committed to saving lives. Brady was a policeman. Kitty had known him all her life. She was more inclined to believe his version of events. In his personal opinion it was possible a disgruntled Landlord found a way of clearing out their property. Brady's version, one to be believed, made Kitty thank the Lord her parents earned the money to buy their cottage. They saved hard, and took up the opportunity to purchase the year before she was born.

For goodness sake, get your mind onto something cheerful.

Kitty straightened her body and carried on walking. Her lungs levelled to a normal breathing rate.

'All right my beauty? ' Kitty, startled by a male voice turned to find a short, squat man stood in her path. His crumpled, threadbare jacket was tight across his protruding belly. Kitty noticed his trousers did not match the jacket, and were short in the leg. There was nothing either fashionable or attractive about his appearance. In other circumstances she would have found him comical.

He smoothed long unkempt sideburns, and ran a finger across unruly eyebrows. She turned around and continued walking. He rushed in front of her, and again stood in her way. The alley lamplight flashed against something in his hand; a knife.

Shock prevented her from moving. Although she was taller than he was, the thought of trying to fend him off with a knife frightened her. She tried to speak, but her throat constricted.

'Pretty Ladybird, time for you' n' me to get acquainted. I got summit for ya.' Spittle ran down his chin while he fumbled with his clothing.

Kitty saw her opportunity to escape. She pushed against him with as much force as she could muster.

'Get out of my way, you great oaf. *Move.*'

She rushed past him but he regained his balance and snatched at her shawl. She swung her arm outwards to fend him off and he grabbed it. The man pulled her wrist, and twisted her body until her back pressed against his chest. He yanked her upper body back and she screamed. A voice echoed from the depths of the alley.

'Oi, you had better not be bleedin' working girl. I warned you, this is my patch'. It was with relief Kitty recognised the voice as that belonging the woman who had threatened her.

Kitty screamed out again, but the man tightened his grip.

'Help me. Please hel...'

'Shut it.' The man placed the blade the width of her throat. 'You will do as I tell you. Understand?'

Kitty felt the point rake across her windpipe, and grunted out what she hoped sounded like a yes. She dared not swallow or move. All around became silent, aside from his heavy breathing below her ear. There were no footsteps, nothing. Much to Kitty's disappointment the woman decided against investigating their activities.

Nervous of her situation, Kitty knew she needed to pacify the man while she worked out what to do. Her body trembled, and tears threatened but she could not let him get the upper hand.

Still the cold blade rested against her windpipe; she barely dared to breathe. He fumbled behind her back with his free hand; she could feel her gown moving. His intentions were clear. Fighting nausea Kitty refused to give into his fumbling. The more she tried to wriggle free, the harder he pressed into her.

Think, Kitty, think.

Her heart and head pounded. Frantic thoughts of succumbing to a murderer at last gave her renewed energy.

Kitty took her chance and with one swift movement, grabbed the arm with the knife. At the same time pushed her body back into his. She heard the tinny echo when knife hit the cobblestones.

'*Bitch.*' The man cursed loudly as Kitty knocked him to the floor.

She kicked the knife away amongst a pile of rubbish, lifted her skirts, and ran. She continued running until her lungs could take no more.

At last the end of the tunnel became evident. Grey smog swirling around a lamp, and distant voices told her she was close to the exit onto the main road. A vast dark space opened before her. Kitty glanced over her shoulder. She was relieved to see the outline of the man kneeling on the floor. Tears ran down her face and she used the sleeve of her gown to wipe them away. It was time to compose herself and get out of the alley.

The large courtyard she stepped into looked different at night. The buildings were the back entrances of shops and their storage yards formed a large square. Wooden barrels stacked against the grocery store wall created sinister shapes with misshapen shadows. In the daylight when she walked around the shops and through the alley, the barrels were a burned honey shade with black metal bands, far more pleasant to the eye. It was also evident the greengrocer threw old vegetables behind the barrels. The smell around her was disgusting and rats crawled everywhere.

Father would skin me alive if he knew I had taken this route home.

Ripped Genes

(Book II Ripper Romance Suspense)

Sequel to: Ripper, My Love.

A new world with old memories. Will life ever be the same again?

Kitty Harper, a young seamstress from Whitechapel, London, fell victim to the notorious murderer, Jack the Ripper. She did not die. One part of him simply broke her heart, and the other destroyed her life. He took what was precious and killed her dreams.

Her closest friend rescued her from her torment, and shame. They escaped the horrors of England, and set up a new life in America.

Luck stood beside them, until the past brought trouble to her door, and once again, Kitty found herself fighting for survival. Love never left her side, yet it took death for her to see who truly held the key to her heart.

This sequel to Ripper My Love is brilliantly written and a real page turner. Like the first book I just couldn't put it down. Amazon Review

The Penny Portrait

(Victorian Romance)

Harwich 1865

When Elle Buchanan is abandoned by her parents in her sixteenth year, she has no choice but to run from the leering eyes of their landlord. Earlham's beach in the town of Dovercourt, holds memories of her childhood and becomes her home. Hiding out in a rundown shepherd shack she takes stock of her life, and finds friendship in the form of a crippled male, Stanley.

Through various friendships she is able to follow her love of art and earn from her skill. Under the guidance of Angus Argyle, a local art tutor, she thrives. His sharp eye spots a charcoal drawing in her portfolio, and knows the naked man Elle etched. She tells of how they met, and Angus sells the drawing to its model with the promise that they would say nothing.

Elle struggles with the loss of friends, friendship, and love. Growing up alone she is naïve, and her innocence loses her a love she so desperately seeks.
Will Elle have to give up her dream for love or will love find a way into her life?

The Penny Portrait

Chapter 1
A Misunderstanding

'No!' Elle screamed,' it should not be like this.' She pushed the man from her body and he slid ungraciously from the bed. He tried to snatch at the bedclothes but missed. The floundering moves he made as he fell back onto the floor would, under normal circumstances, be classed as comical. However, Elle sensed he was not amused. Before she had chance to try and make light of the matter, he had gathered his wits and gently pushed her back onto the bed.

'What do you think you are doing? You are sent to please not tease. Now lie down like a good girl and let me enjoy you'.

Elle struggled to sit upright but he had a heavy build. The more she wiggled and writhed, the more he took it as a sign she was a willing victim to his lusty desires. Frustration fought frustration, and Elle made one last push for freedom. Once she freed herself Elle stood beside the bed. She straightened the thin cotton gown she wore, and pulled her lank honey-gold hair from her face.

'Sir, I am sorry, so sorry. I am not teasing you, but I do need to leave. Sadly I fear a misunderstanding.' She lowered her head, and hoped the giant of a man would note her innocence. His voice had an authoritative tone with a distinctive sound of upper-class breeding. His voice also had a softness, and despite his size she could tell he was a gentle character. Not once had he been rough with her. Guilt made her falter but deep down she knew she could never lay with this man. She had been brought to the room by a valet, not fully understanding what was wanted from her, and at no point did she think this would be the outcome, it had crossed her mind she might have to clean a room but never to be entertainment for a gentleman. Her sixteen years of innocence, living in a quiet village, had never encountered such a situation. She was indeed in a desperate state but not desperate enough to share her body

Prior to his waking, she sat watching him sleep, and her artistic inner-being could not resist etching him. Her greatest joy was to sit with charcoal and draw. She captured his likeness well, and opted to tuck the drawing in her pocket, in her opinion it was too good to throw onto the coals burning in the grate. She scribbled, *The Man in Room Eighteen*, in the right-hand, bottom corner. It would be put into her box of drawings when she returned home. A quick glance at his clothing laid over the ornate rosewood chair, told Elle he was a man of means and like many, followed the fashion of Prince Albert, Queen Victoria's consort. The chances of him ignoring a shabbily dressed girl in her sixteenth year were minimal. Most people with money overruled the working class.

Think, Elle. Think!

Elle stared at the thick, plush carpet; blood red; crimson. An idea flashed through her frantic brain; one that might just save her from the awkward and frightening situation in which she found herself. She clutched at her lower belly and groaned.

The man sat up and stared at her. 'What's the matter with you? Are you sick?'

'No sir, I am in pain. I suffer from my monthly curse, I …'

The plan worked, the man jumped from the bed. As Elle was well aware, the highly improper conversation topic proved an embarrassment to him. The man hastily draped the sheet around his body, no longer emboldened in manly needs, he showed himself flaccid, and irritated. A shiver of fear triggered a sense of survival in Elle, and she realised the need to act swiftly, despite her gut instinct telling her the man would do her no harm. There was something about him, a kind aura, yet Elle decided not to take any chances.

She screwed up her nose to indicate more pain. 'I am afraid I would be unclean for you to bed me, sir.'

He shook his head.

'Damn you women and your monthly excuses.' He moved towards her and towered over her. Nervous, Elle, sure the fear inside must shine through her eyes, remained in humbled status.

Please do not let him see my fear. Do not give him power over me.

He tilted her chin upwards. 'Pity. I would have enjoyed you. Pretty thing. Come back to me when you are next free. I will make it worth your while. Here, take this, you look in need.' He handed her a coin. 'Find our mutual friend, and inform him to send another to take your place.' The man flopped onto the bed and folded his arms behind his head. She had been dismissed. With relief Elle let herself out of the room and into the corridor, she ran the full length and down one flight of stairs. The coin, hot in her hands as she gripped tight, was too precious to lose. It had become her lifeline. As was a small charcoal drawing. Both items were her only possessions. She tucked the coin into her pocket alongside the picture.

At the bottom of the stairs she stopped to take in her surroundings. Ahead, by the door that led out onto the main street, stood a man in a uniform. Another man in a smart, gold braided suit stood behind a large desk.

Elle panicked. This area did not appear familiar at all. She could not remember coming through such a plush entrance. She moved behind a large planter with a vast amount of greenery overhanging and watched people mill around the vast reception area. Elle was in awe of the clothing worn by obvious members of the gentry. Jewellery adorned the necks of young and old women.

When the valet had sneaked her upstairs the place had been silent. She shifted from foot to foot. Nature added to the urgency of the moment.

'What are you doing behind there? Get out this instant.'

A large hand and deep voice startled Elle. She looked up to see a grim face smothered with whiskers staring down at her.

'I um-I'

'Get out from behind the plant and remove yourself from the building. This place is not for the likes of you. Now clear off.' The concierge pulled her to her feet and pointed towards the back exit. 'Out.'

Elle didn't need to be told twice but not wishing to bump into the man from the night before in fear he might have other guests to entertain, she ran for the main doors. She brushed past silk gowns and inhaled wafts of rose water perfume. She sensed their contemptuous eyes on the back of her neck as she headed out through large glass doors edged in gold. An atmosphere of combined forces willed her to leave their sumptuous surroundings and Elle had no desire to stay. They outclassed her tenfold.

Terrified, she ran for several streets before the need to rest her lungs and empty her bladder became imperative. She leaned against a wall and took stock of her situation. She craved sleep, and needed somewhere to rest for the night but was reluctant to use her precious coin. Exhaustion took over and she slipped behind a large building. Several doors led out onto the dark alley she found herself in, and Elle glanced around for a corner to relieve herself. Her body was short of energy and she needed a place to rest. Smells and a warm glow from lights from one doorway tempted her over to investigate further. Beside the door stood two large containers and Elle slid between them. She tugged her shawl around her shoulders and curled into a ball. Tiredness washed over her, her body- pushed to its limits- trembled. Elle had spent days walking. Her only release came when she had been approached by the valet at the hotel she passed by several hours ago. Confused by his intentions but in need of sustenance, Elle had allowed herself to be drawn into his suggestion. She was to entertain a gentleman in room eighteen, in exchange she would be given hot milk, and the man himself would pay her a coin. On arrival to his room the valet had motioned to the sleeping man in the large four poster bed.

'When he awakes he will have need of you. 'Wash over there and be quiet', were the only instructions given.

While Elle waited she was drawn to the features of the sleeping mound. Large plump lips, coal-black hair with a wisp of grey here and there, and long dark eyelashes; all attractive and indicative of a well-groomed male. His olive skin and even-arched eyebrows made his features a pleasure to look at, and his shaven chin looked soft enough for Elle to want to reach out and touch him. Instead she broke off a piece of charcoal from the fire place and found a scrap of paper in a nearby waste basket. She spent forty-five minutes frantically sketching the image before her. Elle, too scared to leave, and not so innocent of what lay before her, did not wish this moment to be tainted in any way. She had seen men and women fornicate in alleyways and questioned her mother as to what was their purpose. Her mother informed her, and warned her of the consequences of such activity. The ticking clock, the crackle of the fire and the gentle snores of a handsome man made new memories for Elle. The whole scene mesmerised her and her natural instinct captured the peaceful innocence in the only way she knew how; by using her talent. Elle often used drawing as a way to release fear or joy when words failed her. Her parents had encouraged her gift but lack of money meant Elle went without the paper supplies she secretly desired. Her dream to own paints and canvas were just that; a dream. Even more nowadays.

'Please let it be warmer tonight'.

Elle whispered to the night sky as it took over from the twilight. She pulled her legs to her chest and huddled down for sleep. Her stomach growled. She had eaten nothing for two days. One glass of milk and a sweetmeat taken from a plate in the hotel room, are all that had passed her lips.

Tomorrow I will eat. Tomorrow I will return home.

Chapter 2

Heading home

The following morning rain drizzled down on Elle, the sky as grey as her mood. Rats disturbed her during the night and hunger gnawed at her insides. She stretched out the aches in her limbs and leaned against the wall to regain her balance. White flakes floated in front of her eyes and giddiness took over. Blackness followed as she lost control of her body and slumped to the floor.

***

'What's this, a mangy stray dog for the pot, Bill?' A gruff male voice accompanied a floating sensation as Elle came around from her faint.

'No. Some scrap of a girl I found by the bins. Fetch a blanket from the back room for me.' Another deep voice reached her ears; a softer, more caring tone.

'Old Burgess finds her there will be hell to play. You are too soft for your own good.' The gruff voice grumbled on becoming fainter as the man moved out of the room.

Elle tried to move.

'Stay still, there's a girl. My old back is groaning. Hurry with that blanket, Jack. My back is nigh on killing me. There. By the fire. Quick, warm some milk. Stop staring at me like I have lost my mind. Move man.'

Elle felt herself being lowered into a chair and a warmth surrounded her. Her eyelids refused to lift. She so wanted to see face behind the kind voice.

'Here lass. Drink this. Not too fast or you'll throw it back. Well done. Slowly.'

The rim of a warm mug touched her lips and she supped at the honeyed milk.

'There. Well done. All finished. Good girl. Now get some rest while I fetch you a slice and bread.'

'A slice and bread? Are you crazy man? Burgess will have you out of here with one flick of his wrist.' The gravelled voice of the other man in the room vibrated Elle's ears but still she was too weak to move.

'Hush your mouth. Burgess is in Chelmsford with his missus today. Besides, I shall use my allowance, I will eat less supper. Now get on with the shoe shine and take them up to Major Sharp. You know he hates waiting. Leave me to do what I want. If she were my girl I would want someone to do the same.' Elle noted the voice soften with a hint of sadness.

'Ah. Now we come to the nub of the matter. Your girl runs away and you take in strays. Let's hope your girl is as lucky as this whippersnapper. Her arms are so thin, they will break with one movement. Bonny though. Pretty when cleaned up, I'll wager.' The voice disappeared out of the room and pots and pans clattered in the background. A clock ticked and gradually the aroma of bacon filled the room. Her mouth watered and saliva trickled from the corners of her mouth. What she wouldn't give for a slice.

'Well now. Can you manage to sit up?' A tug at her sleeve startled Elle, and realised she was being addressed. She gave a weak nod of her head and slowly opened her eyes.

A pair of kind twinkling faded with age, blue ones stared back into hers. Creases around them indicated the man was smiling. She attempted to wiggle upright in the large horsehair seat. Stray wisps of rough hair scratched at her legs as she moved. The room began to spin and she inhaled deeply.

'That's it. Nice and steady. Old Bill has time to wait. Mind the bread and slice might get cold. Fried in dripping and dipped in egg for you, little one. Come on get some down you. Do you good.'

Elle couldn't believe her ears. So much kindness from one human being. She reached out for the plate where her prize sat waiting to be devoured. The first bite was chewed and swallowed with such haste she nearly choked. Bill sat down beside her and offered her the mug at regular intervals. Each mouthful was washed down with more milk. She wiped the plate clean with the last piece of crust.

'Thank you.' The words came out as a whisper. Elle wiggled further up the chair and enjoyed the fullness of her belly. A belch escaped her lips and she put her hand to her mouth. Embarrassed she glanced at the man. His large whiskered mouth curved upwards and he gave a loud guffaw of a laugh.

'There's all the thanks I need. A satisfied stomach.' He pulled the blanket up to her chin. 'I can't keep you here indefinitely. Get some sleep for an hour and I will wake you when my chores are finished. We will talk more after.'

End of Sample.

A Collection of Free Stories

Cinderfella

The world rushed by at a rapid pace, baggage trolleys, staff and travellers moved at an incredible speed, and for Ellis, it was quite breath-taking. Ellis Lancaster, felt his pulse racing and his chest tightened.

Why he put himself through the agonies of flying was only a question he could answer. Settling into a seat that looked out at the runway, Ellis took a sip of his latte and reflected on the meeting he had been called to the previous day. He had been asked to represent the company and present his latest project to an interested party in Paris.

Ellis was a shoe designer, and this project if accepted, would put Soled Out on the map. It was a major breakthrough and was the opportunity he had been waiting for. Ellis had worked for fifteen years for the company, he was a quiet, loyal employee, who started as the tea boy and worked his way close to the top. At last his hard work and loyalty was now paying off, he was on his way to Paris, the epicentre of fashion.

'Excuse me, is this seat taken?'

Ellis looked up and responded to the owner of the voice with a shake of his head, he took another sip of coffee and continued reading his outline for the meeting in Paris.

'Are you flying or waiting for someone?' the female voice continued with its chatter, much to the annoyance of Ellis.

He continued reading, and pretended he hadn't heard.

'I'm Tessa, by the way.'

Ellis could not ignore the well-manicured hand dangling across his papers. He looked up to see an attractive woman, obviously wanting him to shake hands. He obliged, all the while thinking how forward the woman was, he was a complete stranger.

He was not sure how to handle the situation but could not ignore the woman completely.

'I'm Ellis, nice to meet you. I'm on my way to Paris'.

Tessa expressed great interest and for some unknown reason, Ellis found himself telling her about his business trip, and his life before he rose to the top.

'I hope you didn't mind me interrupting your reading only you looked so worried, and dare I say, nervous? I felt a distraction would help you.'

Ellis gave an embarrassed nod, and muttered his thanks. He no longer wanted to continue idle chatter and picked up his file to indicate the end of conversation. Tessa, ignored the hint and carried on talking to the back of Ellis's project papers.

'I am always nervous when I fly, I talk too much I am sure. I am off to Paris. I love the buzz of a busy airport, the kiosks and the people rushing about, it excites me'.

Then came a brief pause in the chatter and Ellis drew his breath.

'Forgive my rudeness. I've never been to Paris and am on a tight schedule of planning a meeting. Nice to have met you.'

He picked up his belongings and headed off to the check in desk, leaving behind Tessa and the cafe.

The flight to Paris left at midnight and was a smooth comfortable journey. His hotel was a comfortable one overlooking the Seine. After a good investigation of the room and hotel facilities, Ellis decided he had all the creature comforts he could wish for, and opted to stay in his room for the evening.

He poured himself a generous whisky, sat in a comfortable chair and continued reading over his presentation, there were no alterations required thanks to Jenny the efficient office secretary.

Leaning his head back in the winged leather armchair, Ellis began to relax and unwind. He chanted out his speech word for word. He was ready. Tomorrow would see him climb another step up the ladder of success. He folded away his papers and sipped his drink. Life was good.

A sharp knock at the bedroom door brought him out of his dreamy state, and slightly disgruntled at being disturbed, he crossed the room and pulled open the door. Before he could grasp who was standing there, a voice he recognised launched into conversation at speed.

'I'm sorry to disturb you, only I wanted to return something you dropped at the airport. I know it's late or early whatever way you want to look at it, being's it is after twelve.' To Ellis amusement it was Tessa, and she wore the widest smile. She held out a brown, leather shoe, the reason for her tracking him down.

'I had dreadful visions of you hopping around Paris tomorrow. The shoe is such a smart one, you were bound to be wearing it for your important meeting. I debated and finally, I thought I had better find you. I knew where you were staying as I noted the name of your hotel on your bags. I couldn't believe my luck when I found it was the same place as me! I overheard your name and room number and well, the rest is history as they say.' She giggled and waggled the shoe in his face.

Ellis laughed at the picture she had painted.

'You certainly have been thoughtful in your quest. It is rather late to offer you a thank you drink. Would you care to join me downstairs for breakfast in a few hours?'

Tessa nodded enthusiastically as she accepted the offer.

'Oh, that would be lovely. By the way, I picked your shoe up at midnight; does that make you my Cinderfella?' She giggled.

Ellis smiled. He knew the shoe would never fit as it was a single, one-off design. A sample for the presentation, he then decided that this trip to Paris might not be so bad after all, he had a sneaking feeling that Cinderfella had found his princess.

Her Barren Womb

The groceries dropped to the floor as Jane ran forward down the hallway. She knew before she reached Tim that he was dead. The angle of his body, the gaping mouth and staring eyes, told the facts.

She could hear someone screaming and wished they would stop; they needed to be in control, not panicking. On reaching his body she dropped to her knees, and to her surprise tears dripped onto his face. She touched them, his skin was cold and clammy. She touched her own face and found it wet with tears. There was a hush about the place; the screaming had stopped. She cradled him to her and muttered his name over and over, willing him back to life. She prized a letter from his cold hand.

'This isn't how it's done, Tim. We are supposed to be together forever, remember?'

She and Tim met one summer, it was so long ago that the many years just roll into one, they were lovers, best friends and occasional enemies, their life was, and had been, good.

Each day since retirement was spent reflecting on their past successes and failures. Failures in Jane's life were few, she failed to stop the paperboy delivering the wrong paper once, she failed to see the step at church one Sunday and spent the next few months on crutches, a broken ankle proof that the fall was a hard one, and she failed to produce a child. Her biggest failure of all, she knew it disappointed her husband.

Oh how they had tried, every moment of every day until nature decided time was no longer a friend of Mrs. Devon's womb: Jane was barren.

She hated the word, the way it looked on paper and the way it sounded to her ears. Useless v barren, no contest, they were equal as far as she was concerned.

Tim never turned from her, he said he saw only her, he was happy with his life and if they were not meant to be parents they would be good to those who had been blessed. Jane knew he hid his disappointment well, and was grateful he still loved her. She arranged many events and eventually they found a joint project that gave them a rich, fulfilled life. Their time was spent at single mother groups, helping young girls cope with their lives as being a single mum.

Jane admitted she was envious but her nature was such that she saw this as her gift from God, the chance to ensure children got a good start in life. Tim made toys from wood and she sewed for the babies, she made maternity dresses for the girls, and they soon had a large family in the community, they were loved.

Jane went through the motions, police, ambulance, family, friends and funeral services were all contacted.

They took Tim away. He was gone. No more gentle whistles as she smoothed down a new dress, no more admiring glances, just nothing - no more - a void.

The funeral was a good one. Jane considered funerals had their good and bad points, Tim's was as perfect as one could make it. The flowers, food and funeral necessities were perfect.

Standing by a tree she noticed a young man, tall, slim and the same hair colouring as Tim, she excused herself from the mourners and walked towards him.

'Hello, how are you?' She asked. He nodded and smiled, his sad eyes looking downward. It broke her heart to see such sadness in one face.

'She's here you know, can you see her?' Jane pointed to a young woman across the cemetery. 'She's pretty don't you think?' Again the young man nodded a silent agreement.

'I told her she could come and stay for a while but she feels a little awkward. I really don't see why, I have only just met her and have had no reason to make her feel that way. Perhaps I will convince her later.' Still the young man said nothing. Jane continued, she spoke softly and clearly, the words clung to her tongue like a heavy brick, 'I'm glad you came today. I hope you understand my love cannot be reclaimed. It died and was buried today.' She remained composed as she watched the wordless young man walk away.

Jane had always known she could see the dead, she had done so since she was a child, but nothing had prepared her for seeing Tim at his own funeral. He looked just as he had done the day they first met. So healthy and fit. She hoped she had done him proud and he approved of his day but he needed to know, she no longer loved him. Her heart was as barren as her womb.

A tired Jane saw off the last of the mourners and well-wishers, all that remained were the remnants of an afternoon tea. After an hour of false conversation, she told everyone to leave, she wanted to be alone, she really couldn't cope with their good intentions and clichés.

She kicked off her shoes, peeled off her black cardigan, and gathered up crockery dotted around the room. She moved them into the kitchen with the intention of clearing up in the morning. An evening of peace with a large brandy was all she wanted.

'Can I help you with that?' The voice made Jane turn, she didn't jump and she wasn't scared, she knew the voice. 'Thank you, yes that would be a great help.'

'It was a pleasant day. Tim liked pleasant days.' The voice continued, Jane agreed but was a little annoyed now by the last statement, should she react or should she stay quiet?

'Tim always said he liked pleasant days and had many in his life. I know.'

This time Jane was not prepared to let the statement go, she slammed down the plate in her hand, the bell like sound rang tinny around the kitchen.

'Young lady, I know my husband enjoyed pleasant days. We had those pleasant days together for many years. Unfortunately, it appears he had a pleasant day that did not involve me and the result is standing in front of me now. Please do not say any more about pleasant days. I suggest you leave and never return, you did what you had to do, you have said goodbye to your father, now please leave. I am sorry you didn't get to say hello but well, that is life, full of the unexpected.' With no words, to Jane's surprise, the girl turned around and left.

Tim visited that evening, he moved around the home, he was looking for something. Jane watched, tormented by the love they once shared, and by the knowledge that he had cheated on her eighteen years before, a pain that would not leave her heart.

As he moved from room to room, she knew what he was looking for; a letter. The hateful letter that had poured pain into her heart with every word. The letter declaring that he was a name on a birth certificate and the owner wanted to get in touch. The letter that probably caused Tim to stumble on the stairs. He was searching for the letter that killed him.

Jane knew he wouldn't find it, and remained silent. It was to be his torment while she endured hers. She had destroyed the letter after calling the telephone number of the writer, gave the news of Tim's death and the date of the funeral.

The writer came and went. Tim's child came and went, they'd both seen her and been tormented by her in different ways. Jane's love died the day she read the words, *you are my father and I want to meet you.*

I Want That Job!

Life hit her - smack right in the face - the mirror threw back an image Lucy recognised but despised. Her life had become a blackened painting, lifeless and she was so alone. Her family rejected her, they despised what she had become and told her to move away, find friends who would guide her along the right path. Sadly, her friends no longer called and most were in loving relationships. To add to her sadness she struggled daily within the work place.

One of her colleagues received an anonymous phone call and Lucy guessed they had been told her secret. She noticed the atmosphere changed during the course of the day, they had been told before she could explain to them herself. Each time one of them glanced her way she sensed a wave of cold fear whip through her veins. One guy slammed the photocopier lid shut and walked out of the room when she entered, another made coffee for the team except Lucy, and they made it obvious she was now an outsider. Even her desk had been moved from prime position near the window. She was informed it was due to furniture fading issues. She said nothing.

Why do I fear them? What harm can they do? It is my secret not my shame!

During the month of rejection upon rejection from her colleagues, Lucy's mood changed. She lost clients to other members of the sales board, and her temper rose.

I am being punished for being me? Who let the cat out of the bag? My ex? My dad?

After one particular nasty remark by a male with an arrogant air about him, her adrenalin pumped through her veins. It was time to take action. She left her written notice on the boss's desk, turned heel and emptied her desk, she walked towards the exit and took a deep breath knowing she would never return. Even the MD had taken to turning his back whenever she walked into the room. It was time to leave.

***

Simon straightened his tie. He loved his image in the mirror and he stared at himself with pride. Courage and energy smiled back. His interview was at ten fifteen and he was ready.

This is the job I've always wanted!

He arrived at the entrance of the building with minutes to spare and took the elevator to the appropriate floor. He announced his arrival and waited. Nerves flipped his stomach and he fought to remain calm, to prevent his hands from shaking.

I need this job. Keep calm. Breathe.

The managing director and the interview board were impressed with his knowledge of the product and the company. The interview was a relaxed affair after a few moments of formal discussion. Golf, motorsport and other topics were touched upon. It turned out he was a member of the same golf club as the MD and he was offered the job on the spot. He was delighted, there was an increase in the salary and was very welcome as the new apartment he had his eye on was a little over his previous budget.

His new apartment was ideal, the location for work and nightlife was within walking distance, and he had a feeling he was going to enjoy his new life. Simon spent a month preparing his move and today he walked into the building to start work with a briefcase full of enthusiasm.

He entered the office and his new colleagues rallied round. His desk was in prime position by the window, and a steaming coffee was handed over. Everyone was so friendly. They'd welcomed him into the fold and Simon was delighted.

I was right to apply for this position. It's the job I've always wanted.

After work they invited him to join them for a drink, he accepted the offer and spent the evening hearing about his predecessor. Apparently she was a lesbian and left when her secret was found out, it was a shame as apparently his co- workers really liked her. Simon listened and smiled inwardly. He knew every one of them inside and out. Their lies about trying to get Lucy to stay rolled off their tongues and he wanted to let them in on his little secret. Lucy no longer existed, she was not a lesbian just a female trapped inside a body she despised.

She was now Simon - who worked in a job they'd always wanted.

***

Poetry by Glynis

When Imagination Sleeps

Head on pillow away I sail,
Along the night time sleepy trail-
Contented heart and heavy eyes,
Breathing softly, night time sighs,
Dragons, Witches and Fairy dust
Elves, Pixies, no Goblin trust.

Wings, wispy, drenched in moonbeam lace,
Beautiful, evil, fire and grace -
Silver hair, forked tail and large black cat.

Dainty shoes, clawed toes and pointed hat,
Flying, fighting, sparkling wings.
Roaring, cackling, softly sings,
Gentle touch, breathing fire and warty skin -
Let my childhood dreams begin.

The Flame of You

A stumble is not a fall, nor a weakness.
"Dreams move us forward" is not fact, sometimes - in the darkness - they hold us firm - a cement of fear with chains - coated in insecurity.
Cloaks of esteem fail to keep out the chill of, "I am good for nothing - for no one person," and yet, in a tunnel of confused emotions - in the darkness - lingers hope, holding out the candle of future light.
A flicker of power, the flame of who you are, burns brightest for others in their hour of need - one day let it glow for you, let the mantle of esteem find self, and walk out of the tunnel knowing this is your time - your time to shine - fan the flames of you and keep the fire of positive burning.

Dedicated to those who allow me to live my life as I wish, to those who defend our shores, to all who serve the countries they love.

Admiration and Gratitude

Admiration and gratitude, I walk in the sun -
You are unknown to me, yet in the world we are one.
I am beholding to you, I offer you these things -
my thanks as I hear the sweet tune a bird sings.
Concern and thoughts I have a few
I sit and listen and share a view.
Allowing me that gift, giving my life chance
is a stranger and never will we share a glance.
I have never suffered but owe you my life -
you allow me to live as mother and wife.
Each day you are in my mind
Unknown Soldier I hope peace you find.
I hope that soon you are on homeland shores
and you are with loved ones, free from wars.
Please know this stranger prays
for those who allow me perfect days.
To you I give thanks for my daily chores -
my gratitude and admiration are all yours.

Know Me in History

You move as elegantly as a swan
Gliding on the river -
Your bustle swishes silently
Your boots and buttons shimmer -
Silks and stays are of the finest
Your graceful elegance
Your manners perfect-
You are rhythm in a dance.
Aloof, entrancing, quietly aware
Your beautiful Victorian face
Causes many a man to stare.
History is how I know you,
I could not fill your shoes –

Nor you mine when listening to the blues -
Haunting, melancholy singer
Your life sung in a song,
I see you sitting on your back porch
Your life hard your day long.
History is how I know you
I read about your life -
There are many others
Who intrigue me
With their elegance and their strife.
I live in a modern world
One that I know well
And one day someone
Will know me in History as well.

Dignity's Last Tango

Without warning it crumples to the floor -
dignity loses its foothold,
slithers across the stony ground of humble,
and flounders; crying out for music.
It cries out for a rhythm to revive feet
with the desire -the need- to dance again,
but bones, straddled by scrawny skin,
can no longer complete la Salida.
Dignity dances only inside an addled mind,
and in a much smaller world than before.
Before the stony ground of humble rose, and became a hill,
no longer the ballroom of life around which dignity once danced.

Temptation's Plate

Chocolate cream, stuff it in,
Overflowing garbage bin,
Do not waste that wedge of pie,
Starving children, daily die.

Nuts and chips and chocolate drops,
Clearing after Christmas never stops.
New Year's Eve and drink the drink,
Noooo, don't waste it down the sink!

Second day of the brand new year,
Diet day is upon me never fear!
Lettuce leaf, and tuna melt,
The best this year so far I've felt.

Oh no! From the corner of my eye,
I spot a piece of week old pie.
The crust is hard and not appealing,
But I cannot ignore the feeling.

Now the diet has lost its grip,
A glass of wine I gently sip.
Tomorrow is the diet day,
Now temptation's plate is cleared away.

Ashes of Our Past

This place is empty now, the disarray of tangled stems
cling to hedge and tree,
the flesh tingles as the past swirls the fogs of time around,
whose blood has mixed with sod and stone?
Who has history lying here? Is there a hidden part of me?
A broken cross and angel lay upon the dewy path,
a name that has no meaning,
a place with no life or soul,
the warm flesh is mine and the ashes from our past are
yours,
no longer body whole.
Step by careful step
the walk I take is calm
the still flesh no more, who are you all?
It tantalises curiosity this place,
I hear your memories call.
The whispers of time surround me-
as do the ashes of our past.

Repeat 'I Do'

Clip, clack, here comes the bride,
Teddy and Dolly by my side,
Mama's curtains for a train,
Old stilettos take the strain.

Clack, clip, there's the groom,
Marrying me, decades too soon.
Clip, clack, Vicar Bear said to kiss,
But we're too shy so our lips miss.

Clack, clip, down the path,
Why do the adults always laugh?
Clip, clack, here comes the bride,
Two best friends by my side,
Mama's veil and lacy train,
The groom and I get married again.

These last two poems were written for my eldest daughter and my son. They were married six weeks apart so my brain went into overdrive!

Ivory Tulle and Lace

(Nicola's Poem)

Where are the days past?
When as a child I saw you,
Those days did not last,
When into Ivory tulle you grew.

Ivory tulle and lace before me,
Eyelashes on a cheek,
You raise you head to see-
A waiting bride so meek.

I leave you now with a man,
One I love and adore,
I walk away as Mother,
And your Father takes the floor.

He will slowly walk you,
Towards the man you chose,
He will hand you over,
And that family page will close.

Your own page is written now,

As you accept his ring,
You will offer up your vow,
And joy to him you bring.

Ivory tulle will be packed away,
And memories we will store,
Life will move day to day,
When as a wife you walk the floor.

Two Children of Our Hearts

(Darren's Poem)

Entwined hearts beat as one,
At last life's adventure flows,
Friendship and trust… foundations,
Upon which a marriage grows.

Embrace your unique chemistry
Take love firmly by the hand,
Support the one you've chosen,
United you must stand.

Explore the mind of your lover
And find the inner core,
Take note of the little things,
And set the past behind the door.

Use the quiet moments
To let love's hand unfold,
Never rest your head, to sleep
Exposing shoulder cold.

Truthful love will solid be,
When doubt knocks upon the door,
May open heart and honesty
Be with you ever more.

The love you share together
Will stand the test of time,
When both hearts understand,
The other's beating rhyme.

The path will not be easy,
You may stumble along the way,
When times are hard and life unkind,
Recall your vows declared today.

Take with you our sincerest blessings,
As your married life now starts,
Know that we love and support you,
Two children of our hearts.

Due for Release Late 2015

Heels and Hearts

Medical Romance

As the practice manager of a local clinic, Jessica Daniels, is coping with her new co-worker but only just, and it opens her eyes to her emotional well-being.

Hurt during a work romance and vowed never again to mix business with pleasure, Doctor Andreas Konstantinou, is a distraction Jessica could do without. The Greek Cypriot doctor is quite a looker and she finds it a struggle to focus.

After a celebratory drinks evening with his new colleagues, Andreas confesses his pleasure, he loves a pretty feminine leg in a heeled shoe. Although not a fetish, it is something he learned to appreciate as a young lad.

Jessica takes a close look at herself and realises she is dowdy and has neglected her life. A new pair of shoes, a change of clothing, a new job and a seminar abroad, all alter her pathways and she sees the doctor in a new light. Unfortunately, they always find a way to hurt each other and love never quite grasps their desire for each other.

Three serious medical events bring them together, but

Jessica is still unwilling to let loose her love for Andreas—until shoes and a kitten persuade her otherwise.

Chapter One Sample …

Chapter 1

'Welcome to the practice, Doctor Konstantinou.' Jessica Daniels raised her glass to toast the handsome male across the table. She, and other members of the local medical centre, called out a hearty greeting. The busy Black Bull pub in Skepping town was often the place they gathered for their monthly team-building meets and voted a natural choice for the introduction of their new GP. The low-beamed building benefited the group with its comfortable seats and large oak tables in private booth-style areas. The team of ten enjoyed a supper of pub grub and beverages of their choosing and many chose to enjoy several beverages. It was a lively crowd who echoed their boss's sentiments by chinking glasses with spoons or stomping feet.

'We wish you happiness in your new job and look forward to a great future together.' Jessica smiled at the new member of staff and sat down to enjoy the general chit-chat buzzing around the table. Their old doctor had been literally that, old. Too old to practice according to the board and the new arrival with the physique of a Greek god, promised to be a breath of fresh air for all concerned.

'Stiniyia mas – to our good health. Thank you all. I look forward to working with those of you I haven't met before, and of course, meeting my patients.' He smiled at all around the table then across at her; and Jessica shifted in her seat.

Oh, you are hot. Too hot to handle, but just the thought of running my fingers through that dark hair…

As Practice Manager, she met him first during interview stage and considered him a fine specimen of a man - extremely sexy. They had worked together during his orientation days and he'd already met several staff, however, it was decided to have an informal night prior to his official working day.

Tonight, whether it was because he was more relaxed that sexiness oozed from him by the bucket load. Jessica aimed to keep up her standard by never mixing business with pleasure - and he sure would be pleasure. Good-looking and desirable, he was everything Jessica looked for in a man – visually. Cypriot blood fired through a body of tanned muscular hotness, at least she guessed he wore his Mediterranean tan all over, his darkened arms and opened collar hinted as much. His facial hair was merely a hint around an angular jawline. Handsome. Body trembling handsome.

After formalities were over the majority of the group headed home. The place held a party atmosphere and the remainder of the team were in good spirits and kept their eyes firmly fixed upon their new colleague. Born in southern Cyprus, educated in America, and finally taking his place at medical university in England, Andreas Konstantinou brought with him an exciting combination of cosmopolitan living and cultural differences.

Wine flowed and so did flirtatious looks from the receptionist Tanya. To Jessica's relief, the new doctor appeared not to notice.

'Please, can I get you all another drink?' Andreas Konstantinou took their orders and made his way to the bar, unaware several female – and possibly a few males- watched his rear saunter across the room. The rest of his body went with him: his rear the main feature. A deep sigh went up when he bent down to retrieve a dropped coin.

'My god, he's ace!' Tanya declared and gave a low whistle, 'that hint of an accent could be the downfall of me by the week's end and as for his ass …'

'Control yourself, Tanya. He is a work colleague not a playboy'. Muriel, the eldest amongst the team, made her feelings clear with a sharp reprimand. She had a prudish outlook on relationships, for Muriel, sex only happened after the marriage and then probably only on the wedding night out of duty. At fifty-two she was the mother hen of the office, and sometimes the younger team members found her staid ways annoying. However, this time Jessica agreed. Tanya was a man-eater, a demon for stealing men from friends. Goodness knows how many dates she'd been on that week and she would think nothing of snatching away Jessica's new fantasy- not that she knew he was her fantasy.

Both she and Jessica were twenty-six but Tanya had exceeded her life limit of one night stands, while Jessica had enjoyed a few flings and two good relationships – well, good until both left her for Tanya.

'Muriel is right, Tanya. Control is the keyword here. He is to be our colleague. Agreed, he is a hunk of a man and we will be dealing with him on a daily basis, a far cry from old Doc Moore but there is a fine line we must not cross. Watch out, he's coming back.'

'Yes. My latest heels are Jimmy Chou's. Cost me an arm and a leg.' Tanya launched into new conversation and lifting her leg higher than decency allowed, showing off a length of finely tuned thigh. Jessica grinned at Muriel who sat with a disapproving frown.

'High heels are not good for your legs. Don't you agree doctor?' Muriel directed her question at Andreas as he attempted to squeeze through a gap between the black faux-leather   seats and heavy oak table that threatened to land him upon Tanya's lap. Jessica sensed the girl had manoeuvred forward to make the space even tighter.

'Err, yes – no. Excuse me – sorry. High heels. The stiletto? They are not good for the foot but good for the soul of a man,' a ripple of laughter rang out and he grinned a wide white smile, 'I did not mean the joke, what I mean is, for me, a lady can turn a pair of heeled shoes into something of beauty. Although, a fat leg squeezed into a pair is not something I enjoy, I will confess. This man finds a curved calf can be sexy with heels attached.' His infectious laugh echoed around the pub and heads turned their way. People smiled over at the table, women put their heads together and whispered and Jessica decided Doctor Andreas (his newly given name to make it easier for patients), might well be an asset to the practice. His laidback, friendly attitude was just what was needed after the starchiness of their previous colleague. Likewise, his good looks might be a hindrance and appointments would have to be scrutinised carefully for timewasters. Doctor Andreas Konstantinou was most definitely the most interesting thing that had entered the sleepy town for a long time.

I could waste many hours on him, that's a fact. So, heels turn him on ...

***

The walk home to her two-bed Victorian end of terrace cottage took no more than five minutes. Everything she needed from the small town was a five minute walk away. Jessica did not care for driving. Her life centred round her neat home – her pride and joy. She shared it with Fred and enjoyed the peace and quiet he instilled in the place. Only the gentle hum from his water filter greeted her upon her arrival. Fred the Goldfish expected nothing more than fresh water, oxygen and a daily pinch of food. Jessica's life was simple. No boyfriend complicated things.

Her last, Simon, proved his loyalty by hiding the fact he also dated Tanya. Her colleague played the "I was unaware and am as shocked as you," card but Jessica knew otherwise. Muriel knew and her face always expressed her thoughts, she never needed to speak them out loud. Simon came to work at the practice on a temporary basis, he was an IT whizz and set up a new system. The after-hours chats he and Jessica enjoyed soon became a semi-serious relationship. Then, for Jessica, it became serious. He'd hooked her heart, and with no remorse, in one act of betrayal, he shattered it into tiny pieces. After their relationship folded, Jessica vowed never to mix business with pleasure, and never get caught up in a workplace romance. Her heart was too fragile, no man would ever benefit from the love she could share. Simon had taken it all and crushed it with his insensitivity and lies. She cried for weeks, her weight dropped to a dangerous low, and she concentrated so hard at her job she lost her social life.

When the house came on the market, it captured her attention in the local estate agent window. An impulsive request to view, and a feeling of comfort once she stepped through the front door, Jessica knew it was the distraction she needed. Months of DIY therapy and she never again looked back at what might have been with Simon.

Once inside her home, Jessica kicked off her sensible work shoes and shoved her feet into her red fluffy boot style slippers. It was all about comfort and practicalities with her. She clicked on the music channel and allowed the music to wash over her as she shrugged on her red fleece onesie. She rocked to the love angst words of a song while she waited for the milk to boil in readiness for her cocoa. Her mind wandered to Andreas and she had a one hundred percent power surge of need rush through her body.

Oh he'd really want you in your sexy outfit tonight. He is quite a catch. Shake your hair down girl, look at you. Tight bun, minimum makeup and brogues. Big turn on – not.

She lounged across the sofa, sipping her drink and allowing the peace of her home bring her to a stage of calm. Her mind started at the top of the head of her vision and ended mid-chest. Her muse entered a conversation about their fantasy man and Jessica's relaxed state became an intimate moment of realisation.

End of Sample

Printed in Great Britain
by Amazon